# THE BALLAD
### *of*
# TOM DOOLEY

## Also by Sharyn McCrumb

# THE BALLAD

## *of*

# TOM DOOLEY

## A BALLAD NOVEL

# SHARYN

# McCRUMB

THOMAS DUNNE BOOKS
St. Martin's Griffin
New York

# ZEBULON VANCE

✦━━◦◯◦━━✦

**W**hat did I know about murder cases that a man's life should lie in my hands? I had spent the whole of my adult life in politics, except for a few years on a mountain circuit court, a decade before that trial. A war ago.

This tale is not a penny-dreadful thriller, penned by the likes of Mr. Wilkie Collins. Look elsewhere for clues and footprints and the trappings of a puzzle story—*and go to the devil if you try to make this tale into one.*

A case of law is a chess game for those who make their living at it, and a great sorrow for those who get caught up in its web.

A man died bravely, doing perhaps the only noble thing he ever achieved in his brutal, useless life. Another fifty years of living would not have improved him, for he had only a minute's worth of courage, and he spent that.

That is the burden of this story, and it would shine brighter if there were a good woman at hand with the heart and the wit to tell it well. But we have no good woman to speak out for the doomed man— only a vain and selfish ditch rose, who rightly feared for her own life, and a raddled slut who delighted in the destruction she wrought single-handed. One of those wretched women is also my client, for the pair was arrested together, and bound over to stand trial for the same crime, but I had deemed it better for all concerned that they be tried separately for this deed, and I vowed to ask for severance as soon as I was able.

The young soldier was the first to face the judge, and it was he that I was concerned with at the outset. I would do what I could for him.

People will tell this story for a century, though I'm damned if I know why. There's little enough to it. No doubt they will sing about it, and spin fanciful tales, and act it out, turning all its principals into Sunday-school sweethearts and black-hearted villains. It will all be nonsense. At least I remember what was real.

*I remember.*

I am weary and garrulous in my old age, sitting by the fire in my fine Washington home, and thinking back twenty-odd years, to when I was domiciled here in the old Capitol Prison, instead of in the United States Senate, where I have been nigh on ever since. I have been paging through my personal papers, idly speculating about whether I should like to write my memoirs someday. They would make interesting reading, though I do say so myself. One might trace my progress from backwoods farm boy to country lawyer, to Congressman, and then to Colonel of the 26th North Carolina during the War. I saw action on the front lines in Virginia. That was about as much soldiering as I cared to experience, so when the opportunity arose, I got myself elected Governor. From the Governor's Palace in Raleigh, I sat out the remainder of the hostilities, skirmishing with bureaucrats and trying to protect the people of my state from both armies. They clapped me in prison here in Washington at the War's end, for my trouble, but I didn't take it personally—all the governors were there, so I did not lack for society. In a few weeks, they let us all out again, and I went home to a state made so desolate by war that my own personal ruin hardly mattered. I began again.

I had to practice a little law after the War ended, before those same trifling government bureaucrats saw fit to let me back into the congress I had unwillingly left when my home state seceded. I do not mean to ever leave Congress again. I shall die here, protecting the interests of my fellow Tarheels for as long as God grants me breath and strength.

A fine row house in the District of Columbia city is a far cry from my birthplace—a log cabin in the Carolina backcountry—but from my boyhood I could see my way clear to getting here as surely as I could see that blue haze of mountains that walled us off from the state of Tennessee. I come of good stock, though you might not think it, for we looked no more prosperous or cultured than most of our frontier neighbors, but my father's father had fought in the Revolution. He wintered at Valley Forge with General Washington, and fought alongside him at Brandywine, Germantown, and Monmouth. I am proudest, though, of the fact that he fought closer to home—at King's Mountain on the South Carolina border, just west of Charlotte. In 1780 a group of backcountry volunteers, calling themselves The Overmountain Men, engaged the British forces there, and defeated them in an hour, killing their commander, and proving that untrained colonials could defeat the mighty British army. George Washington's troops were losing the War to the north, and that little victory on a Carolina hillside proved to the rest of the country that winning was possible. It was the turning point of the War, and I was proud that my family had been part of it.

On that little mountain farm where I grew up, we plowed furrows, and slopped hogs, and hewed firewood, but we were never allowed to forget that we were destined for greater things. My grandfather had left a library of five hundred books, and my mother read to us each night when the chores were done. My father died young, though, and so the way to prosperity was a steep and thorny path for us. I got some schooling over in Tennessee at Washington College, so that I had the rudiments of Latin, and composition, debate, and ancient history, but my father's death ended that idyll, and before long I was clerking in a fine resort hotel in Warm Springs. That, too, was an education, though. It was a zoo for the aristocracy, and I learned to pass muster as one of them.

I read law in Asheville, and then begged and borrowed the funds to take me to the University of North Carolina for the formal study of law. I meant to get elected to something before long, and so I did, but for a few years in my youth I practiced law on the circuit court out of Asheville. There was little in those experiences worth mentioning in a senator's memoirs.

But this Wilkes County case . . . That came later in my career, and in it, I was defending a man on trial for his life. I had thought of including the tale in my memoirs, because it became quite a celebrated trial. *The New York Herald* even sent a reporter down to cover it. But the public finds it hard to recognize success or skill if one ultimately loses the case, so perhaps I will not include it, after all. I have had enough adventures for two lifetimes, without telling that sad little tale.

That Wilkes County court case constituted my brief hiatus from public life, falling in 1866, when, having been the Confederate Governor of North Carolina, I was barred from running for public office yet awhile, so, when they let me out of Capitol Prison with the rest of the Rebel governors, I bided my time and supported Harriette and the boys by returning to the practice of law. Perhaps I thought that my renown and popularity would make up for any deficiencies I might have in my long-disused courtroom skills.

The law was never much more than a means to an end for me, anyhow. I was always happy to help people escape what was coming to them, which is mostly what a defense attorney does, but from the very beginning I was only marking time until I got elected to something. But for the War, I would have never looked back.

A frail girl was stabbed to death in the foothills of Wilkes County, and nigh on everybody there knows who did it. Well, I didn't know. I was practicing law in Charlotte, some ninety miles away, and I was only called in to defend the man they had arrested, a complete stranger to me, despite what people have said to the contrary over the years. He was a Confederate veteran, as was I, but we never served together, and would not have been acquainted even if we had, for I began and ended my military service as a colonel, and he stayed a sickly private and a drummer boy. We were worlds apart, except perhaps to people who looked at our lives on paper.

This twenty-two-year-old former soldier got himself arrested, and I in my infinite wisdom got the trial moved to the next county, where nobody knew any more about it than I did. My intentions were good. And I suppose I could not have done otherwise, even if I had been more in possession of the facts. In the end, a lawyer must do his client's bidding, and I did that.

God help us both. I did that.

I expect that in years to come there will be more people wondering why I took this case than there will be wondering if he did it.

Oh, why did I agree to represent a man, generally accorded by my learned colleagues in the legal profession to be guilty, who could not have paid for a shot of whiskey, much less an attorney for his defense? An idle, amoral Confederate veteran, accused of stabbing a young girl to death and burying her body in the woods.

Well, *somebody* had to represent him. Any country lawyer will tell you that. If we managed to get Satan himself into a courtroom, it would be some lawyer's lot to defend him, and to argue, no doubt, that he is a hard-working fellow.

*But why me?*

I don't know that I had any choice in the matter. The Wilkes County judge appointed me, and ordered me to defend this young man pro bono. It is a fine sentiment, pro bono. For the public good and in the interest of justice, a lawyer can be assigned to an indigent defendant, and he must represent his client completely without charge. This ensures that the poor are accorded a defense, but it can be hard lines on a struggling attorney, and I expect that the temptation would be great to rush through the case, and move on to more lucrative matters. A man's life is at stake, though; if I shirked my duty in so grave a matter as this, I would never sleep again.

I don't suppose the judge pulled my name out of a hat. He could have found lawyers a-plenty in the surrounding counties without reaching all the way to Charlotte to fetch one. Perhaps he intended the appointment as a favor. Here was I forced to practice law, but lacking in experience, and perhaps he thought that a notorious murder trial would set my name before the general public, so that people would queue up to retain my services for their legal requirements.

I am sensible of the honor, but I could scarcely afford the opportunity. There I was, former Governor of the state of North Carolina, and before that a U.S. Congressman, and, in-between, for a few ill-considered months, a colonel in the Army of the Confederacy, and, only incidentally, an attorney licensed to practice law in my home state. I never thought I'd be called upon to do so again after all the loftier honors I had achieved. Indeed, I hoped not, but our fortunes shift like the tides, and the fall of the Confederacy had left me high and dry, penniless, jobless, and free only on the sufferance of the United States President. In those days I was rich only in friends.

From the corridors of power to a stuffy little courtroom in a town in Iredell County that is only on the map two days a week. When I charted the course of my life, that was an unforeseen development, but there I was.

If I should ever have the ear of posterity, it would take me a good many words to talk my way out of that one. But I am both a lawyer and a politician. Words are my stock in trade. This story, though, will be omitted from my memoirs. After all, for all the protracted nature of the legal proceedings, the case only took up a few days of my time, and its outcome did me no credit. It is a mere footnote in the long and illustrious history of a dedicated public servant. I shall not speak of it.

From time to time, though, that poor wretch crosses my mind, and before I force my thoughts on to other things, I repress a shudder, and think, "There but for the grace of God, go I."

I was born beyond the pale of gentrified civilization, as was that young man in the dock on trial for his life. You might think that coincidence of circumstance would have made for common ground between him and me, but the truth is that we could not have been farther apart had one of us been born on the moon. My childhood poverty was only in material want, but in heritage, intellect, learning, and morality, my family had wealth beyond avarice.

For reasons I am at a loss to explain, this Wilkes County case became a cause celebre among the national press, and I fear that whenever people read about the sordid circumstances of these wretched people, they will attempt to tar all the inhabitants of the Carolina mountains with the same brush, which is hard lines on the honest and educated people who choose to live in those mountains. In defense of my fellow countrymen, I offer up the example of my own life.

# PAULINE FOSTER
## *March 1866*

———⊙———

W ilkes County, North Carolina. Why, I wouldn't go back
there again to save my life.

That's why I went in the first place, though.

On account of Dr. George Carter being there, and him being a
real doctor, and not just some old besom practicing root medicine
and faith healing. I had tried the other kind, and I wasn't getting any
better, and folk kept saying that maybe Dr. Carter down in the foothills could cure what ailed me with a bluestone or maybe a salve of
lard and quicksilver.

I had kin over there in Wilkes, which is how I heard tell of him in
the first place, and that was what set me on going, even if I had to walk
the forty miles to get there.

Nobody up home seemed to know the cure for what I had, but they
all knew how I got it right enough.

The old woman I went to was the one who birthed the babies
hereabouts, and she made poultices and tonics for them as took sick,
so at the end of February, 1866, when I couldn't stand it any longer, I
went along to her. Not at first, when I found the sore, because when

you're young and strong, you just ignore little aches and pains, figuring that soon enough they will go away by themselves. Only this one didn't.

By and by, when my throat got sore and my head commenced to ache, I wrapped up some butter I had churned fresh that morning, so as not to be beholden for the favor I was asking, and I walked across the brown grass streaked with rime until I reached her forlorn little cabin at the edge of the woods, same as everybody around here did when they hurt bad enough.

Nobody knew how old she was, but the old folks remembered her as a widow woman, and she was still spry as any of them, so it was thought that her potions must work, else how would she still be quick and well after so many years. I would not have gone to her for beauty treatments, though, for her face was as brown and wrinkled as snits, which is what she called pieces of dried apple, so she was not from these parts to begin with. Nobody from here said that word. I think she may have come over from Tennessee, and there are those that would tell you that she had the Sight, but I never set much store by talk such as that. *Sufficient unto the day is the evil thereof*, not that I take much stock of the Bible neither, but I did agree with St. Matthew about that. We all of us have the same fate coming by and by, and I was never inclined to rush out to meet it. But she talked like she knew things, and people fought shy of her on that account, for fear of what she might tell them that they'd rather not know.

I had no need of her fortune-telling, and not much for her beauty salves, neither, I'd judge. Despite my sickness, I am a likely-looking woman, mostly because I am young. At least I am little and needle thin, which makes my eyes look big as a calf's. I have a good hank of coarse dark hair, a short straight nose, and a pale heart-shaped face. I'd show better with a dusting of rice powder and a dab of rouge to smarten me up, but there were no complaints about my looks, not even now when the War took men more'n the five miles from home they used to travel in search of a wife. I reckon that to a scared and lonesome soldier any scrawny gal of twenty can pass for a beauty, though there is real handsomeness in the Foster line that some say I got just a touch of.

One of my Wilkes County cousins is such a beauty that she puts the rest of us in the shade, though it makes her a devil for pride and sloth and willfulness. I never lacked for admirers, or at least for them that was happy to take what I was willing to give, but I reckon men would rather be tormented by a hell-bent beauty than settle for a plainer girl with a will to work and an even temper. Leastways, my cousin Ann was married at fifteen, and I had already reached twenty without having anybody want me any longer than a week. I don't know that I'd a-wanted any of them, neither, but nowadays, knowing I am ailing, thinking back on being spurned is like holding a hot coal between my breasts. I had suffered the sleights of false-hearted lovers, and I had spent their coins, and now I was sickening from their attentions, branded as a loose woman for what the War had made of me. It was hard lines, all round, but I had no one to complain to. I must shift for myself, as ever.

After the old woman set my offering of butter into a bowl on a wet rag, she bade me lay back on the pine table near the fire, and, while I stared up at the roof beams, she hoisted up my dew-soaked skirts, and spraddled my legs. She looked at the chancre on my private parts, more for form's sake than to tell what I had, for I reckon she knew that afore I had spoken ten words. But she squinted into my mouth, too, and, when she saw the white flesh where it ought to have been pink, she nodded, looking more satisfied than sorry.

" 'Tis pox."

Well, I was sorry indeed, but I was no more surprised than she was, staring up at her over my belly. "I judged that it was. Can you cure it?"

She locked eyes with me for a long moment, and then she spat on the floor. "I reckon I can tell you how you came by it. You was bit by a trouser snake."

She saw my puzzled look and cackled. "I say you have been a-laying with all and sundry. And I reckon that you have been paid for your wickedness with the wages of sin. Going with just the one man will make a girl fall pregnant, like as not, and that can be attended to if need be, but spreading your favors amongst the drovers and trappers and soldiers like you done will get you poxed sooner or later, and so it has done for you. And that is a graver matter than a swollen belly."

I met her eyes with a stare as bold as brass, for if she was looking for me to hang my head and weep for my waywardness, she'd be a long time waiting to see it. She was as old and dried up as broom straw, and I reckon she had forgotten what it was like to be young, and, anyhow, when she was in my time of life, there weren't no war on, and that makes a world of difference to the course of a life.

I was sixteen when the War commenced. It didn't reach us right away, tucked up in the mountain fastness like we are. There is not much up here worth fighting over, and not enough flat ground or spare provender to accommodate a big army, anyhow, but within a year or so, we began to hear about battles flickering just beyond our boundaries, and we knew that at any moment the war might flare up and engulf us in its flames.

Before the War ever came to us, the young men went away to it. Mostly they didn't want to, though, except for the fools who thought they were heading off to a grand adventure. The rest were caught in the net of a law called Conscription, that said unless you could pay your way out of the army, or else managed a big plantation or a hospital or suchlike, then you had to go and serve in the Confederate army, on account of North Carolina having left the Union. But they never asked our opinion about secession, and most folks up here said it was a rich man's war and a poor man's fight.

When the bureaucrats enforcing Conscription started hauling our young men out of the mountains, I had just turned eighteen, and I was hoping for a spell of dancing and courting to sweeten my salad days, before I settled down to a lifetime of farm work and childbirth, and all the cares of growing old. But I was done out of that youthful dalliance by the War.

Before I could have any fun, all the likely young men went off to the flatlands where the fighting was, and the young girls all wept to see them go, knowing they might not ever come back. So they said good-bye as hard as they could. Being young and knowing you might not live to grow old makes a nonsense of all those silly rules about virtue and chastity—anyhow, that's how it struck me, and the soldiers were happy enough to take memories of a sweetheart away to war. Some of them came back now and again, sent home to recuperate from war wounds, or maybe they just walked away from an encampment one night and hightailed it home, and they weren't shy boys anymore, after what they'd seen and done, and I welcomed them home as well. It wasn't a love match, really, or if it was, it was them being in love with the whole idea of soldiering and danger and sorrow—not just taking a shine to one young woman. When you see a baby-faced young fellow eying you like a starving dog, and you know that he may not live to see another spring, he wants you to give him all the springtimes he's ever going to miss in one gulp. He doesn't mind parting with his money for the consolation, neither, and mostly I lived on that.

Then, of course, in '64, the War finally found us here in the hills, and suddenly food was scarce, and soldiers were burning farms and making our lives a misery, and then it became a practical matter to give a man what he wanted for a slab of meat or a warm blanket. Whatever you have to do to survive shouldn't count as a sin. It don't seem fair to me that soldiers get forgiven their trespasses after the peace treaty is signed, but that the rest of us are condemned to eternal guilt by the long memories of our neighbors.

I figured it was my war wound, that touch of pox that I got along with the meat scraps and the blankets the soldiers give me. I wish I had some warm memories of love and joy to salve the affliction and make me think it was a fair exchange, but I never had that. I took what the soldiers had, and they did likewise, and, if they cheated me in the bargain, they are mostly dead and buried by now at Antietam or the Wilderness or Chickamauga, past being revenged upon. Dead or alive, I reckon they have all forgot me now, and I never cared now what happened to any of them.

I am alone.

I wasn't about to fall to weeping in front of a judgmental biddy like this granny woman, but her words froze my belly to my backbone nonetheless, for I had seen men afflicted with pox, and that they had died raving was not the worst of it. Before it came to that, the skin of the sufferer would curdle and crust with fearsome sores, bubbling and running like salt pork in a hot iron skillet, so that not even the bravest Christian could stand to go near them.

I was not afraid of what would come to me, but I was angry that I could not see my way out of this trap. And I was only twenty-two. Too young to be looking at such a fate. I reckon most girls would be scared enough to fall to praying, only I didn't believe there was anybody out there to hear me, and, if there was, He had let this happen, so I didn't see no use in begging favors of Him now. Didn't nobody in this world give a tinker's dam for me, and I didn't hold out much hope for mercy in the next one, either. I had to shift for myself, same as always, and let the rest of the world beware.

"Mayhap, salts of mercury will help you some," the old woman said. "A doctor could give you that." She laughed and recited that old jest I'd heard a time or two from the soldiers: *"One night with Venus, and a lifetime with Mercury."*

I scowled at her as I hitched down my skirts and clambered off the table. Then and there I made up my mind that I would go elsewhere to find a doctor, for I would get neither cure nor sympathy from the root doctor biddies up there. I had no qualms about leaving Watauga County. I'd be no more alone anywhere else than I was there. But freedom costs money, and I had none.

"I reckon there's a doctor down the mountain in Wilkes County," I said. "I have people down there, and I believe I will go to them."

The fire blazed up just then as a new bit of dry wood caught alight atop the logs. The old woman's eyes lit up as well, and she fixed me with a narrow gaze. "If you up and go to Wilkes County, nothing will come of it but sorrow."

I shrugged. "I don't see how it could be any worse down there than where I'm at right now."

She shook her head. "There's no hope for you anywhere. Better if you was to die here, without troubling anybody. It's you that carries the sorrow within you, and if you venture down into Wilkes County, you will take death and dishonor right along with you, and you'll spread them like the pox that brands you."

"On other people, you mean?" I laughed. "Why, that ain't nothing to me. I'd see the whole world pole-axed in one blow if it would make me well and happy. Or even if it wouldn't."

"Nothing will make you well. The death you will bring to others may gladden your heart, though. That is a greater sickness than the pox, and it, too, is beyond my power to cure."

"Oh, I don't want cured of that," I told her as I wrapped up in my shawls and made for the cabin door. "If my body has to hurt, I think it is a blessing that my heart never will. It don't even the score, but it helps."

For the next day or two, whenever I had occasion to speak with anyone, I led the conversation around to doctors, hoping for one that I could get to without much travel or money, and I asked in particular about Wilkes County. By and by somebody mentioned that there was indeed a good one by the name of Carter down the mountain in Wilkes. As soon as I heard that, I made up my mind to choose that doctor, on account of the kinfolk I had there, not that I thought they'd be overmuch glad to see me. My father came from Wilkes, and he had left a brother and cousins back there when he moved the forty miles west up to the ridgetops near Blowing Rock, but he had never married my mother, so they took no notice of me, those Fosters, for all that I called myself one.

The Fosters are not a close family, nor a clan that can be counted upon to rush to one another's aid in time of trouble, any more than I'd have bestirred myself to help them. I would not be welcomed with open arms by my Wilkes County cousins. But I reckoned if I made it worth their while, and added a dollop of guilt into the brew, then one of them would be bound to take me in. Best not to tell them I was coming, though, or they'd put me off for certain.

When the end of February came and the wind let up a little, I packed my clothes in a canvas poke, and, come sun-up, without so much as a good-bye to anybody, I set off along the trace that led east and down the mountain.

It takes most of a week to get over to Wilkes County, following the old buffalo trace, first along Lewis Fork Creek, and then down into flatter country along the Elk Creek Road that leads to Wilkes County, where my people had come from before the War. Walking from Watauga County to Wilkes is a long, bitter journey to make in the tail end of winter, but miserable ain't the same as important, so there's no use making a tale of my six-day walk back to the family seat. The war years brought so much suffering to the folks in these mountains that for me to complain about any hardships on my journey would be like spitting in a well. I've known worse. Everybody around here has.

Back in a cold winter of the War, when times were hard and food was scarce, my daddy took sick of the fever and inside of a week, he was dead. Didn't none of his people come up for the funeral. Maybe the message never reached them, and with bushwhackers prowling the roads, such a perilous journey wasn't to be thought of anyhow, but I don't believe they would have come even in the best of times. They don't exactly consider us kin. We didn't grieve for him ourselves, and maybe his Wilkes relatives mourned him even less. The Fosters keep to themselves, but just because we didn't live in one another's pockets didn't mean I couldn't find them when I needed them. They all lived in some proximity to Dr. George Carter, and that was all they were good for.

But I had to go somewhere. My daddy was dead, and Mama had no use for me. Times was hard, and I was past eighteen and on my own. But for the War, I might have had a husband and two young'uns by now, but the Confederacy turned most of our young men into worm food, and I didn't care to make a match of it with the old men and the maimed veterans who were left.

My grandfather's niece, Lotty Foster, had herself a cabin and some scrub land alongside of a creek called Reedy Branch, maybe a mile before it empties into the Yadkin River. I reckon she might have taken me in: any woman that has borne five bastards hasn't had much practice saying no to anybody, but the family all said that Lotty was bad to drink, and, despite having that grown-up daughter Ann, the family beauty, out and gone, she had four other young'uns still at home. No use putting myself there, I thought. I would end up tending children as well as doing all the chores and, like as not, spending my evenings being expected to nursemaid the old sot herself. I wasn't feeling well enough for such a burden as that, and I was by no means sure her little cabin would have room for me nohow. Best seek an easier place to begin with, and leave Lotty's cabin for a last resort.

I didn't have far to go to seek other lodging. Across the road from Lotty's cabin was a steep hill with a little house and some outbuilding on the top of it: James Melton's land. My handsome cousin Ann had married him before the War, and the chores there were likely to be fewer, though not because Ann was doing a hand's turn of work, for it was gospel in the family that she never had and never would. We were near to the same age, but I had not set eyes on her since we were children, and she was pretty enough then, but proud and bossy with it, too. I did not expect to find her much improved.

They call that part of Wilkes County "Happy Valley," though I couldn't see that the folks there were any better off than the rest of us. There were fine houses scattered here and there, same as anywhere else, but between the showplaces were ramshackle cabins and ordinary houses—again, same as anywhere else.

The one thing I did notice when I got there on the first day of March: it was warmer down there than it was up on the mountain. Though the hillside forests were still bare, new leaves with a yellow tint to the green were budding on the valley oaks and chestnuts, so I judged that Wilkes County was a week closer to spring than where I had just left. The road was muddier, though, and the wind was still sharp. I'd be glad to get shut of the foul weather, and sit down by somebody's fireside, for my cheeks felt like snowballs.

I asked the way a time or two of the farm folk who gave me shelter in the course of my journey, not wanting to spend any more time in the wind than I had to, mindful that I was sick, but since the road followed the Elk Creek, it was simple enough to find my way to the Stony Fork Road. By late afternoon I was standing on the dirt track, looking up that long hill toward the farmhouse where my cousin Ann lived now. I had heard tell that there were fine plantations down in the bottom land around the Yadkin, and that may be so, but I had not fetched up on the doorstep of one of them. The Elkville community could boast of no river mansions with colored servants to wait on you hand and foot, though I heard tell there were such places in Wilkes, owned by the likes of the Isbells and the Carters. Not my Foster kin, though, and not the Meltons, either, from the look of this place. Ann's husband's property was a shabby hill farm that would be hard-pressed to feed the owner's family, much less anybody else around the place. I was used to such as that, though. Thanks to the War, we were all schooled in doing without.

The wood frame house had no upstairs, no fancy pillars or porches, and its steps were two flat stones set in the dirt. It could have used a lick of paint, too. It was a toad of a house, squatting on its hilltop under bare trees in a yard of scraggly brown grass. A thin wisp of smoke drifting out of the stone chimney told me it was no warmer inside the house than out. Still, Cousin Lotty's place was no more grand or kept-up than this, and hers was child-infested to boot, so I reckoned I had better make the best of things here, if they'd have me, which I reckoned they would.

I did not have the charm of Cousin Ann, but I have a knack of knowing what folk want, and for being that, as long as it suits me.

I wasn't used to much in the way of comfort up home, either. Beggars cannot be choosers, and beggar I was, so I picked up my bundle of clothes, and waded uphill through the dry grass to the door.

By the time I got there, a couple of scrawny hounds had crawled out from under a shed, and were yapping and baying at my heels, but I gave the littlest one a hard kick with my boot, and they thought better of trying to light into me. Them dogs didn't worry me none. They'd have to have the teeth of a handsaw to get through two petticoats, a wool skirt and my old leather boots, and when they saw no fear in me, they gave up, and slunk back under the porch. But I was hungry and shivering from my journey, and I could have done with less noise. Nobody came to see what all the commotion was about, so I rapped hard on the door with bare knuckles numb from cold, hoping they wouldn't keep me standing out there in the sharp wind for too much longer.

By and by the door opened a crack, and a tall, gaunt man peered out at me, neither angry nor welcoming, but looking as if he had only opened the door to stop the knocking. He didn't say a word—just stared out at me, waiting, I guess, to be told what I had come about.

"I'm Pauline Foster," I said, investing in a smile. "If you be Mr. James Melton, I am blood kin to your wife. I come to see her." Without giving him time to answer back, I picked up my sack of clothes, and shouldered my way past him into the house, calling out for Ann. He stood aside and let me pass without a word. I reckoned James Melton was the kind of man that nobody paid any mind to, so maybe he was used to it.

I saw then that there weren't no use to be hollering, for Ann could not help but hear me. The inside of the house was one great room with a fireplace at one end, and a pine table and a bench seat set back a few feet from the hearth. At the other end of the room two narrow beds stood side by side on a rag rug. At the foot of one bed was a wooden trunk, its lid open, and clothes were spilling out of it and onto the floor, so that told me where Ann slept. The walls of the cabin were wide chestnut logs, chinked with clay to keep out the wind, and there was one little square window set in the far wall, but in the dusk of a gray winter day, it didn't let in enough light to do much good. That was just as well. Brighter light would have showed the dirt and untidiness of the place, which was bad enough as it was.

Ann was sitting on a stool near the fire, and the flames made shadows on her face 'til I didn't hardly recognize her, but once I got up close I could see that the kinfolk's tales were true. She had grown up to be a rare beauty, right enough. She had big dark eyes, set in a heart-shaped face, and her black hair was drawn back in a bun so that you could see the sharp line of her jaw and the cheekbone ridges that made her a wonder to look at. Her mouth was thin, and gave her a peevish look of discontent. When she got old it would wrinkle like a draw-string purse, but for now she was just past twenty, and not even an uncertain temper could mar those looks. I wondered why she had settled for James Melton, who was tolerable to look at but still un-prosperous, when her perfect face surely would have taken her higher than that. I made up my mind to ask her about her choice of a husband, but not just yet; not until I had settled in as one of the household.

She sat there on her stool, looking up at me with an expression of mild curiosity, like she didn't know who I was and didn't care over-much, either. I didn't think Ann ever had much use for other women, nor they for her. But speaking my mind would not get me bed and board, so I knelt down, all smiles, and threw my arms around her, as if she were my dearest friend in the world.

"Why, Ann, it's Pauline. My daddy, rest his soul, was first cousin to your mama, and I have just come down from the mountain to see my kinfolks here."

Ann shrugged. "Well, you're a scrawny little thing, ain't you, Pau-line? And you don't have much of the Foster looks about you. I'd not have knowed you. But you had better sit yourself down here by me. Your cheek feels like ice. —James! This fire needs another log!"

He got up without a word to do her bidding, and, as he was shov-ing fresh wood into the blaze, I saw him close up in the firelight, and I revised my estimate of his age. What I had taken for gray hair in the dim light turned out to be naturally fair hair that shone like bronze when he was kneeling by the fire. He stood tall and straight, his face and hands were free of veins and creases. Why, he couldn't be much past our age from the look of him, for all that he acted twice that. I wondered if he was ill himself, or if the War had sapped his vitals, or—I stole a glance at Ann, staring drowsily into the fire— maybe living with her just drained the life out of him. I wasn't sorry for him, though. Any man who insists on taking up with a beautiful wife ought to pay dearly for the purchase. I could see that he had.

Ann had taken the pins out of her hair, and she shook her head to let it fall about her shoulders. From the folds of her skirt, she drew out a wooden comb and began to brush the tangles out of her black curls.

I summoned a smile and held out my hand for the comb. "I'd be glad to do that for you, Ann. It's hard to reach there in the back."

She frowned a little, but then she gave a little shrug and handed over the comb. I was sure she was accustomed to accepting kindnesses from the male sex, but that it was a rarity for a woman to offer her anything. "What is it you came for, again?" she said.

I had it in my mind to lie about the purpose of my journey, but I could see that Ann Melton was not one to be swayed by fine words about sentiment and family feeling. She had no use for relatives, nor for the society of a woman friend. What *did* she have a use for? I looked again around the shabby room that stank of stale food and unemptied chamber pots.

"I was hoping you could use a hired girl," I said, making even strokes with the comb through the thicket of hair. It could have used a wash with soap and lavender water more than a brushing, but the weather was mortal cold, and most women would rather have greasy hair than risk the chills and fever that could come from washing it afore spring. Anybody else would have looked scraggly and foul with lank, dirty hair, but it hardly took the shine off Cousin Ann, lit up in the firelight like Jacob's angel.

"I can cook and do the washing and mending. Scrub floors. Bake bread. See to the chamber pots. And I reckon I can do farm chores. I'll work cheap enough."

She pushed her hair out of her eyes, and turned to study me now, her interest captured at last. "You want to work here? As a hired girl? What for?"

"I came down here to see the doctor," I said. Best go with the truth. Ann Melton understood selfishness. "I'm sick, and I need to stay close by for a couple of months while I get treatment for my ailment."

She pulled away from me then, making the comb jerk against her hair, and she swore and snatched it back from me. "What's the matter with you, then? Consumption?"

I could hear the alarm in her voice. Consumption took young healthy people in a matter of months, and your very breath might spread the contagion to a healthy household. I forced myself to laugh and to keep my voice steady. "Naw, it ain't that. I'm fit enough to work like a mule. Mostly, I don't even feel sick. I am just feeling poorly is all." I pointed somewhere between my stomach and my knees and made a face.

After I said it, I glanced over at James Melton, but he was just gazing off into the fire like he hadn't heard a word we said, or else he didn't care. Ann gave me a moment's shocked stare, and then a harsh laugh. "Reckon *somebody* made her little old self the Soldier's Joy these past few months." She hummed a little snatch of the tune, ending in a fit of giggles.

Well, that was true enough, so I laughed with her, because getting mad about the taunt wouldn't get me what I wanted, and anyhow it was better to laugh than to think of dying in a raddled, festering lump before I reached thirty. Either way, the joke was on me. I just wish whoever give me that dose of poison in our coupling had been worth dying for. But nary one of them was.

Ann's giggles tailed off, and she began to twirl a hank of that greasy hair while she thought about what I said. Then she leaned in close, watching my face while she spoke, but I didn't move a muscle. "It ain't a baby, is it?"

"No," I said, trotting out the lie that I had made ready for just that question. "I got shut of one and that's why I'm ailing."

Ann nodded, satisfied. It was the answer she expected to hear. "I wish I had thought of doing that. James and me have got two." She pointed to a cradle set in a corner of the room. "My mama keeps them half the time, though."

"It's good to have her close like she is."

Ann nodded. "And too drunk mostly to make the climb up the hill to see us. But I take the babies to her, so that's all right. —So, Pauline, you're aiming to stay here for a couple of months while you are seeing our Dr. Carter for physick, and you are wanting to board with us, and to pay for your keep by being the hired girl. Is that right?"

I nodded. It was simple enough to state the facts, but I thought that living through the bargain itself was likely to be the longest spell of my life. I looked at them, more masters than kinfolk, that was sure. All James Melton seemed to want was a quiet life, which was all right with me. I wouldn't add to his troubles, but I doubted if I'd take much away from them, either. I wondered what Ann wanted. Not a woman chum—I could see that. Of course she'd want somebody to do a hand's turn of work around the place, which was more than she ever did, but there was something else besides.

"So you'll do all the cooking and cleaning here, and you'll help James in the fields besides?"

I nodded. I would have promised her anything to get leave to stay. If it got too harsh around the place for me, then I could take my time and find somewhere else to light, but for now I needed to stay.

She gave no sign of yea or nay, and she was still watching me through narrowed eyes, maybe trying to satisfy herself that she was getting the best end of the deal. "Would you want paying?"

I hesitated. This was the part that had to be got over, before I could be sure of my place. "I would. That's only right, for as I have said, I will work as hard as a man for my keep."

James Melton looked away from the fire then. "We must give her wages if her work is satisfactory. I'll not have it said that I did otherwise."

"I need the money to pay the doctor for my care. Just enough for that. But I don't eat overmuch, and I'm not particular about where I bed down, long as it ain't out in the cold."

A look passed between them, for however separate the ways of man and wife, they can still speak without words before outsiders. Ann glanced back at me, and shrugged. "If she works in the house and the fields, all summer long, mind you, I reckon we could pay her something, so she can buy her medicine."

James Melton nodded mournfully. "Doctors ain't cheap."

"But remember we are giving her room and board besides."

"Well, if I have somebody to help with the chores and the farming, I'll be able to do some more shoemaking and wagon building. That will bring in a little money, and that's worth something."

I looked hopefully at James Melton, trying to keep my face a blank, so as not to push him into reconsidering. If I looked at all pleased, he might doubt that he was getting the best end of the deal.

"I think we could run to ten or eleven cents a day," he said at last. "Would that suit?"

I stared at the floor, thinking of working from sun-up until dark for a penny an hour. Why, I could make more than that in an hour with soldiers and drovers, but the armies were gone and drovers were scarce in winter. Beggars cannot be choosers, and beggar I was. But I could see that they didn't have much to spare. Times were hard for everybody in this winter after the War, and I saw that he meant to be kind. There were plenty of people who would have expected more from me and offered less. And to me working for paltry wages was cheaper than having to pay lip service with gratitude for my keep.

"Thankee. It will do me just fine," I said, summoning up a smile.

# PAULINE FOSTER

## *Early March 1866*

If you ever take a notion to hire yourself out as a maid of all work, I advise you not to go hat in hand to any relatives you may have, for your kinfolks will treat you worse than ten strangers ever would, and they'll think themselves charitable while they are doing it.

I settled in to the household, peculiar as it was, and I suppose it might have been worse. Since I did the cooking and the washing up, there was no question of begrudging me food. I ate same as they did. And they didn't expect me to sleep in the barn, though when the weather turned warm, it crossed my mind a time or two.

That first night we sat up by the fire for another hour or so, not saying much, and finally when Ann began to yawn, I said, "Where do you want me to sleep?"

"With me, I reckon," she said, pushing her stool back from the fire.

I looked over at the two narrow beds, set a few feet apart, for I had been hoping to have one to myself. I glanced over at James Melton, who was sitting at the pine table, with his shoemaker's tools in front of him, and he was crafting the leather sole of a lady's slipper. "But what about him?"

"One bed is his'n and one's mine," said Ann. "You can take your pick I reckon."

So man and wife didn't sleep together. Well, that was interesting. But I didn't want him no more than she did, and it was no part of the work I had bargained for, so I said, "I'd as lief share with you, cousin."

"That will do—but not every night." She gave me a little cat-in-the-cream-jug smile, and added, "Some nights I might have company."

I had judged right about Ann's attitude toward work—which was that she never did any if she could avoid it, and mostly she could. Every morning at daybreak I dragged myself out from under the pile of quilts, taking no care at all to be quiet about it, but that lump under the covers next to me might as well've been a log for all it ever moved at that hour.

A while later, once I had built the fire back up from embers, when the milk gravy was hot in the skillet, the biscuits were near done, and the scrawny winter apples from the storeroom were stewing back to sweet plumpness in hot water, why then, with many a yawn and groan, Miss Ann would hoist herself out from her warm burrow, and throw on her day clothes in time to be the first one at the table. By then James would have brought in more wood, and most days he'd fetch me a pail of water for cooking while he was outside, so the both of us had done an hour's work before the tip of Ann's perfect nose ever poked out from under the covers. The way I saw it, part of my eleven cents a day was wages to keep my opinions to myself about such as this, but I couldn't help thinking that I was here in the first place because I was sick, and I minded having to work so hard in the shadow of a spoilt little poppet, who couldn't even spare a thank you for them that kept her fed and warm. If I ever meet another woman as handsome as Ann Melton, I mean to ask her: *"Do you think you can treat everyone in the world as your servant, just on account of your fine face?"* I really would like to know what goes on in the scullery behind such a splendid countenance.

Her husband never acted like he minded her idleness, though. He must have thought it the most natural thing in the world for me to go out to milk the cows and slop the hogs, and empty the chamber pots, and scour the pans, while she sat there at the table, picking at her food, or chattering away at me as I went past with my mop and pail.

Since it was still bleak winter when I started working, there was little enough to do beyond the household chores, and once I got the cabin scrubbed and tidied, I could put it to rights in an hour or so, if I put my mind to it. There was sewing to be done, for Ann could never be bothered to mend her own clothes, much less those of her husband, but I could do that chore by firelight after supper, and, even then, no more clothes than they had, I soon had that done as well.

After a couple of days, Ann got used to me about the place, and she wasn't particular enough about housekeeping or cooking to find much fault with the way I did things, so we got along tolerably well. She would never be a woman's woman, but it pleased her to have someone to talk to, although she cared little enough to hear anything back from me. Mostly, I think, she just wanted to think out loud, and I was the excuse for it. Some people like the society of people who work for them, so that they can have their own way all the time, and so that there'll be no backchat or fault-finding, whatever they care to say. I figured that being Ann's devoted companion was just another chore, and I did it, same as I did the rest.

I did not think about whether Ann Melton was happy. To my mind, she had more than most women in this world ever get: beauty, a meek and uncomplaining husband, a home of her own, and little enough asked of her in return. It seemed enough to me, for I had never had any of those things.

A few days after I settled in, though, when the sky had cleared to a watery blue, and the wind died down a notch, I saw my cousin Ann as if she were somebody else altogether. I was outside, about to wring the neck of a chicken for our dinner, when Ann strode into the hen yard, all cloaked and bonneted as if she meant to be outdoors for more than her usual run to the privy.

"James is doing a spell of shoe-making now, so he can tend the fire. We could go off visiting this afternoon, since the weather broke."

I wondered who she aimed to call on, since nary a soul had come to the cabin in all the days I had been there, but before I could ask who she intended to grace with her presence, she froze in her tracks, looking past me, and her whole face lit up like firelight.

She was taking no more notice of me at all, so I turned to see what had left her dumbstruck, thinking maybe she had caught sight of a rainbow up over the hills. I was still looking for that rainbow a few seconds later, when it finally hit me that the wonder she had beheld wasn't nothing but a scrawny dark-haired fellow in an old brown coat coming toward us out of the pine woods.

In a couple of heartbeats she had collected her wits about her again, and I don't believe the young man even noticed it, but I never forgot that look, for it set me to wishing that I could want anything in this world as bad as my cousin Ann must have wanted this blue-eyed boy.

As he got closer I could see that he was handsome enough, about the same age as we were, and he wasn't lame or missing an arm, or missing an eye. The War had been over for a year now, and them that was coming home had already made it back, but the fighting had left its mark on most of them one way or another. If this boy had been in the War, he looked as if the last four years had touched him but lightly, and I wondered how that could be, for I did not think he had the makings of an officer. Nothing about his clothes or his countenance made me think he came from the gentry. I had known officers in my time, and there was an air of command about them that this fellow didn't have.

There wasn't much meat on him, but that was true of everybody in these lean times, and in his case it just sharpened his cheekbones, and made him look taller than he was. I glanced past him at the clabbered sky above the pine woods. Today, his eyes truly were bluer than the sky. He was nice enough to look at, I'll give him that, but I didn't see anything about him that should set a woman's face alight, the way Ann's did when she caught sight of him. He wasn't a rich man, if his boots and hands were anything to go by. He looked like an ordinary dirt farmer, fortunate in his looks at twenty, but another decade or so of drink and hard work would put paid to that, as it would to Ann's. I told myself that there is some satisfaction in having less to lose.

Before he got within a civil speaking distance of us, Ann had pushed past me, and run out of the hen yard, flinging herself in his arms, and calling out, "Tom!"

*So that's the way of it,* I thought, following her out.

He held her close for a minute, before he caught sight of me, and then he let her go, still watching me warily, the way a stray dog does, to see if you are going to shy rocks at him. We neither one of us smiled. I don't like anybody unless they give me a reason to, which mostly they don't. Maybe he was the same.

After a minute or two of stroking his cheek with her hand and ruffling his hair, she grabbed his hand and led him back to where I was standing. "This here's my cousin Pauline," she told him. "She has come to work on the farm a spell while she's getting treated by Dr. Carter."

He nodded at me, but didn't smile, so for spite I said, "Would you be Ann's brother, sir?"

They smiled at one another then, but they could not fault me for asking, for Ann did have a brother named Tom, but I'll bet she was never half so glad to see him as she was to see this fellow.

Ann said, "He's Tom Dula, Pauline. Lives with his mama 'bout a mile from my mama's place on Reedy Branch."

"You have the look of a soldier," I said, not because it was true, but because men seemed to take that as a compliment.

He nodded. "Well, the 42nd North Carolina tried hard enough to make me one."

Ann had linked arms with him, and she was leaning against him now, looking as proud as if he had won the War all by himself, instead of losing it in company with a hundred thousand other ragged souls.

"Tom was at Petersburg, and Cold Harbor," she said.

"I went in as a company drummer, but by the end of it, the army needed fighters more than drummers."

Ann hugged him closer to her. "And he got took prisoner at Kinston near the end, and finished up in a prison camp up in Maryland. Took him nigh on two months to make it home, and with me out here watching the road for him every day and worrying if he was safe, until my tears turned the dust on my cheeks to mud."

Tom Dula turned to look at the empty road, and it was a moment or two before he spoke again. "I was lucky, I reckon. I lived through the Yankee prison camp, and I finally did get home. That's more than John and Leny did."

Ann nodded. "Strange to think of it that way, Tom. Them being dead and gone. And you were the youngest. I know your mother was near as thankful to have you back as I was."

I just kept looking at the pair of them, neither one seeming to remember that I was standing right beside them. I kept quiet, because there wasn't much I could think of to say, except to congratulate this fellow for outliving his brothers, which didn't seem fitten. Besides, I was more interested in how the land lay between him and Cousin Ann, for I had not seen her sparkle with warmth or joy at all until this Rebel boy walked out of the woods.

"How long have you been back?" I said, thinking he must have arrived yesterday, from the way Ann was carrying on.

"It'll be a year midsummer," said Ann, but her smile faded as she looked at me, for my speaking up had reminded her that I was watching them. She narrowed her eyes, and said, "Well, this standing around isn't getting your chores done, Pauline. When you see to that hen, there's washing to be done." She looked up at Tom. "James is in the house, cobbling right now. Let's you and I go talk in the barn where it's warmer."

I went back into the hen yard, watching them hurry, arm in arm, toward the barn, and I was thinking, "It'll be warm enough wherever the two of you fetch up." But it was all the same to me who Ann chose to carry on with. I couldn't see anything special about this boy, worth making such a fuss over. But a minute or two later, as I wrung that chicken's neck, I found myself thinking of the two of them entwined together in the hayloft, and, when the wind eased up a bit, I fancied I could hear laughter and soft voices.

We finally did get around to visiting the neighbors. The early March weather was still harsh, but it was a fallow time for farms, and people were naturally tired of having been cooped up all winter. They began to host get-togethers at one house or another through the rest of the winter. These occasions weren't fancy parties: just a couple of old fellows sawing away on a homemade fiddle or a mandolin, while jugs of corn liquor, clear as water, passed from hand to hand, to fuel the talking. There was dancing, too, but not enough young men to make much of a go of it. People wore their ordinary everyday clothes: there were no fancy ball gowns or silk cravats to be seen at a Happy Valley party. Why, even the soldiers' uniforms I'd seen at a dance or two back during the War had been more elegant than this, and the gaiety seemed a notch below the soldiers' merry-making, too, but I understood that. The soldiers were drowning out thoughts of the morrow, knowing that they might be dancing their last reel, or seeing a willing girl for the last time. Such darkness as that had forced them to raucous revelry. The fever pitch was lacking in the festivities of a winter gathering in a world that was now peaceful, but poor—and missing some of those boys who would never come home.

I wore my best calico, which was clean but faded, and had seen me through most of the War. There were some women better turned out than me, but I am twenty and tiny, which counts for much. I did not lack for partners when I cared to dance. Even the fat old ladies and the scrawny war widows were not left wallflowers, for there was no belle of this ball, except my cousin Ann, who was no favorite among her own sex, but by the menfolk she was much desired. I don't say they thought well of her, but they would have taken any favor from her she cared to bestow, and no one seemed to mind James Melton's presence among the watchers.

I did meet the other Tom—Ann's brother, Tom Foster—among the congregation at the dance. This Tom was a gawky, raw-boned boy, a couple of years younger than Ann, and not a patch on her in looks, but then, knowing the reputation of Lotty Foster, their mother, the two of them might have had different fathers to account for the lack of family resemblance.

When the dancing commenced, Tom Dula played the fiddle alongside the mandolin player for a reel or two, which called to my mind that he had been a company musician in the army. He played well enough, I suppose, but not as if he'd practiced or cared much for the skill of it, but only because music-making happened to be a thing that came easily to him. I don't think he ever bothered with anything that didn't come easy. He didn't keep at it long, and he seemed to prefer the moonshine to the merry-making, same as I did. I spent most of the evening within arm's reach of the whiskey jug, and sitting on a bench with a gaggle of older ladies, because I wanted to know more about Cousin Ann, and I judged that not much went on in the settlement that those old cats didn't know about, so I sipped 'shine and listened, and every now and then I would drop a word into the stream of talk, to set the current off in the right direction.

Once, when Ann hauled Tom to his feet and made him partner her in a quadrille, I remarked to no one in particular, "They make a fine pair, do they not? What a shame that Ann did not meet Tom Dula soon enough to make a match of it."

With a short bark of laughter, the white-haired lady beside me said, "Why, they had ample opportunity. Those two have knowed each other all their lives."

"And been sweet on one another near 'bout that long," said Betsy Scott. "Lotty Foster used to tell about the time she caught Tom Dula buck naked in Ann's bed. She said she run him off with a broom."

The two old ladies looked at each other across me, and I could hear them thinking, *"Lotty Foster is a fine one to be upholding chastity,"* for it was common knowledge in the settlement that Lotty herself could be had for the price of a drink. I had been thinking that Ann married young to get away from the sight of that at home, but now I thought I might have been wrong about that.

The ladies were still reminiscing about the long and close acquaintance of Tom Dula and Ann Foster. "When Lotty caught them in bed . . . that would have been before the War, wouldn't it, Betsy? Yes, I thought as much. So Tom he couldn't have been much more than fourteen."

As the talk flowed around me, I watched the two of them, Tom and Ann, laughing, as they clasped hands and skittered down the row of dancers to take their place at the end of the line. Ann's face was alight with the heat of dancing, or perhaps with the joy of being partnered with Tom. I had never seen such a look about her in the vicinity of James Melton.

"Why didn't she marry up with him, then?" I wondered aloud.

Mrs. Scott shook her head. "Marry a boy of fifteen? Why, it was not to be thought of. James Melton had land and a roof over his head. At fifteen Tom Dula had none of that, and lo these seven years later, I am bound to say he still doesn't."

"And never will," said her companion in scandal.

Mrs. Scott nodded. "Like as not. Ann wanted to get shut of her mother's house, with all of those young'uns underfoot. If she had married Tom, she might still be stuck living with her mama—or with his'n, and where's the escape in that?"

The white-haired woman laughed. "Anyhow, I don't reckon Ann Melton would have to marry Tom Dula to get what he's good for. Any woman in these parts can have *that* for the asking. And there have been enough of them ready to ask—including Ann herself, to this day."

I kept staring at the dancers. The fiddlers had taken up another tune, and Tom and Ann, still hand in hand, had set off dancing again. I looked around the room, trying to spot Ann's husband in the crowd, and, by and by, I placed him over in the corner, sitting with the older men who favored drinking over dancing.

I nudged Mrs. Scott, and nodded my head toward James Melton. "He doesn't mind?"

"Does he mind?" Mrs. Scott turned to stare at me, as if I was a mule she was looking to buy. "You'd know that as well as anybody, wouldn't you, Pauline? Aren't you working over to their place these days? How does it strike you?"

I shrugged. "Like he hardly knows what's going on around him," I said. "I got to wondering if he had ever got kicked in the head by a mule."

Betsy Scott laughed. "Better if he had been. He is so far under the spell of your pretty cousin Ann that some folks around here are saying she's a witch."

She got up to fill her cup just then, but I kept turning her question over in my mind. Ann and James Melton. They got along well enough, as married people do—like two yoked mules, obliged to plow the field together. They get along by getting on with the work, and not worrying about what their feelings may be toward one another. But, as far as I could see, that's all there was between them—two yoked people getting on with the work of living. Keeping body and soul together on a scraggly hill farm in the aftermath of that war was enough to keep anybody's mind set on the furrow straight ahead, for neither food nor money was easy to come by these days. I'd have thought no more about it, if I hadn't seen the way Ann looked at Tom—a look that said being cold and starving were trifling matters compared to the fever of wanting him.

All right, then. If she felt that fierce about Tom Dula, why was she still with James Melton at all? It isn't as if James Melton had any money or position to speak of, and Ann had little enough reputation to ruin, so what kept her bound?

There was some sense in her stopping there as long as the War lasted, for Tom was away in the fighting, and where else could she go? But next month would mark a year's time since the War had ended, and Tom had finally got shut of the army, and walked home from that prison camp in Maryland last summer. They had told me all that themselves. And yet, here was Ann, nine months after Tom came home, still being wife to another man, still "Mrs. Melton," to all the world. What kept her there? Those babies might have tied another woman to hearth and home, but I never saw Ann pay any mind to hers.

To see her and Tom together, you'd think that as soon as she saw him walking down the road, she'd have thrown her clothes in a flour sack, and took off after him, no matter what.

The fiddlers swung into a new tune just then, as if they were reading my mind.

*If I had a needle,*
*As fine as I could sew;*
*I'd sew that gal to my coattails,*
*And down the road I'd go.*

I tapped my foot in time to *Shady Grove*, thinking I might get up and dance after another cup or two of whiskey. "Why didn't she go off with Tom when he came back from the War?" I wondered aloud.

"Like as not, she wasn't asked," said Mrs. Scott.

I puzzled over that riddle for a good many days afterward, but I knew the answer would come to me. The Bible says that not a sparrow falls but what the Lord knows about it. In Happy Valley the fate of sparrows might go unremarked, but every human being in the settlement was watched and judged and commented upon on a daily basis, it seemed to me, and not out of Christian concern, either. There was little else to talk about, I reckon. Once you have done with the weather, and who was sick, how the crops were faring, and all the birthing and dying news, then what was left, except to tabulate the sins and follies of your neighbors?

I was a nine days' wonder back when I first arrived. Every old cat in the settlement was itching to find out what business I had in Wilkes County, and, when they learned that I was here to see Dr. Carter, they tried even harder to nose up the reason for it. The first thing that leaps to any old biddy's mind when a single woman turns up in the settlement is: "Is she in the family way?" Though a moment's thought would tell them that pregnancy was hardly a reason to consult a doctor. An unwed girl might well leave her own community to birth her baby elsewhere, but she'd not trouble a doctor to help her do it when there were midwives a-plenty to be had. What would a man doctor know about bringing babies into the world anyhow?

They used every neighborly visit and settlement social as a chance to look me over, but there was no telltale bulge beneath my apron, and the rest of me was as scrawny as ever.

Finally, though I'm sure it pained those gossips to do it, they gave up all hope that I might be a wayward woman saddled with a bastard child. Well, I was a wayward woman, if they but knew, and I wish they had been right in their first guess. I'd rather have paid for my sins with a brat than with the pox. It would be a deal easier to get rid of a babe, for one thing. A dose of pennyroyal tea, or a corset cinched as tight as it will go—and if that fails, you can smother the newborn with a cloth and tell folk that it died in the night. There's plenty that do. I'd fall pregnant a dozen times if it would rid me of this pox.

Is it not a wonder that the human race goes on at all? All men give you is pain and sorrow, and I cannot see why any woman would have aught to do with them. Young girls prate enough about love, but that doesn't seem to last as long as pox, either. I suppose they do it for their keep, for when you are turned out of your mama's house, it is better to go and be someone's wife than to hire out as a servant. And for the rest, the girls who cannot or will not make a match with some fellow, then laying with men is an easy way to get money: selling yourself for a few minutes to some randy young lout, who is foolish enough to waste good drinking money on a roll in the hay. I make eleven cents a day laboring hours in the fields; servicing strangers pays better than that. Anyhow, a girl must live.

Since all that is true, I could not see what it was that Ann wanted with Tom Dula. She had her house and her keep, thanks to that husband of hers, and I reckon Tom Dula wasn't paying her nothing for her favors, for I never saw that he had a penny to bless himself with. He was living at home with his mama, and doing less work than anybody I ever saw, and I don't think he ever figured on doing anything else. The future to him was just going to be a succession of days as similar to one another as glass beads on a string. Ann couldn't go off with Tom, because Tom wasn't studying on going anywhere—*ever.* So I didn't see that she had any call to shine like a candle flame whenever he came in sight. As far as I could tell he was just another poor, no-account ex-Rebel, and if he wasn't bad to look at, time would take care of that soon enough. Maybe my cousin was love-smitten with Tom Dula, but that was one pox I did not get.

"People are talking about Tom and me."

It was near dusk, a few days after the party, and Ann had followed me out to the yard, so she could talk to me while I went on with my chores. The days were getting milder now, as March wore on, but I knew that that only meant there was more work ahead on the farm. I was taking the dry clothes off the line, and setting them in the woven basket to bring in. Those that were not all the way dry yet could hang up by the fireplace. It had been a gray day, always threatening to spit rain, but never quite doing it.

I stopped, holding one of her petticoats in midair. "Talking about the pair of you?" I started to laugh. "I don't reckon they're resorting to telling lies, Cousin Ann. I know what goes on the nights you turn me out of the bed."

A couple of nights a week, Ann would make up a pallet on the floor, and tell me to sleep there. I crawled under the quilts, but I did not sleep. I lay awake there in the dark, listening to the raspy snores of James Melton, alone as always in his bed, and in the dead of night, I'd feel the cold draft from the door as someone came in, walking slow and quiet, trying not to make a sound. Then the soft footfalls would stop on the side of Ann's bed, and I could hear a sigh and a moan, and then the sound of the covers being drawn back, and the soft thump of boots hitting the floor.

The first time it happened, I lay there real still, wondering if somebody had come to cut our throats in the night—the War had not been over long enough for such fears as that to subside. But before a minute had passed, I heard a sigh and a giggle, and an answering grunt, and then the rustling of the bed covers, and I knew what was going on in the bed. Ann had banished me to a pallet on the floor, because she knew that Tom Dula would be paying her a visit.

I raised up a little, trying to peer through the darkness over at that other bed—the one where James Melton lay asleep. If Tom coming in had woke me up, how did he sleep through it? Did he really hear nothing in the bed a broom's length from his, or did he not care what Ann did? I shook my head in the darkness. If he had been seventy, there might have been some sense to it, but James Melton hadn't reached thirty yet. I puzzled over it a few minutes more, until the weariness of the day's work pulled me under again, and when I woke up at cock crow, Ann was sleeping peacefully in her bed alone.

Now here she was, standing there red-cheeked and shivering in the yard, telling me that folk were beginning to talk about her and Tom Dula. So help me, I laughed in her face.

She got all squinty-eyed at me then, and her mouth cinched up. "You are forgetting yourself, Pauline," she said, spitting out the words. She wobbled a little where she stood, and I could smell the whiskey on her breath. We had both had a drop or two of likker to keep out the cold that afternoon, and to make the hours pass quicker. "We are letting you stay here so you can keep going to the doctor. I'll thank you not to laugh at me."

I shrugged. "I ain't said nothing to nobody. Folk can't help seeing what's put right in front of their noses." *Excepting, maybe, your husband*, I thought. But I didn't want her to turn me out in the cold, and I was not drunk enough to speak my mind, so I said, all sweetness and sympathy, "I reckon what you feel for Tom just shines through, and you can't help people noticing it."

She shook her head. "It ain't that. People have been remarking on how much he comes by here."

I couldn't see what she was het up about. The people in Happy Valley said worse things about her than that. I hadn't been here a month, and already I'd heard sneering whispers about Ann selling her favors to the passing cattle drovers, for a pint of spirits or a likely bit of cloth. And I didn't see why she should care what people around here thought of her, anyhow. Ann Foster Melton was no fine lady with a reputation to protect. Her mother was the next thing to a harlot, and, if that drover story was true, the apple had not fallen far from the tree. But Ann was a beauty, and she already had her a husband, so what could she lose if they blackened her name? What could they take away from her? Hurt her feelings? I never cared what people said behind my back, and I couldn't see why she should, either.

I went back to taking James Melton's drawers off the line, moving slow and careful so as not to drop the clean clothes in the mud, for my head was spinning a little from the whiskey. "Well, it is true, Ann. So let them talk."

"No." She shook her head in that slow, deliberate way that folk do when they're drunk. "Let them think he comes here for another reason."

"Like what?"

She stepped back and looked at me, the way you'd size up a calf at market. "You're a spinster, Pauline. I reckon he could come courting you."

"Well, you can put that lie about, for all I care," I said. "I won't dispute it, if Tom was to say it's so."

"Tom is no good at telling lies. He's too lazy to remember them. So it has to be true. I need you to sleep with Tom."

# PAULINE FOSTER
## Mid-March 1866

✦⟶══○══⟵✦

All I know about love comes from watching them that is afflicted by it, but what Ann was asking of me did not square with what I'd seen of that ailment before now. I finished taking the clothes off the line, stuffed them in the basket, and headed for the barn, out of the rain-speckled wind, and out of earshot of James Melton, on the off chance that he would mind about any of this.

Ann followed me in, and sat herself down on a hay bale, patting it for me to sit down beside her.

"You are a-wanting me to bed down with Tom Dula," I said, saying each word as slow as a Bible oath, and watching her face while I said it.

She looked away from me, shrugging a little, and she pulled a blade of straw out of the hay bale and began to twist it in her fingers. "People are talking," she said, so soft that I could barely hear her.

"Those that aren't deaf and blind, you mean. The way you two carry on, it's a wonder the whole world hasn't heard the tales about the pair of you."

Ann giggled, and looked back at me, blinking real slow, and I wondered if she was going to throw up or pass out, but she took a few gulps of cold air, and seemed to steady herself. "I never could hide my feelings, Pauline."

"Well, people may talk, but that won't kill you. Why do you care? I ain't heard your husband complaining."

Ann shrugged. "He don't care. But if people keep talking, he might."

I said again. "You're a-wanting me to do it with Tom?"

She nodded.

I laughed. "You're drunker than I thought, then, Cousin. I thought you loved Tom Dula. Not that I can see why."

She nodded again.

I stared at her, trying to see what the angle was in all this. I was ready to believe that love was only a fairy tale, like saying that the stork brought babies or that there was gold at the end of a rainbow, but Ann's eyes glittered with unshed tears. She looked sorrowful enough to be suffering from something, and I couldn't make sense of it. "You don't talk like any lovestruck body that I ever heard tell of," I told her. "Most women would scratch my eyes out if I was to lay with their man. So how come you're so ready to foist him off on me? Like you're throwing him away."

Ann reached for another wisp of hay, not looking back at me. Her dark hair had come loose from its bindings, and it curtained off her face to where I couldn't see her expression, but her voice was steady when she finally answered me. "Sex ain't nothing. If you're thirsty, it don't matter which cup you drink out of, does it? What Tom does in the hay, that don't change what we have, or what we are to one another. He loved me afore he went to war, and he came back loving me. He will always love me, no matter what. Nothing he does with you will change that. He'll never quit me."

None of that made a lick of sense to me. As far as I could tell, once a man bedded a new woman, he abandoned the old one. As often as men went looking for a new woman on their own, I thought it was foolish of her to encourage it. I could see her wanting to get rid of him, because he had no prospects and I didn't see what use he was to her, anyhow, but if she did still want him, then she ought to be worried about losing him to the next girl in the straw. I wasn't a believer in true love, but I'd take my oath that anger and envy were real enough. I had felt those things firsthand. If I did as she asked, then sooner or later jealousy would take hold of her, and I didn't want to lose my place here when she thought better of what she wanted me to do.

I pretended to think it over. "How do you know Tom is willing?"

She laughed. "Oh, Tom don't care. He'll do anything I ask him to do. And bedding some woman is about as pleasant a chore as he could think of, especially if you get him likkered up first. You aren't bad to look at, Pauline. You're skin and bones, but he'll be happy to oblige you all the same."

"He won't be doing me no favor," I told her, and it made me sore that she might think so. "I don't feel a thing for Mr. Tom Dula. I can't see nothing special about him at all. But if you want him serviced, I'll do it. Same as I milk the cow and slop the hogs. It's all one to me."

"Good. It's better if you don't like it too much."

"But how is that supposed to keep folks from suspecting you and Tom?"

"Oh, he'll brag about it afterward. Men always do. Word will get around, but I don't reckon you care about that. I reckon you had your share of soldiers back up the mountain."

"Not 'cause I liked it overmuch," I said.

"But you'll do it?"

I shrugged. "As long as you don't regret it afterward and turn me out."

"No. It has to be done." She peered up at me, turning things over in her mind, and then she said. "I don't expect you to do it for nothing. There's a jug of whiskey in it for you."

"Good," I said. "I'll drink half of it first."

I was still puzzling, though, over how she could bear to see him go off with another woman, if she loved him as much as she said she did. Now that her being with Tom was no secret from me, one night as I peeled potatoes for supper, I felt emboldened to ask her how it came about—her and Tom.

Ann smiled. "I can't remember a time when he wasn't there. The Dulas didn't live any distance at all from my mama's place, and we used to meet up—him and his brothers and some of us Fosters, and we'd all play Indian in the woods. He was a tough little boy, young as he was. He never cried or ran from anything.

"I remember one time this little dog of his had got to chasing a rabbit, and it went down a hole near the edge of the creek. I guess it got trapped in there, because we could hear it whimpering, but it wouldn't come back out. That hole was so deep we couldn't even see the pup, and I was crying thinking it would be dead for sure. It might have been a snake hole, even. When we knelt on the bank and looked down in it, we could see some broken tree roots, but the pup must have been eight feet down or more.

"Well, Tom told me to hush, and he dropped down on his knees beside that muddy hole in the creek bank, and listened for a minute. I was about to tell him that I'd run get his daddy and brothers to bring axes to help him widen the hole, but before I could say a word, Tom shot forward headfirst into that hole, shinnying down it until I couldn't even see his feet anymore, and then I started to cry even louder. But a couple of minutes later, that dog clambered out of the hole, caked in red mud. And I looked down to see if Tom was following him, but the dog had made such a stir getting out that the hole was caving in. I started digging with my bare hands, and down at the bottom Tom was digging upward, and after what seemed like an hour, I saw his muddy hand clawing up through the dirt. I grabbed him and kept pulling until he was free. He looked like a gingerbread man, all caked with mud like he was, but he didn't care. He kept saying, 'I saved my dog. Done it all by myself.'"

Ann smiled, remembering that day on the creek bank. "He never did thank *me* for saving *him*, but I never forgot what happened. Tom loved that little no-account dog, and he was bound and determined to save it, no matter what. I knew then that if Tom Dula loved you, he'd do anything in the world for you."

As long as it didn't take too long, I thought, setting the paring knife at another potato skin. Tom Dula was lazy. I never saw him do a lick of work if he could help it. I thought that if Tom was to like you enough, then he might do some brave, quick thing—like risking his own skin to pull you out of a hole, or snatch you out of a burning house. Yes, he might do that. He was brave enough. But if that dog had been stuck in the hole for, say, a month, and Tom'd had to bring it food and water every single day without fail—why, I reckon that dog wouldn't have lasted a week. He had a quick kind of courage, but not the slow, steady kind that would last you a lifetime.

I dropped another potato skin in the pail for the hogs. "So that's when you set your heart on Tom, then?"

Ann shook her head. "He wasn't more than eight when that happened. He was just one of the gaggle of young'uns to me for the longest time, and then one day—he wasn't. I don't know how he came to look different to me after all that time, but we had a long snowbound winter when I was fourteen, and I didn't see him for a month or more, and then, come spring, when he turned up again, I just looked at him coming through the field, and I thought, *There you are.* Not like you'd think that about some neighbor who happened to drop by, but a stranger feeling, as if you had been looking all your life for a lost treasure, and suddenly you had stumbled upon it. I found him then, and I knew we were meant for one another.

"He knew it, too." She laughed. "We just came together like a compass needle points to north. I don't even think we said much. Tom ain't one for talking overmuch anyhow, but his eyes were so deep and blue when he looked at me, I liked to drown in them."

"You started young," I said, for I knew that Tom was a year younger than Ann, so he'd have been thirteen.

She laughed. "I showed him how. He weren't my first. But being with him was like nothing else for me before or since. Oh, we were in rut that spring, him and me, worse than the rabbits. We'd sneak off together every chance we got. Mama even caught us one time in her bed, and she run Tom off with a broom, and then laid into me with a razor strap. We kept to the woods thereafter, Tom and me. Oh, that was a fine summer."

I understood the words to what she was saying, but not the tune. Never in my life had I felt much of anything for anybody. For me one person was the same as all the rest, and all of them let you down sooner or later. Trusting people was just asking for trouble. I tried to figure out what folk wanted, and I'd give it to them, as long as it got me what I needed, but I never put any feelings into it. It was just a way to get along in this world. Whenever I heard somebody talk about this deep feeling they had for someone they said they loved, I thought I must be missing something, but I didn't know what it was. It never seemed to profit them that had it, though, so I reckoned I was better off without. And maybe they were only fooling themselves, anyhow, for I couldn't see that love made any difference in how they acted—not in the long run.

"But even though you are saying how much you loved Tom, you went and married James Melton," I said to Ann. "Right soon after that rutting spring, and well before Tom went off to war. You were fifteen when you wed, didn't you tell me?"

She nodded. "It didn't change anything, though. Tom knew that. I reckon James Melton knew it, too. But he would hang around me, looking like a starving dog in a smokehouse, wanting me so bad he could taste it. And I said no a time or two, but then I got to thinking about it. What else was there? James had a little land and a house of his own, and he made some money by being a cobbler and wagon-making. He works hard, and he's good at making things, I'll give him that. Tom never had anything, and I couldn't see that he ever would. Tom doesn't care to work, and he never seems to want much. If his belly is full, he is happy to pass the time doing whatever he takes a notion to, be it fishing or fiddling, or just walking in the woods. That's fine for a lone boy, I reckon, but it's no way to keep a wife. So I figured to marry James, so that I'd have a home, and mayhap if James was to die, why, then I could marry Tom, and he could live there on the farm with me. He'd never make a farmer, but I could take care of him, anyhow. That mama of his won't live forever."

"I guess you didn't figure on the War coming."

"No." She sighed. "That liked to kill me."

"Tom going off to fight, and James staying home?" I said.

"Well, no. It wasn't like that. James joined up in the summer of '61, long before he had to. Tom didn't go till the following spring, when they were making the men go to fight. I don't reckon he wanted to go. But James did. So I had most of nine months here with Tom still at home and James gone. They were in different regiments, too, so I did all my waiting and worrying twice over. Well, thrice, I reckon. My brother Pinkney fought, too. He and James were both in the 26th North Carolina. Most of what I know about James's time in the army came from him."

"I didn't even know your husband was in the War." It didn't square somehow with that quiet shadow of a man I'd known nigh on a month now.

"He don't talk about the War. He's not the same since he came back. He just works and keeps to himself. He was lucky to come back at all, Pink says."

"Why?"

"Well, he was all right for the first two years, but then the 26th fought at Gettysburg, and James was wounded—left shoulder and right leg. He still limps a little. You might'a seen that."

I nodded. "He got shot at Gettysburg?"

"Yes. It's no wonder. Pink says James volunteered to carry the regimental colors into battle. So everybody else is shooting bullets, and he's carrying a damn flag. Of course he got shot. Never a thought for me. What was I supposed to do if he got himself killed?"

"Marry Tom, I reckon. Maybe he thought he would be doing you a favor if he got killed in the War."

"But what if Tom had got killed, too? Then where would I be? I used to ask myself sometimes, if only one of them was to come back, which one would I want it to be?"

Anybody with any sense would have picked James Melton in an instant, but that bundle of twigs and feathers and scraps of bright cloth that passed for Ann Melton's mind probably thought otherwise. "And you were hoping for Tom?"

She nodded. "Tom and me—we've been together all our lives. We loved each other as children."

I laughed. "I would have thought you'd had enough of him."

"Well, that was before I married up with James. I'm not sorry about it, though. I knew I couldn't be marrying up with Tom. It would have been a waste not to lay with the one person in the world I truly did love. I'm glad we did. I hadn't any business to marry James, I reckon, but he had land and a trade, and I needed so bad to get away from home. I couldn't stand it another day—mama with her likker and her endless stream of men, and another baby every year. So I let James take me away, because he so much wanted to. I reckon he's sorry now."

That was exactly what I was thinking, but I took care not to show it. "He seems like a good man, though. You didn't love him a bit?"

"Of course I do. He's kind and he works hard, and he was wonderful brave in the War. I wish I could be like him, Pauline, but I'm not. I could never be that steady and good. I'm just like Tom. Good-looking and lazy, but passionate, too, to those we truly love—to each other—and able to laugh and have fun, instead of thinking all the time about working and saving up some money. We're just the same, Tom and me. We come from the same place, and we're made of the same clay. And maybe the devil spit in it before God made us, but at least we belong together, him and me."

"It seems hard lines on your husband, you feeling like that."

"I love them both, Pauline, but not in the same way. My love for James is like that field out there that he spends half his time plowing and sowing and weeding, and all. It will change. The crops die in the winter, or dry up in a summer drought, or the soil gives out, so that you must let it lie fallow for a time and let the weeds take it. It comes and goes, that field. But Tom . . . Tom is like that green mountain you can see rising there in the west, holding up the sky. It never changes. It will be just the same forever."

"Well, you're not the same, are you? You up and married somebody else the first chance you got."

"That didn't change anything! If I had married Tom, where would it have got us? Starving in a ditch somewhere? I thought maybe if I married a man with land and prospects, then I could do something for Tom. Maybe we could help him get a place of him own, or maybe James could hire him on to help build the wagons."

"Even I know Tom Dula better than *that.*"

"Well, it's true. He isn't interested in taking up a trade. I misjudged how much I could push him into doing something. But I'll not forsake him, whatever he comes to be. If this whole state had been laid waste by fire and cannons, and Tom had lived on, then I'd be content to keep going. But if not a single foot of Carolina soil had been touched in the War, but Tom had died in battle, then this world would be a desert to me, and I'd quit it as quick as I could."

I shook my head, for none of it made a bit of sense to me. "Well, you were luckier than most women. Luckier than you deserved to be. Both your men went to war, and both of them came back."

"A thousand times I wished the War had made my choice for me. In a way, though, Tom's going off to fight helped me live through it.

I didn't mind when we had to drink chicory instead of coffee, and do without meat 'cause bushwhackers stole all our chickens, because I knew that, wherever he was, Tom was going hungry, too, and it made me feel closer to him."

From the sound of it, James Melton had suffered a deal more than Tom had, but he wasn't the sort of man who lets on about his troubles or his sorrows, so I guess Ann never knew or cared what he went through. I wondered about it, but there was no use trying to explain any of that to Ann. Instead I told her, "There was a woman up home in the Globe that dressed up like a boy and followed her man off to war. You ever think of that?"

"I heard about her. She and her man were in the same regiment as James and my brother. But I don't reckon I could pass for a boy, do you?" Ann smiled and touched her breasts. "Anyhow, if I had gone, Tom would have ended up having to look out for me, and so I'd have been a danger to him. It was better for me to wait here. I never had no word from him, of course. Even if he could write, I couldn't read a letter. But all the same, if he had died, I would have known. The instant it happened, I would have known."

"So now he is back. What happens now?"

"I don't know," said Ann. "Whatever he wants to happen, I reckon."

There was one person in Wilkes County who could keep a secret, apparently. Dr. George Carter wasn't bruiting it about that his patient Pauline Foster had the pox. *Sy-phi-lis*, he called it, when he spoke to me about it, but he didn't talk about it to nobody else. Or if he did, it didn't reach the ears of the ordinary folk in the settlement, for Dr. Carter did not associate with the likes of them. He went to elegant parties with the quality folk, up at Colonel Isbell's fine house, drinking wine out of crystal goblets, and dancing on polished oak floors under a crystal chandelier. I had never seen the inside of such a place, but some of the women had been inside the Isbells' house on some errand or other, and they never tired of singing its praises.

Maybe I didn't matter enough for him to talk about.

Whatever the reason, the real story of Pauline Foster's shameful ailment did not get threshed out in the gossip mills of Happy Valley. They figured me for consumption, I think, as pale and scrawny as I was, and I never told them any different.

There are some that would say that I should have told Ann what my illness really was. When she bade me to lay with her lover Tom Dula, I might have spoke up then, and told her that I had the pox, and that if she threw us together, she was condemning Tom and a raft of other people—including herself—to share my affliction. I'll bet she would have thought twice about her plan then. But I never gave her the chance to reconsider—and why should I? If you ask me, Ann Melton was already blessed enough in this world. She had the sort of beauty that made men tongue-tied to look at her—worse than that, they thought she had the look of a fine lady. "An *aristocratic beauty*." Her that would lay with a drover for a sack of coffee beans. And she had a house and a husband, and two men that loved her.

What did I ever have? What did this world ever give me, except pain, and hunger, hard work, and finally a deadly affliction, that would carry me off, like as not, afore I ever saw thirty. And sick as I was, I washed Ann Melton's drawers after she had been with her lover; and I cooked her food, and scrubbed her floor, and emptied the slop jars every morning. What charity did I owe her? It seemed to me that she had been given too much already. And perhaps it was up to me to even the score a little, for all the plain, unloved women who must trudge through life in bone-weary misery. Pretty, selfish, stupid Ann had it coming, for she never gave a thought to anyone's needs but her own. And if Tom Dula was brought low in my trap to ensnare Ann, that was too bad. Back during the War I had seen enough of soldiers to know that they showed little enough mercy to others, and I was satisfied to pay one back in kind when I could.

I was as good as my word—that time, anyhow. One evening that week as we drowsed by the fire, after a supper of salt-crock beans and corn bread, I managed to put away half a jug of that clear-as-water whiskey they made in copper stills in these parts. By the time Ann got to yawning, and James Melton, bone-weary from a day of wagon-building, stumbled off to bed, I was swimmy-headed and beginning to nod off myself.

Ann poked me in the ribs. "Stay awake, Pauline! Tom is coming by any time now."

The drink had loosened my tongue. "Do I get the bed tonight then?" I asked, grinning up at her.

Her face clouded over, and she raised her hand to slap me, but seeing the look on my face, she let it fall again. "You asked for this," I said.

"Don't mean I want to watch it happen, though. Take him along to the barn loft."

The fire had burned low, and I had been listening to James Melton's snores for a good while when the door opened on a gust of cold wind, and a shadow fell over the threshold. I glanced over at Ann's bed, but she was buried deep under the pile of quilts, as still as a hollow log.

I'd bet she wasn't asleep, though. For all that she insisted on this being done, I knew she minded about it. —*Good*.

I stood up, and wrapped a thick wool shawl around my shoulders, waiting to see if Tom was going to come over to me, but he just stood there in the open doorway. He glanced over at Ann's bed for a long moment, and then back over at me, jerked his head like he expected me to follow him. Then he backed out, and let the door close softly behind him.

I got up, a little wobbly on my feet, and went out into the yard. The night air was a little milder now that we were well in to March, but there was still enough of a chill to shake the whiskey glow off me. The moon shone like a gold locket through the branches of the white oak tree, and the black shape of the barn loomed before me.

I shivered a little from the wind, but I wasn't scared. What we was fixing to do—why, I had done it a hundred times before, and Tom Dula didn't look like the best or the worst of them. I didn't feel much of anything. Good or bad, I didn't figure it would last long, and it wouldn't mean any more to either of us than partnering for a reel at a settlement dance. Less, in fact, for there'd be no one watching us.

I could see him standing just inside the barn, leaning against the wall, and watching me, with a funny half-smile on his face. I wondered if he was happy about getting a roll in the hay, or if it pleased him that I didn't want to. Some men are like that. I didn't know what Tom Dula was like, behind that handsome face and the easy smile.

He tried to take my arm, but I shook him off. "Let's get this over with."

·  ·  ·

He held the ladder while I climbed up into the hayloft, but I didn't bother to thank him for it. If I was to fall and break my neck, it would have done him out of his fun, that was all. He didn't kiss me, but I could still smell the whiskey on his breath, and I knew that he had been making a night of it somewhere else, before he ever came here. Not a word passed between us. Tom didn't talk much anyhow, and I didn't care to make things any more pleasant for him than I had to, so I just hitched up my skirts and lay back in the straw and let him get on with it, hoping the whiskey in my belly would keep me from minding too much.

I spent the few minutes it took him to get done with it wondering what Ann Melton saw in Tom Dula that I never did. Well, I've had worse. He wasn't old or fat or toothless, but the others had given me something for my trouble—a few coins or a drop of whiskey. I reckon he thought he was doing me a favor, being as young and likely-looking as he was. I didn't get nothing at all from Tom Dula that night, not even so much as a kind word or a thank you. But I smiled and hugged myself in the cold darkness of that hayloft, knowing that I sure as hell gave *him* something that night.

I am trying to think back on when I first encountered my other cousin, Laura Foster, but it's not the kind of thing I'd be likely to re-member. Laura Foster wasn't the sort of girl who sticks in your mind. Had I met her once when we were children, long before the War? Maybe. I remember Ann from those days, running around like a wild Indian, with her black hair flying loose and not a stitch on under her dress, but if one of that horde of barefoot young'uns had been six-year-old Cousin Laura, it had slipped from my memory. I think of her now in the faded colors of early fall, when the green leaves are going yellowish and the fields of goldenrod fade to a muddy brown. That was Laura Foster . . . small and sallow-skinned, with broom-sedge hair and witch-hazel eyes, so quiet and colorless that if you blinked she might disappear.

She was old Wilson Foster's oldest girl. We were kin somehow or other, but since I was not a legal child, I never bothered to learn the rights of it. Her daddy tenant-farmed over at German's Hill, maybe five miles from the Meltons' and the Dulas' farms. Laura's mother took sick and died sometime before the War ended, leaving Laura to look after her three brothers and a baby sister. Well, they didn't any of them starve to death or die of cholera, and that's the best that can be said of the care she took of them. Mostly, she went her own way, same as Ann did, except that Ann married young to get out of having to tend to her mama's brood, while Laura went on living at home in German's Hill, likely because there was no other place for her to go.

She and Ann, both cousins to me, were chalk and cheese. Where Laura whispered and wavered, Ann carried herself like the Queen of Sheba—all fire and rolling thunder. She burned you where you stood with her bright beauty of tumbling black hair and dark, flashing eyes. By being more alive than anybody else, she squeezed your heart until you never forgot her for an instant. I didn't say you would love her, though I reckon there was more than one man that did. Wanted her, anyhow. But no woman I ever knew could stand her. She made no pretense of caring a fig for anybody but herself, not even troubling to ask after anybody's health or family, and when an older woman tried to converse with her, she was bored and she showed it, tapping her foot or gazing about the room, looking for some man to charm or something better to do than be talked at. The women all knew her reputation, too. None of them liked Ann enough to protect her from the scandalmongers, who were only telling the truth, after all. A woman who makes free with any man she pleases has no friends among her own sex, but Ann never cared about that, either. Tom Dula was all the society she ever wanted, and the rest of us she barely tolerated, if she noticed us at all.

I had no more use for the settlement's old biddies than Ann did, but I took care to keep in with them, because it seemed foolish to make enemies when you didn't have to. Those respectable old women might be useful one day, though I never tried to make Ann see that. You couldn't reason with Ann.

She was like pokeberries, Ann was—bright and tempting to look at, but pure poison through and through. I suppose jealousy was part of the reason women hated her so much, but then Ann never took the trouble to make anybody like her. I guess she figured that the sight of her was all she ever needed to give. You never knew which way the wind would be blowing with her. One day she might be all smiles and sweetness, asking after your health and wanting to hold your new baby, and the next day she'd breeze past you on the road, taking no more notice of you than she would a stray guinea fowl.

Since I had to stay in the same house with her, I used to watch her, trying to figure out the rhythm of her moods, for my peace of mind depended upon keeping on her good side. But if there was ever any rhyme or reason to the weather of Ann Melton's humors, I never found it. I ended up thinking that she was doing it simply to keep folks off balance around her, trying to guess at her mood, as if she was calling the tune. It gave her the upper hand—I worked that out—but I soon decided that I did not care to dance to her fiddling. I began to act just the same whether she behaved fair or foul, and pretty soon I began to see less of her moodiness, though she gave it in full force to everyone else. Except Tom Dula, of course. He always saw the sunny side of Ann.

Or at least, he did until he took up with Laura Foster, come spring.

It wasn't as if she found out in some underhanded way. Tom never troubled to lie. I always thought he was too lazy to exert himself by trying to remember some falsehood. Besides, he cared as little as she did what anybody thought of him. He was young and handsome, and people seem to find it easy to forgive a man like that.

Tom came over to the house one evening in late March, in time to cadge a bite of supper with us. He sat there by the fire, spooning rabbit stew into his mouth, and, for once, Ann was not all smiles and sweetness. She sat huddled up on the floor next to his stool, holding his cup of water for him, and leaning her body against his leg, smiling into the firelight like a satisfied cat. I had the sewing in my lap, and I was seated in the cane chair, a ways back from the hearth, pretending not to listen to what they were saying.

"Are you coming back later?" she murmured softly to Tom, glancing over at James Melton, who was at the table, nodding in his chair.

Tom sat very still. "Not tonight, darlin'. I'm headed over to German's Hill in a little bit."

Ann stiffened, and turned to look up at him. "That's a long walk on a dark night. What do you want to go over there for?"

"I just feel like it." He was keeping his voice light, as if the conversation was of no consequence at all, but the air felt the way it does when the leaves turn over on the trees, about an hour ahead of the thunderstorm, and there was that same quiet that comes right before all hell breaks loose.

"Well, you must be fixing to go visit somebody," said Ann, still speaking so softly that you could have heard a snake rattle in the log pile.

Tom shrugged, and, from the look on his face, I judged he was wishing he had thought up a lie when she asked him, but anybody who had fought his way through Petersburg and lived through a Yankee prison camp does not run from a fight—and maybe that was what Ann liked best about him: that she couldn't run roughshod over him, like she did over most everybody else. I never saw James Melton cross her once. I worked beside him every day in the fields for months, but I think I knew him less than I ever knew anybody.

Tom was smiling down at Ann, like he was daring her to keep hectoring him, and presently he said, "Why, I didn't know I had to answer to anybody about where I go and what I do."

"You don't need to tell me. I know. You're going to see my own cousin Laura Foster," said Ann.

He laughed. "Well, now, she wouldn't be the first of your cousins that I was acquainted with, would she now, Pauline?"

I glanced up from my sewing and met his eyes with a blank stare. There was a mocking glint to them, and although he was smiling, I didn't think he was happy about anything.

That flicked Ann raw, though, for she could hardly object to him seeing Laura Foster when she had foisted him off on me not even a month ago.

"After all, Ann, it ain't like Laura is married or anything, is it?" He was looking over at James Melton, who was still in his chair, awake now, and intent upon mending a harness, and paying us no mind. "It ain't like we care who beds with who?"

From the way Ann's eyes glittered, I thought she was going to break out into a storm of weeping, but she just kept staring up at Tom, taking his measure, and finally she shrugged and turned back to the fire. "Please yourself, Tom. I doubt you'll get much joy out of that stringy little mud hen."

Tom stood up and set his tin plate on his stool. He patted Ann on the head and winked at me, like I shared a joke with him, "Well, Ann," he said, heading for the door, "maybe I can teach her a thing or two."

That night I slept in a pallet on the floor, because Ann's bed shook with her sobbing.

# PAULINE FOSTER
## *Late March 1866*

✧⟞⟝⊙⟞⟝✧

S o we hunkered down and waited on spring, and it seemed a long time in coming, and nothing much happened in the meantime. When the weather was foul, James Melton occupied himself with mending shoes. I did the cooking and the washing, and what farm chores there were to be done while the weather held cold.

Once a week, I would plod up the muddy road to the place where the doctor saw his Elkville patients, and I took the bluestone medicine what he give me, but I felt little better for it. Some days I was tolerable and some days worse, but there seemed no rhyme or reason to it. Ann mostly slept the days away under her pile of quilts, or else she paced that cabin like a penned-up bull.

"It would take your mind off your troubles if you was to help me make the biscuits," I told her one afternoon, when I judged she would wear a path in the plank floor if she was to keep pacing.

She shot me a scorching look with those black eyes of her. "I don't want to take my mind off it. I want to feel every second of misery I'm

67

having so that I can give it back to Tom with interest when I see him."

"I thought you said it didn't mean nothing—him being with anybody else. And, anyhow, it means folk aren't gossiping about the two of you anymore."

She snatched up an unmended shoe and shied it in my direction, but she was so wide of the mark that I just stood there and watched it thump against the wall, and fall to the floor.

"I reckon you heard the new gossip," I said, fixing to hurt her a lot more than that slipper would have hurt me. "They do say that old Wilson Foster caught Tom in bed with Laura the other week, but he's not so particular as your mama was. The word is that he let them be. Of course, Laura is twenty-one, not fourteen like you was."

"Tom don't care," said Ann, plopping down with her elbows in the flour where I was kneading dough. "Nobody thinks less of a man for doing what comes naturally. More fool the woman that lets him. If Laura thinks he's going to marry her on account of it, she has another think coming."

"Unless there's a baby on the way."

Ann shrugged. "No telling whose it would be, though. Tom wasn't her first, not by a long chalk. If you haven't heard the other tales told about our cousin Laura, then let me tell you I have."

"Must run in the family," I said, laughing, because name-calling never bothered me none. "And there are stories a-plenty about you, too, Ann. You and the cattle drovers. They say you'd sell your favors for a jug of whiskey or a scrap of cloth."

She gave me one of her black looks. "I lived through the War, didn't I?"

. . .

As the days grew longer and the wind quit howling, and the world slowly began to turn green again, I found I was feeling better, and I thought that perhaps Dr. Carter had cured me after all. My rash and my fever went away, and I began to feel less miserable than I had in many a month. I was still a forlorn hired girl, with no prospects and no one to look out for me, but at least I was still young and spry, and the fine weather made it easier to go calling on folk. I didn't like any of them much, but listening to them talk was better than fetching and carrying for Ann every waking minute. Besides, you never know when some little nugget of scandal will repay you the trouble of listening for it.

One afternoon in late March I was walking up the road in search of something to do besides farm chores, when Wash Anderson hailed me from the edge of the woods. He had a blanket slung across his shoulder, and he was whooping and waving an earthenware jug up over his head, like a damned fool.

I hitched up my skirts, and plowed through the tall grass over to where he was standing. Wash Anderson is another young buck who lives with his widowed mama and his sister Eliza, just down the hill from the Meltons' place. He hangs around the settlement without being good for much, same as Tom. It's a wonder these fellows don't miss the War, as bored as they all seem to be with peacetime, and them never doing any work if they can help it. If I was a man and I had my health again, I believe I'd amount to more than they did. He is an amiable enough fellow, is Wash. Always good for a tune or a jest, and good enough company if you've nothing better to do, but he wasn't a patch on his buddy Tom for looks: round-faced and tow-headed, with a foolish grin, and though he wasn't yet thirty, he had a gut on him that spoke to his fondness for likker and food. I had no use for Wash Anderson in the ordinary way of things, but I take care never to get on the outs with anybody, and, besides, Wash Anderson brandishing a full jug of whiskey was a tolerable sight.

"What do you want?" I asked him, hands on my hips, and showing him that I wouldn't put up with any sass from the likes of him.

"How do, Pauline," he said, making a mock bow, as if I was a fine lady, but the smirk on his face put a sting to it. "Me and Tom Dula are fixing to lay out in the woods this evening with this here jug, and another one just like it, and make us a party of it. We would be right glad if you was to join us."

I could smell his breath from two feet away, and I flapped my hand to stir the stench away from my nose. "Seems like you have already started in on that jug without us."

He gave me a wobbly grin and reached for my arm. "Just feeling the spirit move us, Pauline. Come on."

I let him lead me into the woods then, keeping my eye on the whiskey jug to make sure he didn't trip over a log and spill it out on the ground. I didn't care if Wash Anderson broke his fool neck, but it would be a shame to waste good whiskey. Anyhow, I had nothing better to do that evening. I had much rather call on Wash's sister, Mrs. Scott, or walk over to Miz Gilbert's to spend the evening and maybe cadge a bite of supper, but if either of them had any gossip it would keep, and I'd just as soon pass the time with a jug as eat, even if it meant putting up with the likes of Wash and Tom Dula. I could suffer them well enough, for the sake of their whiskey. I reckoned they might try to make me pay for my share by letting them lay with me, but if I could put it off long enough, they might be too drunk to manage.

As soon as we had gone a ways into the woods, where the evening light was green, a-shining slant-wise through the leaves, I began to hear faint, shrill sounds, and I stopped in my tracks, thinking at first that it was the cry of a bobcat. But as I stood and listened, the screeching stopped, and then the sounds came together and made a tune, and then I knew that Tom Dula had already beat us to the meeting place, and that he was amusing himself on his fiddle while he waited.

I am not much of a music lover, though I suppose I like a lively dance as well as the next girl. It's just that the tunes all sound more or less the same to me, and if the fiddler is an indifferent player, they all sound like scalded cats. I started forward again, following the sound, and it was a likely melody, though I did not know its name. I judged that he played it well, for the sound of it did not set my teeth on edge. I decided that Tom was a better fiddler than most I'd heard. I suppose he ought to be, though. It ain't like he ever let work get in the way of his practicing.

We found him sitting on a fallen log with his back up against an oak tree, eyes closed and wrapped up in the tune he was playing. I held back for a moment watching him, because the way he moved with that bow in his hand showed more grace than I had ever seen in him before. A shock of hair slipped down across his forehead, and he glowed with the fever of his playing. For a moment there I thought I could see how Ann could be so taken with him. He was so handsome sitting there, lost in his fiddling, that he could have been one of those magic creatures they tell about in fairy tales, sitting there in the woods in twilight, conjuring up music. Funny, I felt closer to him then than I had back there in the barn when he had his pants down.

The music didn't cut any ice with Wash Anderson, though. Maybe he was already too drunk to notice. He staggered right on past me and plopped down on the log next to Tom, jostling his elbow with his shoulder, and, even though Tom was playing a sad, slow tune, Wash stamped his feet and let out a "*Woo-eee!*" to spur himself into a reveling frame of mind, I reckon.

Tom opened his eyes, looked from one of us to the other, and then he sighed and set the fiddle down behind the log, well away from Wash and his muddy boots. I sat down on the other side of Tom, almost shy at seeing this new side of him. "That was fine playing you was doing just now," I told him.

Wash whooped again. "Didn't you know, Pauline? Why, that was Tom's job during the War. He was a musician for the mighty Confederacy. We was in it together."

"What regiment were you in, then?" I said, hoping to take a long turn at the jug while they went maudlin with memories of the War.

"Company K, 42nd North Carolina," Tom muttered, looking none too pleased to have the matter brought up. I never had heard him talk much about soldiering.

I turned to look at him. "They had a fiddler in the army? What for? Did you play for the officer's dances?"

His frown deepened to a furrow. "I was a drummer, that's all. It wasn't music they wanted; it was somebody to mark time for the marching. When the army wasn't getting itself shot to pieces at Petersburg and Cold Harbor, they liked to pass the time in camp by making us do drills. They had us beating out the cadence for that. And during a battle we'd beat out the regiment's commands—charge or retreat. Like a code. There wasn't much music to it. Just keeping time."

Wash had spread out the blanket in the clearing in front of the log, and he began to tap a cadence on the side of the whiskey jug, but nobody paid him any mind. I nodded my head toward him. "Was he a musician, too?"

Tom shook his head. "Naw, he was just another warm body put out there to get shot at, same as everybody else."

"I hear you got took prisoner."

I felt Tom shiver when I said that. "Yeah, but it didn't spare me much. I lasted until a month before the armistice, and after that I was just waiting until it got to be my turn to go home. They let us out by state—in the order that our states had left the union. First one to secede was the last to get to go home. Hard luck on those South Carolina boys."

"So you made it right up to the end of the War before you got captured?"

"Yeah. March of '65. That was only last year, wasn't it? Seems like a lifetime ago. I got took at Kinston, when we went up against General Cox's Federals. They got more than a thousand of us in one fell swoop. I shouldn't have been there at all. I was sick with the fever off and on through my whole enlistment. I'd go to the hospital and start to get better, and they'd send me back to the line again, and the fever would come right back. If I'd a-been a Federal soldier, they'd have sent me home for good, but the Confederates would have kept the dead in the ranks if they could have figured out a way to keep them standing up."

"And they wouldn't have smelled any worse than the rest of us," said Wash, hooting and slapping his thigh. Then he scooted down off the log, and sprawled out flat on his back, with his arm curled up around the jug. He lay there, peering up at us from the blanket, and the sight of his whiskery face, upside-down in the fading light, put me in mind of a goblin, except he didn't scare me none. Drunks and fools—I was used to both by now.

I leaned down and wrenched the jug out from under his arm, and then I knocked back a long, burning draught of whiskey. It was raw and strong, and burned my throat all the way down to my stomach. I had tasted better stuff. This was rotgut—good for nothing except getting a body drunk, but that was all right with me, because that's all I required. I figured that if I kept the two of them talking, they wouldn't take their turn on the jug too often, and I couldn't think of anything worth hearing from Wash, drunk as he was, so I said to Tom, "I never met anybody who had been in a prison camp before."

He shrugged. "Yeah, you have."

"What do you mean?"

"Well, I reckon you know James Melton, since you're living at his place. He was there."

I could barely see his face in the fading light, and I wondered if he was making a joke, but his voice was quiet and steady, like he meant every word.

"I never knew that. He never talks about the War. Did he serve with you?"

"Same war, same army—that's about all. He joined up early, in the summer of '61, the 26th North Carolina, same as Ann's brother Pinkney. Wash and I went into the 42nd, in the spring of '62. He had a hard war, did James. He was tomfool brave, too."

I resolved to find out more about that, for it didn't square with what I had seen of him. "Funny to think of you and James Melton being neighbors both here and there. Did the two of you stick together there in the prison camp?"

He shook his head. "I never saw him at all. We were in different regiments, and him being wounded might have made a difference in where they put him. I don't know. We have talked about it since, him and me, and we reckon that I was already in there a month before he got taken prisoner in Richmond—early April, that was. And he didn't reach Point Lookout until early May. They let me out a couple of weeks before him, too. I was already home three weeks before he got back."

"What was it like, then, being a prisoner?"

He was quiet there in the darkness for so long, I didn't think he was going to answer me at all, but finally he said, "I saw the ocean."

I never had, of course, being born up the mountain two hundred miles from the Carolina coast. "The ocean. Well! What's it like?"

Tom nodded toward Wash, sprawled out on his back and trying to keep a leaf in the air with his breath. "It's like that there blanket, only wet."

"The Federals kept you penned up by the seashore? That sounds all right. I have heard tell that rich folk go to the shore for pleasure, of a summer."

"Not like this they don't." He was fairly spitting out the words. "I never want to smell salt in the air again as long as I live. The Federals packed a thousand of us in like cord wood on a train to Maryland, and when we got there they stuck us on a godforsaken spit of land caught between the Potomac River and the Chesapeake Bay. We were penned in like hogs on a stretch of dirty sand, crammed into tents that gave us no relief at all from the weather. Like *hogs*."

"I reckon it was crowded then?"

"More people than you've ever seen in your life, Pauline. Maybe twenty thousand, I heard somebody say. We had no firewood, and damn little of anything else. The water was so filthy, we could taste the shit in it. All we ever thought about was food."

"I thought the Yankees had plenty of food."

"Maybe they did. But they didn't feel like giving us any of it. When they heard that Yankee prisoners down south were doing without something, they'd take it away from us to get even. They'd turn us loose on a stretch of shore sometimes to wash, and while we were there we'd snatch up what we could find—seaweed or clams and such. But there were thousands of us Rebs and damn few shellfish. I learned how to catch rats, though."

I took another pull from the jug to wash that thought out of my head. "Naw, I couldn't eat rat."

Tom wasn't looking at me. He was staring off into the woods, like he was somewhere other than here. "I reckon we had some boys who couldn't bring themselves to eat rat neither. Most of them didn't make it out of there."

"How long were you shut in there?"

"Long enough. Three months, more or less—March to June. I lost track of the days, but I was spared the bitter winter and the late summer storm season. It was bad, though. When they turned me loose to walk home, my clothes hung off me like I was a scarecrow. Hand over the jug."

I passed him the whiskey and didn't much begrudge it to him. I could see he needed it. "What do you reckon then, Tom? Was that there camp worse than the War itself?"

He wiped his mouth on his sleeve, and looked down at Wash, who was laying there with his eyes shut. "The War was different for everybody. Anybody who wasn't there can't be told what it was like. Sometimes it was so dull, I felt like I was sleep walking, and then again sometimes a minute seemed to last most of a day. We saw things that all the whiskey in the world won't wash out of my head. I was sick half the time, too."

"So you said."

"Well, I was." He scowled at me, not liking that I'd said that, making light of his troubles, but men always make a song and dance about the least little bit of suffering. They can't tolerate half of what a woman endures as a matter of course.

"I thought I'd never get enough to eat again," he said. "Even now—and I have been home ten months—my mama lets me have a hunk of corn bread to put by my bed in the night. I dream sometimes that I am back there in the War, or penned up in that infernal camp, and I wake in a cold sweat. The bread laying there within reach reminds me that I'm home safe again."

"Well, it's over now," I said briskly, for his voice was shaking a little, and I was scared I might laugh at the thought of this big strapping soldier crying out in the night for his mama. Maybe Ann would have felt like comforting him, but I didn't. Besides, I had not come out here to take on any more sorrow. I had enough troubles of my own without having to listen to other people's laments. "Best not to think on it, Tom. It don't seem to be troubling Wash there none. The best way to heal any wound is to pour whiskey on it."

He took another pull on the jug. "I'll tell you this—once I got shut of that war, I decided that I had done all the hard work and doing without that I intended to do in this lifetime. From now on, I'm going to take it easy, and play my fiddle, and take orders from no man."

"Sounds like a fine life," I said. "If you can keep clear of working."

"And another thing. I'll never let them put me in prison again. No more being penned up like a hog. I'd druther be dead."

Wash Anderson had been dozing while we talked, but he sat up all of a sudden, and made a grab for the whiskey. "Play another tune, Tom! All that war talk will just bring you low and spoil the evening for all of us."

Tom gave him a faint smile, and reached back behind the log for his fiddle and bow. After a minute of twiddling with the strings, he began sawing away on a spritely tune, and when he was done, I asked him what it was.

"*Soldier's Joy*," he said softly. "I always wondered what that might be."

He played a few more tunes that evening, but mostly we passed the jug from hand to hand, and by and by they got tired of music, and reached for me instead of the whiskey, but by then they had both got so drunk they couldn't do it but one time each, so I told myself that I got off cheap on that occasion. I got no pleasure from rolling on the cold ground and being pawed at by the likes of them.

I endured it, but when Tom tried to jump me a second time and couldn't manage it, he rolled over beside me and peered at my face in the pale moonlight. He rubbed the back of his hand along my cheek, which was sallow and rough, from the harsh winter. Then he threw back his head and laughed. "Damn, Pauline, it's too bad you ain't pretty like your cousins. That would make it easier to do you. But for plain girls, once is my limit."

I never forgave him for that. From then on, anything that happened to him, I figured he had it coming.

# ZEBULON VANCE

O ur client's husband served with you in the 26th," Captain
Allison told me.

"Melton . . . Melton . . ." I shook my head. "I cannot
place him. There were so many. . . ."

I joined the army early in the War—on May 4, 1861, only weeks
after the firing on Fort Sumter—when there was a carnival atmosphere to the enterprise, with much flag-waving and cheering crowds,
gold braid and shining swords, but I did not stay in the ranks to the
bitter end. As a man of substance in Asheville, I was expected to raise
a company of soldiers and to lead those men off to war in defense of
our home state. I had no more military experience than a blind mule,
but in those heady days in 1861, that was a commonplace. Suddenly
a country that had one well-trained army split into two countries,
with much of that original army going over to the newly formed Confederacy. This schism left vacancies on both sides of the conflict, and
so the officers' ranks were filled with amateurs—like myself.

In order to become a colonel, you needed to round up five hundred men who would agree to serve in your command, and you

needed the means to buy yourself a horse, a sword, and an officer's uniform. That was considered qualification enough for command. For the sake of the common soldier, I can only hope that Providence parceled out the fools equally to both sides—and I hope I was not one of those fools. I do not think I was. Anyhow, I was seldom anywhere important enough to do much harm.

I suppose I could have wrangled a desk job for myself if I had tried. My Harriette would have been overjoyed had I done so, but I wasn't much past thirty, and I had no desire to sit at a desk in Raleigh, firing paper salvos and dodging requisition forms while the War whirled on without me. That was in 1861—early days. We were all fools back then.

They assigned us to the 14th Regiment of North Carolina to begin with, and by the middle of June we had settled in at Camp Bragg, some two and a half miles from the town of Suffolk, Virginia. Twenty-six miles away, in Newport News, the enemy had landed a large force, and, since Camp Bragg straddled the junction of two railroad lines (the Petersburg & Norfolk and the Roanoke & Seaboard), we thought ourselves in some danger of attack. Every night pickets were posted a mile and a half from camp, and the rest of us slept with our weapons at hand. The battle passed us by, though, that time, in favor of another railroad town: Manassas Junction, in proximity to Washington.

A few weeks after that, the government mustered new regiments, some of them comprising troops from the mountain counties. I was gratified, but not entirely surprised, to receive a letter from the Adjutant General of North Carolina's troops, saying that I had been elected colonel of the 26th Regiment, and would I accept the commission?

I delayed just long enough to transfer my old command to another Asheville lawyer, Philetus Roberts, and then I hightailed it down to Raleigh, where I wasted some time trying to persuade the bureaucrats to transfer my original troops, the Rough & Ready Guards, to my newly formed regiment. They thought not, of course, so I had to leave my boys in the 14th, and, after a few weeks' leave at home, I made my way over to Camp Burgwyn, on the Atlantic coast near Morehead City, where we whiled away the waning days of summer watching Yankee sailing ships cruising past, without bothering to waste a shell on our fortifications.

I chafed at the idleness of waiting for the War to find me. I declined an offer to run for the Confederate congress, because I had been so loath to leave the Union in the first place. Then I proposed to go on a recruiting trip back to the mountains to garner more troops, but my deliverance from that seaside monotony came from another quarter: in February 1862, I was ordered to take my regiment to New Bern, where on March 14, the Union forces, under General Ambrose Burnside, attacked.

*Was James Melton there in the swamp with us?*

If he was an enlisted man, I would have no way of remembering him, but I'll wager that we'd have the same nightmares about that day. My regiment was stationed on the right wing, caught between the woods, through which enemy forces were advancing, and a swamp.

About midday we fell back, the last Confederate troops to retreat. When we got within sight of the River Trent, I saw that the railroad bridge was in flames. The other regiments, having made good their escape, had fired the bridge after them—leaving us trapped.

The river itself was impassable, but, fortunately, I knew something of the terrain thereabouts, so I led my men to nearby Briers

Creek, seventy-five yards wide and too deep to wade, but it was our only hope of escape. The only boat to be had was a wooden boat that would hold three men at a time—and we had hundreds of soldiers to ferry across the water.

With the enemy less than a mile away and closing, I spurred my horse into the creek, but midway across he refused to carry me further, and so I was forced to swim for it. One of my men brought the horse ashore, and there I mounted him again, and, accompanied by some of my officers, I rode to the nearest house, where we commandeered three more small boats to effect the evacuation of my troops.

We had to carry the boats back to the creek on our shoulders, and then, amidst shell fire, and clouds of acrid smoke, we set back across the water to rescue the soldiers, a handful at a time. It took all of four hours to get my regiment translated to safety on the other side of Briers Creek, but, except for three poor fellows who were drowned, and those who fell in the redans holding off the enemy, we got the soldiers across.

That was my baptism by fire, and, while I hope I acquitted myself well and did my best for my men, the futility and haphazardness of war were impressed upon me.

The commanding officer in the Battle of New Bern had been my fellow congressman Lawrence Branch. He had taken the rank of colonel about the same time I did, but he had recently been promoted to Brigadier General, though I cannot say I was impressed with his performance in that position. I thought I could do at least as well, and so shortly after the battle, I set about trying to raise a legion—that is: to add twenty additional companies to the ten I already had, plus a complement of cavalry and artillery. If I could amass that number of troops willing to serve under me, I would be promoted to Brigadier General as well.

This venture went nowhere, for shortly after I began my campaign, the Adjutant General informed me that the newly passed Conscription Act had furnished enough soldiers to meet the quota for North Carolina. I am not a lawyer for nothing, though, and I spent a few more weeks trying to find a loophole in the recruiting laws, and thinking up ways to raise my legion in spite of the bureaucrats' efforts to thwart me. It was like trying to swim in molasses. No sooner would I enlist recruits than the generals would assign those men to other people's commands. I could see that they meant to keep me a colonel in perpetuity, so I abandoned the idea of trying to work in the military hierarchy, in favor of going back to the game I could actually play: politics.

The election for governor was coming in August, and the *Raleigh Standard* newspaper was endorsing my candidacy—if I should choose to run. Why, I'd have run for the governorship of purgatory, if the alternative was being outranked by the likes of General Branch and suffering the whims of pettifogging bureaucrats. I had one ace in my hand in this venture: my opponent was not in the military, and soldiers could vote.

The election was not until August, though, and meanwhile I had to soldier on as colonel of the 26th North Carolina, and try to remember that the enemy was the Union army, and not those graven fools in the government back home.

June found me back in Virginia, to join my regiment to Ransom's Brigade for the Seven Days Battle. The Union forces, under the command of General George B. McClellan, had landed on the Virginia peninsula, with the intention of advancing west and taking Richmond. When you are well below the exalted rank of general, you have very little idea what is going on in the campaign, even if you are in the forefront of the fighting. Seen up close, war is all noise and smoke, shouting men, and belching cannons, and through it all the stench of blood and gunpowder. There may have been some grand design conceived by General Lee and his advisors, but it wasn't apparent to those of us in the thick of it. Orders failed to reach the commanders. Reinforcements did not arrive. The fighting seemed sporadic and uncoordinated.

The War was prolonged mainly by the fact that General McClellan was just as bewildered as the rest of us. He didn't seem to know that his army outnumbered the Confederate forces two to one. He didn't realize that he was closer to Richmond than the defending army was. And he hadn't grasped the fact that he was winning.

Instead of pushing on to Richmond and to victory, he pulled his troops back to the James River, planning to load them back on the ships they came in and sail away to safety. We should have given him a parade, but instead we chased him on his way, and at the last piece of high ground before the river, he decided to stand and make a fight of it—at a place called Malvern Hill.

He lined up his artillery on the top of that hill, and he stationed his infantry forces at the ready to engage us in the intervals between bursts of cannon fire.

Our orders were to take that hill.

If I had occasion to meet James Melton, we would not slap each other on the back and reminisce about Malvern Hill. It had none of the golden glory that Shakespeare attributed to Agincourt. It had all the filth and squalor of a hog-killing.

Our orders were to charge that hill and take out McClellan's cannons. To that end, soldiers would charge across the open field, trying to ascend the slope, and a whistling shell would spiral down and blow them to pieces as they ran.

If I am remembered at all for my part in that sorry spectacle, it is for a jest I made in hopes of boosting the morale of my poor beleaguered men. Once when we were pinned down in a hail of bullets, a startled rabbit jumped out of the nearby underbrush and streaked across the field. Seeing this, I shouted, "Run, you sorry rabbit! If I wasn't the governor of North Carolina, I'd run, too!"

Well, I was two months shy of getting elected, but at least I stood my ground at Malvern Hill, and when the time came to cast the ballots, the troops remembered me favorably, so that I won the election by a margin of two to one.

In September I headed back to North Carolina on furlough, for I would take the oath of office before a judge in mid-September. The 26th North Carolina fought on without me, at Antietam Creek in western Maryland, where they say the very air turned red from all the blood shed in that terrible battle. By the end of the fighting, the dead lay stacked like cordwood, a dozen feet deep in the roadbed. General Lee lost a quarter of his army in that one battle, and with it all hope of foreign alliances that might have equipped us to withstand the onslaught of the Union forces.

I was gone from the army for good before Antietam, ensconced in the Governor's Palace in Raleigh, where the battles were fought with forms, and requisitions, and letters couched in diplomatic insolence.

But James Melton had no such escape. He would have staggered on in rags and tattered boots, living on hardtack and homesickness, until the bitter end—which came for him in a Union prison camp many miles from home.

No, I would not reminisce about the War with this veteran of the 26th North Carolina. There was nothing either of us wanted to remember.

# PAULINE FOSTER
## *March 1866*

⊰═◦═⊱

arch finally wore out, and the fields got green again, but all that meant to me was that I'd be working in the fields as well as doing all the household chores. It made it easier to walk the mile or so to a neighbor's place to visit a spell, when I wasn't too tired of an evening to manage it. My fever never did come back, though, and that rash I'd had when I came here had faded away altogether, so I began to think that Dr. Carter's bluestone cure had done its work. He said I had to keep going to see him, though. Some ailments, he said, were like flies in winter—just because you didn't see any around didn't mean they were gone for good.

"I don't think you are well, Pauline," he told me, when he gave me my latest dose of medicine. "And I think you might still be able to pass this disease to someone else if you were intimate with him."

"Oh, I'll be careful," I told him. I meant I'd take care in deciding who it was I wanted to infect. Sometimes I felt like that angel with the flaming sword that drove Adam and Eve out of Eden: I had a God-sent weapon that would bring death to ever who I chose.

. . .

"We have not seen so much of Tom Dula lately," I said to Ann one afternoon. I had spent all day planting corn in the field with James Melton, and when I got in, stiff-backed and bone-weary, Ann had told me to wash her bed sheets before I started on supper. I couldn't refuse for fear of losing my situation, but I figured I owed her a little pain in return, so while I was making biscuits to go with the stew, I made that remark about Tom, as innocent I could make it sound, knowing it would be salt in her wound, and glad of it.

Ann stiffened for a moment, but then she made her voice light, and she said, "Well, it's planting time. Everybody around here has plenty to do right now."

I snickered. "Reckon he's planting something, all right. Over at Wilson Foster's."

Ann slapped me hard, leaving a white handprint on my cheek from the flour. I just smiled at her and went back to kneading the biscuit dough. She wiped her hands on her skirt, but she just kept standing there. Her nose got red, and I saw one solitary tear leak out of the corner of her eye and slide down her cheek.

Finally she said, "He don't care nothing about Laura Foster."

"Well, in case his mama ever dies, I reckon he'll need somebody to look after him. He might be giving some thought to that. Besides, a marriage seldom comes about on account of what a man wants. If I was you, Ann, I'd be studying about what Laura wants."

Ann picked up a ball of dough and began to roll it around in her hand. Then she squashed it flat on the flour cloth and pressed down hard with her palm. "It ain't like he has anything to offer anybody," she said.

"I couldn't say," I said, taking care to keep my voice light and indifferent. "But her mother is dead, leaving a passel of children and Wilson Foster himself needing to be looked after. No love lost between Laura and her father, from what I hear. Now if it was me, I reckon I'd take just about any opportunity to get shut of all those young'uns and an ornery father who used me as a house servant. Did you not find yourself in that self-same situation when you were fifteen?"

She gave me a stricken look then, and I knew I had hit the mark. Ann had married James Melton to get away from a fractious parent and a home life of toil. She must have known as well as I did that Tom Dula was a deal more appealing to a young girl than old sobersides Melton had ever been. Maybe Laura Foster had precious little to gain by marrying Tom Dula, but what did she have to lose?

"It won't change anything," said Ann, pounding another biscuit into the floured cloth. "Tom would never."

I took the dough away from her and rolled it back into a ball. "I expect you're right," I said, keeping my eyes on my work. "Just because he'd have a place of his own, and somebody making him dinner, and waiting to warm his bed, there's no call to think he wouldn't want to hang around here, on the off chance that your husband will drop off to sleep."

Ann edged me away from the table. "Go see her, Pauline. Tonight. After supper. Just pass the time with her this evening and see if you can tell what's on her mind. She may be mixed up with somebody besides Tom."

"Go see her?" I laughed. Ann never thought about anything but what she wanted. "Why, she lives all the way over in German's Hill. Even if I was to stop there only long enough to say how-do and drink a cup of water, I doubt if I could make it back here by sun-up."

Ann stamped her foot. "But I want to know what she's up to! I can't rest until I do. Why don't you go tomorrow after midday and walk over there? I'll tell James to let you."

I thought it over. The prospect of a walk over to see my other Foster cousins was a pleasant thought for me, if the day was fine, and if I had to indulge in tale-bearing at Ann's bidding, I reckoned it would be worth it. Besides, I was curious to see for myself how the land lay between Tom Dula and Laura Foster. I might be stingy with the truth when I got back to Ann, but I'd like to know for my own satisfaction. No use to make it easy on her, though.

"I'll be awful tired tomorrow, Ann. You know I ain't well to begin with. I don't know . . . to make a long walk over to German's Hill, and then to have to walk all the way back here, and get up at the crack of dawn and cook breakfast . . ."

Ann stuck out her lip. "I suppose I could give you a hand with the morning chores, then. But you had better find out something worth telling when you get there, Pauline. If you go over to Wilson Foster's and spend the evening getting drunk and sleeping it off instead of talking to Laura and coming on back, I'll take a switch to you. I swear I will."

I got the half day off, all right. I never once heard James Melton tell his wife "no" about anything. Maybe he was scared to, but I don't reckon he could have been worried about rat poison in his food, for I never saw Ann do that much cooking. So off I went on that next afternoon, while Melton tilled the field alone, with his two milch cows yoked to the plow. I hated to wear out shoe leather trudging through the muddy trace to German's Hill, when I could have got there in an hour or so on horseback, but if James Melton could not afford even a scrub horse, at least he could cobble me a new pair of shoes.

The walk was pleasant enough in the late afternoon, but I decided to stay the night, for spring nights are still bone-chilling cold, and I had no desire to make my way home on foot close to midnight in that weather, especially since this visit was being done as a favor to Ann, and I was disposed to inconvenience myself as little as possible on her account. Why is it that fine-looking folk always think they are doing you a favor by letting you do them one?

We still weren't far enough into spring for there to be much to see on my way to the Fosters' place—a few green leaves on trees here and there, and sprouts of grass amid the mire of rain-soaked fields. The road ran along beside the river, and it was as brown as the fields from the spring rains. I thought it looked like a trail of tobacco spit, not at all like the clear little streams we have up the mountain in Watauga County. I am not much moved by the beauty of nature anyhow, because every place I've ever seen looks about the same. I hoped that the Fosters would have something decent to eat and that they'd offer me some of it, and even more I hoped that there would be a full jug of whiskey and not too many people around to share it with. Whiskey is better than scenery. Better than people, too. It doesn't ask you for anything in return.

I never paid much attention to the *begats* in our family, but as near as I could figure it, Wilson Foster's daddy had been a brother to my grandfather, so we were cousins, same as I was with Ann's mama Lotty Foster. Prosperity did not seem to run in the Wilkes County branch of the family, for Wilson was not much better off than Ann's family. He farmed in German's Hill, but he didn't own the land, just worked as a tenant, so he barely cleared enough from farming to feed his family. Laura was the oldest, of an age with Ann and me, and after her came three boys and a baby girl. Their mama was dead, though, probably birthing that last child, though I hadn't bothered to ask the particulars of it. What cooking and cleaning was done about the place fell to Laura, for there was no money to pay a servant.

It was a dingy white frame house that didn't look big enough to house six people, but I suppose that the little ones all slept piled together somewhere like puppies. It looked like a house that nobody cared about—not Wilson Foster, because he was too shiftless to own it, and not his landlord, because he probably figured that a ramshackle place with a leaky roof was good enough for a tenant farmer's family.

I didn't feel sorry for them, though. They had a roof over their heads, and a woods full of game to put meat on the table, and they had lived through the War. There's many that had to make do with less than that. Besides, the Fosters were not what you would call a close family. We didn't think we owed anything to one another, and we didn't flock together like guinea fowl, preferring our own company to the outside world. Look at Cousin Ann. She didn't take me in out of the kindness of her heart. She let me stay so that she could have a servant for next to nothing. If that is family feeling, you can have my share of it.

I sat looking at the house for a minute, before I approached the door. Before I could hello the house, one of the boys came around from the side of the house, and stood a few feet away from me, staring. I made sure he didn't have a rock in his hand, and then I bade him a good evening, but he just glanced at me wall-eyed, and gave me the barest nod to acknowledge my greeting. Shy around strangers, I thought, and I left him be, and walked on up to the house, wearing a plaster smile, and ready to be the long-lost cousin from the mountains, if that's who they needed me to be.

At first nobody answered my knock, but inside I could hear a child hollering, "Somebody's come a-calling."

I waited, because there's no use in rapping again if they know you are there. By and by, the door opened enough for a small head to peek up at me, and a big-eyed boy stared at me for a moment or two, before he said, "What?"

I gave him a careful smile. "It is all right," I said. "I am kin to you. Which Foster boy are you? James?"

He shook his head. "Naw. I'm John. It was Elbert what brung you up to the door." That got him talking, which is why I pretended to think he was James, who is seventeen. This sorry little pup couldn't have been twelve yet. I knew that the best way to get some folks to talk is to let them correct you. After that, he forgot to be bashful, and I edged past him and headed straight for the fireplace, for it had been a cold walk from the Meltons' place to German's Hill. While I warmed my hands, I glanced around, seeing exactly what I had expected to see: a few sticks of homemade pine furniture, a rag rug on the floor, and some pans and a cast-iron skillet hanging from hooks in the ceiling.

Nobody ever got rich being a tenant farmer, and Wilson Foster was proof of it. After a minute or two my eyes got adjusted to the dim light, and I spied my cousin Laura over next to a cradle, holding a lap-baby in her arms. This must be the youngest of the brood, the one that their mother had probably died giving birth to. That, too, was a commonplace, among poor folk. The women just keep spitting out babies, and wearing themselves out with tending to the brood and doing all the farm chores, until finally one day they birth one baby too many, and die trying. Most men managed to get through at least two wives in a lifetime. The wonder of it was that any woman was ever fool enough to walk into that trap, but most all of them did, sooner or later. I supposed that my cousin Laura would, too, if she ever got the chance, though one baby seemed the same as another to me, and since she had one to tend to as it was, why would she go off to saddle herself with another one?

She was a little thing, Laura was. The top of her head wasn't much higher than a broom handle, and I've seen gourds bigger around than her waist. She had mousy brown hair, and good cheekbones in a heart-shaped face, but she wasn't a patch on Ann, for looks or brains.

When my feet and hands stopped tingling, I left the hearth and went over to the cradle, where Laura was. She had got the baby to sleep now, and she set it down in its old rag quilt, laying a bony finger to her lips to warn me not to wake it with any loud talking. I needed no cautions on that score. The last thing I wanted was to have my visit marred by the bawling of a smelly young'un.

I nodded to Laura to show her that I understood the warning, and pointed for her to come back over to the hearth. We dragged a couple of pine stools up close to the fire, and put our heads together to talk in low voices. I didn't see Wilson Foster anywhere about, and I reck-oned he had not come in from the fields yet, which was fine with me, for I had not come all that way to suffer through idle chit-chat.

"I don't know if you know who I am," I said to Laura.

She nodded. "Yes. You have the look of the Fosters, I reckon, but

I had already heard tell you was working over to the Meltons' place, so I'd a-knowed you anyhow. Not too many strangers about. Leastways, not females."

She didn't seem put out to see me, and I wondered if she had heard the gossip about me and Tom, and whether she cared about it or not. Best not to speak of it right away. "I envy you your home and family, Cousin, for I have none."

She shrugged. "The house is rented, and as for family, I'd as lief give you some of ours, for they are no end of trouble to tend to, night and day. Trying to take care of it all killed my mama."

"I thought I'd heard that the baby there was the cause of her passing."

Laura glanced over at the cradle, where the small assassin slept in peace. "She was worn out, anyhow, and birthing that last child took more strength than she had. I doubt not she was glad to go, in the end."

I mustered the smile I use when I have worked out the right thing to say. "I'm sure it eased her passing to know that her brood was left in your loving sisterly hands." I didn't believe any such thing, but I thought it might please her to hear it said.

"Well, I hope I do my best." Laura looked away and scowled as one of the younger boys ventured into the room. "What is it, John? Get along to bed now! I've no mind to fool with you this evening."

"I'm still hungry, Sister," he said, in a treble voice, on the verge of tears.

Laura sighed and shook her head. "There's cold biscuits in the tin plate in the pie safe. Get you one, and mind you don't make a mess with the crumbs in your bed, for I'll not change it."

The boy snatched his biscuit, and crept away past us. When he had gone, I turned back to my scrawny cousin, beaming in pinchbeck admiration. "Why, all this responsibility for home and children will serve you well when you have a husband and a home of your own."

Laura took up the poker and stirred the fire. "I reckon it will." She didn't seem none too cheered by the sentiment. "But for the War, I'd have been wed long ago, but now there's scarcely enough men to go around, though my spinsterhood is not for want of trying. I reckon I could have set my cap for a fat old widower, but that wouldn't be no different from staying here."

"It can't be as hopeless as that," I said. "After all, you are only just past twenty now, and the War is over, so it may not be long before somebody makes you a bride. I hear tell you have a sweetheart."

She turned on me, still holding the poker, likely forgetting she had it in her hand, but she looked like she'd spied a snake. "What have you heard?"

I laughed. "Oh, not a word about a fat old widower, Cousin. I hear tell that a handsome young soldier is paying court to you."

She sat back down on the stool, and the firelight made shadows on her ashen face, but there was no trace of the pleasure a girl usually shows when you tease her about a beau. She sighed. "Oh, I reckon you're talking about Tom Dula. When Daddy caught us together, I knowed it would get about. Well, Tom is fine to look at, and he is one for sport, right enough, but what would he do with a wife?"

"Why, take her home to the Dula farm, of course. His mother still lives there, but what of that? The rest of the Dula young'uns will be out and gone before too long, and old Miz Dula won't last forever."

"No. But our cousin Ann will. At least it will seem like it to me."

"Ann Melton? Why would she come into it? She has a husband already."

"Some say she has two, and she seems likely to keep them both." Her lip curled, and she twisted a hank of her broom-straw hair. "Don't you wish you were beautiful, Pauline?"

It hurt to be reminded so matter-of-factly that I was not, but I never flinch when I have been stung. "Well, Cousin, if beauty would give me a golden palace to live in, meat and whiskey every day, and servants to do my bidding, I would welcome it, but I cannot see that beauty has given our lovely cousin any more than the lot of an ordinary plain woman: a dull husband and a middling farmstead. Where is the wonder in that?"

Laura shrugged. "More than I ever got, or you either. But it may yet come right for me. There's somebody else who is sweet on me. Folks around here wouldn't think him even as good as that no-account Tom, but leastways he would be proud to have me."

That was the first interesting thing that drab little cousin Laura had said. "Well, who is your suitor then, missy? A bald old farmer or a cripple home from the War?"

She shook her head. "I mustn't say. We cannot have it known. But what about you then, Pauline? Do you have a sweetheart waiting for you back up the mountain?"

"Yes, and his name is legion. I have come down here to get cured of my love sickness. Pox. The wages of sin, folk tell me." I had Cousin Laura's measure by now. She kept to herself, not that she had much choice living so far out from the settlement, and she wasn't the type to tell tales. She was sitting on her own secret like a broody hen, and so I entrusted her with mine—not that I cared anymore who got to know of it. The damage was done, I reckoned.

"I'm very sorry for your trouble," Laura said primly, in a voice so soft I could hardly hear her.

I reckon she was shocked by what I'd said, because her eyes got big, and she leaned a little away from me, like she was a-skeered she might catch it from me. I did not bother to tell her that, like as not, she already had.

# ZEBULON VANCE

I made notes about the case at the time, not because I ever intended to make the details public, but simply because a lawyer must keep track of his cases, and this one stretched out for so many months, while I went on about my life in Charlotte, that I had need of documentation to keep it in my mind. Perhaps I had some thought of turning it into a memoir, for a good deal of my own history intrudes into the story. When all is said and done, more people will be interested in me than in him, poor fellow. I might have kept my own story and thrown out his, if I'd ever had the leisure to pen my autobiography.

I do not know that these jottings do me much credit, but I saw no reason to alter them for posterity. I have told the truth about worse things, so let the story stand as I recorded it at the time.

## October 1866

*I have just returned from a visit to my client, Thomas P. Dula. Tom Dooley (to employ the local vernacular) is a likely-looking lad, a fellow Confederate veteran, and a poor mountaineer born in a Carolina log cabin. I was all those things myself once. But there, I assure you, the*

resemblance ends. Dula is a more handsome man than I ever was, and I
doubt he will ever have the opportunity to run to fat as I fear I am
beginning to, but, aside from that, all the advantages lie with me.

I was appointed by the presiding judge to defend the prisoner, but
since it is a capital case, the poor fellow's fate does not rest in my hands
alone. North Carolina in her wisdom requires that defendants on trial
for their lives must be represented by two members of counsel. Mr. Dula
had three: myself, Captain Richard Allison, and Robert Armfield. I
wondered if the logic behind the multiple-attorney rule was akin to the
tradition used in firing squads, of loading one gun with dummy bullets,
so that each man may believe that he had no hand in the killing of the
prisoner. With three of us attending to Thomas Dula during the trial,
the guilt of the loss is shared amongst us. Thus I hope to use some legal
maneuvering to snatch victory from the jaws of defeat.

Captain Allison is an able fellow, and I'm sure he could have
handled this case without having an out-of-work ex-governor underfoot,
but he was gracious in receiving me, and kind enough to brief me in the
facts of the case, before I went off to interview the client, to determine
the situation for myself.

The prisoner has spent some three months in the Wilkes County jail,
a solid two-story red brick building, sparse of windows, as befits a place
that detains murderers. It sits behind the white-columned brick courthouse, like a ruddy calf in the lee of its stalwart mother, but it is a
pleasant prospect for a prison, with shade trees softening the aspect of
the structures, and a distant line of hills framing the valley now in
autumn tints of gold and scarlet.

I was raised in just such a village, in the towering blue mountains
that lie between Asheville and the border of Tennessee, and I missed

those sheltering hills in my life these days, for I had left their peaceful majesty when I was barely twenty, for the opportunities afforded me by the more prosperous flatlands. First I went to study law at the university in Chapel Hill, and, after a stint in the court system back home in Buncombe County, I set out for Washington to serve in Congress. Though I argued mightily against secession, I was forced to leave the U.S. government when North Carolina did, and, unable to prevent the War, I took my place among the fighting as colonel of the 26th North Carolina, a homegrown regiment. I had no particular military prowess, you understand. In those days, when the continent was trying to mount two armies from the remnants of one, anybody who could get five hundred men to sign up and serve under him was automatically made a colonel, for it was assumed that such a man could afford to buy his own horse and sword.

But the best fighting is politicking. I left the conflict in midstream to take up residence in the Governor's Mansion in Raleigh, and from there, when the Confederacy fell, I found myself back in Washington, this time in a Union prison, along with the rest of the Confederate governors, as the victors seemed intent on collecting the whole set.

A year ago last July, they set me free again, and I took the train back to North Carolina, forbidden to hold political office yet awhile, for, in remaining loyal to my home state, I had rendered myself a traitor to the greater Union. Thus barred from politicking, I was forced to fall back on my original profession—the practice of law, although I had done none of it in a decade, and I doubted that I had either the experience or the inclination to make much headway with it. Still, a man must live, and it was tolerably honest work—well, as much so as being a Congressman is, I reckon.

*The Wilkes County jail, that squat brick building set behind the courthouse, is rather dark inside, and, after the corridors of the Governor's Mansion, it might have struck me as a bit low and cramped, but for my recent stay in similar accommodations in what was again our nation's capital.*

*"We have much in common," I told the prisoner.*

*He sat before me, gaunt, shaggy-haired, and scowling, rubbing at the iron shackles on his wrists, for they had chafed his skin. He gave me an appraising stare with those cold blue eyes, and I wondered if I was looking into the soul of a killer, but I had taken him on as a client, and so, unless he admitted it himself, I must believe him innocent. I wonder, though. When the War came, we took beardless boys out of the cabins, and sent them into the depths of hell, in places like Antietam and the Wilderness, and some of them came back changed. Once a dog has killed a chicken, you might as well shoot him, for you can never trust him again.*

*I was against the War from the beginning, and only incidentally because North Carolina's secession would cost me my seat in Congress. When the Tarheels left the Union, I was on the stump, in my hometown of Mars Hill, orating mightily in favor of staying out of the Confederacy. I had just raised my hand to heaven to emphasize my point when a little towheaded boy came running out of the telegraph office, calling out that Fort Sumter in South Carolina had been fired upon, and that President Lincoln was calling for seventy-five thousand volunteers to put down the insurrection: that is, to invade our sister state, which North Carolinians would never do. Slowly, I let my hand fall.*

*So those who were hell-bent on the War had got it, and as if we had not suffered destruction enough in the four years it lasted, I thought we* might now be getting another kind of retribution. In a generation of young men, we sowed the seeds of violence, and violence we shall reap.

"I thank you for coming to see me," said the prisoner, "but you know I warn't in your regiment, Governor."

"I'm relieved to hear it."

He reddened a little, and nodded, thinking I meant that I would be ashamed to claim him as a comrade because of his current difficulty.

"It isn't that," I assured him. "I have heard that you were taken prisoner near Kinston at the end of the War, but I was long gone from there by then, so your troubles in '65 cannot be charged to my scroll."

"No. You was the Governor by then."

"And I went to jail as well, you know. About the time the Union let you go, they started rounding up all the Southern governors, and so I did three months in a Washington prison, in the congenial company of Governor Letcher of Virginia." I looked around at the bare room with its whitewashed walls and the rough-hewn pine table that separated me from the prisoner. "How does this prison measure up to your Yankee prison camp? It certainly puts me in mind of the one I was in up in Washington."

He shrugged. "It is tolerable, sir. At least here I sleep inside out of the weather, and they do feed me. I miss the taste of whiskey, but that's about all, I ain't used to much in the way of finery, nohow. My mother is a widow woman, and our ridge land don't amount to much. I reckon you know there's no money to pay a lawyer."

"I didn't suppose that there was."

"Yet you come all the way up here from Charlotte, anyhow?"

I smiled, hearing in his question another point of similarity between him and me. Mountain people do not like to feel themselves in anyone's debt. Apparently, judging from my client's troubled eyes, not even if his life depended on it. He had been at pains to make it clear to me that he had not served under me in the War, thus relieving me of a sense of obligation, and now he underscored the point that he could not pay my fee, so if I proceeded to act on his behalf, it was my own decision, and not for duty or for gain. I confess I liked him the better for his forthrightness.

In my younger days, when anybody did me a good turn, I would lie awake nights trying to figure a way to repay his kindness. Later, though, after I had married a member of the Burke County gentry, and became accustomed to the customs of civilization, I learned that obligations are the currency of polite society. You want people to be forever indebted to you for some favor or other, in case you should ever need their power or their influence to advance yourself. This system of influence peddling took some getting used to, but I got the hang of it soon enough. I had been studying rich people most of my life, and if I never got exactly to feeling like one, I reckon I could pass muster amongst them, but the proud independence of my fellow mountaineers still warmed my heart.

"You mustn't feel beholden to me," I assured the shaggy young man. "The money is not an issue. I am obliged for the chance to defend you. The government won't let me run for political office yet, you know, so I must fall back on lawyering to earn my living, but, between the War and my time in Congress, I am years out of practice. So you are my test case, and I hope that you will also prove to be an advertisement of my skill as a defense attorney."

He shrugged. "It'll be uphill work then. They were dead set on hanging me afore they even knew for sure they had a corpse."

I nodded. I knew as much from the briefing I had been given on the case by Captain Allison. "Feeling does seem to be running high against you. We will try to get the case tried in another county, where you may get a more impartial jury. And where I may get one as well. You know, Wilkes County was strong for the Union during the War. Twelve jurors from here might enjoy the chance to give the former Confederate governor one in the eye by convicting you."

"So you want to move me?"

I nodded. "The legal term is a change of venue. I propose to get the case tried just over the line in Iredell County. I lived there after the fall of Raleigh, and I flatter myself that I am well known and liked in Statesville."

"But you ain't on trial, sir."

I smiled. "Sometimes to a lawyer it can feel that way. Juries can be contrary. You can argue yourself blue in the face, and then see your man convicted because those fools in the box didn't like the look of him. But never mind the politics of it. Let us begin with the facts. It would be best if you told me in your own words how you came to be in this jail, charged with this terrible crime."

The cold blue eyes looked into mine, and he looked no more than a boy in his bewilderment. "On account of the women, I reckon," he said at last. "The Bible says that Eve brought death into the world when she ate that apple, and I reckon females have been the death of us ever since."

"And yet, it is a young woman who is the victim in this case, and it is you who are charged with being the serpent bringing death to her."

. . .

He tried to make a gesture, but the shackles clanked, and he let his hand fall again to his side. "Laura Foster," he said. "She didn't count for much. Anybody will tell you that."

I felt a chill when he said that. Did we in our war teach this mere boy that people's lives were of no account? "That sentiment does you no credit," I told him. "And it will not endear you to a jury. Also, it is not how the prosecution will argue it. Whatever this young woman was in life, death will have translated her into an angel of purity and radiance. Even people who knew her will begin to believe it."

He scowled up at me, and the shackles clanked again. "That won't make it true."

"People believing it will make it true. That's as close to truth as we get this side of heaven, son."

I let him turn that over in his mind for a moment or two, and then I said, "Now I know that when the whispering started about you being responsible for this killing, you took off and went over into Tennessee, and that they caught you there and hauled you back. You do see, don't you, that your flight across the state line will make people assume you are guilty?"

A smile flickered across his face. "Well, Governor, don't you believe that, and I reckon it won't be true."

So it seems I have undertaken the defense of a boy soldier, who has no money and who cannot even be bothered to make protestations of innocence. I must be as stubborn as my opponents accuse me of being even to think of pursuing this. And yet I am bound to do it . . . though

*I cannot say what impels me. Is it a case of "There but for the grace of God go I?" I was once a poor mountain boy, with no powerful friends, and too proud to ask favors of anyone. But I don't think I was so very like Thomas Dula, after all. The Lord Almighty may have smiled upon me, but it seems to me that He stood back and let me do most of the scut work of self-improvement all by myself.*

I was born in 1832 in the mountains of Madison County, North Carolina, on a little mountain farm in Reems Creek, a few miles north of Asheville. The President then was Andrew Jackson, a dour backcountry fellow who had once practiced law one mountain and a state line over from there, in Jonesborough, Tennessee. I venture to say that my family's hopes for me ran equally high, for I came of good stock, for all that we were hemmed in by mountains and far removed from the corridors of power.

David Vance, my father's father, had fought with Washington at Brandywine, and froze with him at Valley Forge, before finishing up the War in his native South, alongside Colonel Sevier at the Battle of King's Mountain. I reckon he enjoyed that skirmish more than he did the big battles up in Pennsylvania. I would have.

At King's Mountain those volunteer soldiers, mountain farmers who marched from Tennessee and the hills of Carolina to face down the Redcoats on the South Carolina border, were a sight more successful than General Washington's Continental Army up north. They beat the British in an hour, and walked back home to finish the harvest. So my people were mountain farmers, but they also had education and friends in high places, and they had seen more of the world than the other side of Reems Creek. After the War, my grandfather served in North Carolina's General Assembly, so perhaps the disease of politicking was a hereditary one in my case, but the love of learning was instilled in me at my mother's knee. When my grandfather died, he left a library of five hundred volumes, and my mother put it to good use in the evenings, gathering us children around the hearth, and reading to us, from Shakespeare, the Bible, the commentary of Julius Caesar. These nightly sessions with the classics taught me grammar and oratory, providing me with a wellspring of fine words that I could draw from in later life in my speeches in the courtroom or on the hustings.

When I was six, they sent me and my brother Robert over to Flat Creek, seven miles from home, to board with "Uncle Miah," Nehemiah Blackstock, who was a friend of my grandfather, and, like him, a surveyor. He was also a stern Presbyterian, same as the Vances were, and he brooked no disobedience. Like the recording angel, he kept a list of our failings in his black book, which he would consult when deciding what punishment should be meted out to the young sinners in his care. Many's the time I had been judged and found wanting by Uncle Miah, and he made sure I grew up to be a good and learned man, or else a careful one. But it was thanks to him and the other determined adults who had charge of me in my youth that I got an education and made a lawyer, instead of sitting in a cell like poor Dula.

After my tutelage at Uncle Miah's, I was sent over to Tennessee to Washington College, which was little more than a grammar school, but it was a beacon of culture on the frontier, I suppose, and it smoothed away the rough edges of my primitive state, so that my penchant for arguing became a talent for debate, and my natural loquacity passed for oratory.

My father died when I was eleven, which dampened the family's prosperity, and ended my formal schooling, but by then I had got the gist of education well enough to keep at it on my own, and by then I also had the determination to make myself a successful and prosperous man.

Later in life I learned that the daughters of the well-to-do are sent off to finishing school so that they may learn the proper way to move in polite society: which fork to use, how to make polite conversation, and those arcane passwords of speech and deportment by which the gentry are able to recognize one another as being "the right sort." Without knowing anything of that custom, I set myself on that course at sixteen, when I took a job as a desk clerk at the Warm Springs Hotel, a resort and spa, built to take advantage of the natural mineral springs there in Madison County. The Warm Springs Hotel catered to the Eastern Seaboard gentry, who fled the fevers and miasmas of a southern summer in favor of the cool and bracing mountain air of the Carolina mountains. The guests barely noticed me, of course, for they thought that the denizens of the mountains were ill-bred and savage folk, and to them I was no more than a servant. But to me those rich folks from the flatland were exhibits in my private zoo, and I studied them with the care of a naturalist.

By the time I had finished my sojourn as an employee of the Warm Springs Hotel, I could tell Charleston from Richmond, planter's wife from lawyer's daughter with a glance at their apparel. In that school for society, I learned to speak and dress in a way that would make the gentry accept me as one of their own. I never felt myself to be one of them, though, for there was always an unreconstructed part of my soul that sided with the common man, and understood the pleasures of the jug and fiddle more than that of the decanter and the opera.

Not many of the well-bred Charlotte lawyers of my acquaintance would have taken the case of a penniless illiterate from the hill country, but fighting for the underdog came as naturally to me as breathing. I just hoped for both our sakes that this Dula fellow was innocent, for after the War and the Governor's Mansion I was rusty at the practice of law.

# PAULINE FOSTER

## *Late April 1866*

Listening to Miz Ann Melton blackening the name of her cousin Laura would have made a cat laugh, but, since I had my bed and board to think of, I just kept quiet and let her rave.

"Why, Laura Foster has got no more morals than a mare in heat!" she declared, as if such a thing would disgrace our fine family of Fosters. I had to turn away then, and bite my lip to keep from laughing in her face. Here was Ann with a lover still coming to her bed a couple of nights a week, while her husband slept nearby, and her own mother Lotty, having lost count of the fathers of her young'uns. Then there was me, with a battalion of lovers and a war wound beneath my skirts to prove it. We were fine ones to talk about the sins of little Laura Foster. She couldn't hold a candle to the rest of the family sinners, but you would never catch me saying so to Mistress Ann, to whom I was beholden for my keep. Nor would I be sharing with her the news that drab little Laura claimed to have unearthed another sweetheart besides Ann's beloved Tom. I don't reckon Ann would have believed me anyhow on that score, for nothing would ever convince her that Tom Dula was not the finest, handsomest fellow in all creation.

One man is the same as another to me, except some of them stink more than others, but from the way other women act around this man or that, I can see that they have preferences in the matter of coupling, and, for Ann, the sun rose and set upon Thomas Dula, though I cannot say why this should be so. To my mind, he was no better looking than her husband, and he was a deal less steady and dependable. If you looked at the two of them the way you'd study a horse you were planning to buy, then only a fool would pick Tom.

I used to wonder what she saw when she looked at him. Not what the rest of us saw, which was a lazy, no-account boy with an easy smile and an inclination to go through life like a raft on a river, taking the easiest course as it flowed. If I was to tell Cousin Ann that Laura found some man she liked better than Tom, like as not she would call me a bare-faced liar. Well, I am a liar, but people seldom catch me at it, and, though I had no intention of sharing the news with Ann, I did believe that Laura's affections lay elsewhere.

There are a deal of things a woman might want more than a sunny smile and a strong back in bed: land, money, dependability, honor, the respect of the neighbors. James Melton had all of that. Tom had none of it, and never would. Picking some other man in place of Melton struck me as a foolish choice, whether Ann believed it or not. I resolved to take a close look at the men hereabouts to see if I could tell which one had taken my cousin Laura's fancy. But I would not tell Ann. Let her jealousy simmer a while longer, while I watched the pot boil, and when the time was right, I would let it scald the lot of them.

Spring's cold rains brought the first green shoots of grass, and then deep in the bare woods the redbud trees swelled up like sores that crowned a rosy pink, and then went away, same as mine had. A week or so after the redbud bloomed and withered, Ann was washing herself and found some rosy sores of her own. They were between her legs, where it didn't show, so she was as beautiful as ever, but the affliction took its toll on her temper, which was ragged at the best of times.

She slammed the tin washbowl on to the table, and thrust her face up close into mine, so I could feel the heat of her breath and smell her body, still unwashed, for she had come upon the sores and quit. "I am sick!" she screamed in my face. "And I reckon it is your fault!"

I have one gift from fortune. It is not grace, or beauty, or a fine singing voice, or breeding, but it is a blessing nonetheless. I cannot be moved. Being shouted at does not make me tremble, and neither panic nor insult can tempt me into a display of temper. Inside my head, I am as cold as a creek of snow-melt. Sometimes I wonder what other people feel when they weep or storm, for whatever it is I am not touched by it. While she sobbed and swore, I stood there looking at her, thinking as clearly as if she were humming hymn tunes, and I felt nothing at all.

"Why, Ann, I am sorry you have taken poorly, but it can't have nothing to do with my sickness, can it? I reckon all the world knows how you catch the pox—from laying in sin with them that has it. But whatever else we ever did, you and I, we never did *that*, Cousin."

She stared at me for a moment, letting my words sink in, and perhaps she was too frightened to reason it out, as I had been here a good while before she even took sick. I had no doubt that Ann was poxed, because, though she had not lain with me, I had been tupped by Tom, and so had she, which amounted to the same thing. I was sure of that. I had taken a roundabout way to share my affliction with her, but I had managed it in the end, and it was all I could do not to gloat over my victory. But I generally take the wiser course, and that called for me to force tears into my eyes, and clasp her hand, and say, "Oh, it cannot be my condition that ails you, Cousin! Perhaps you are just liverish."

She shook her head. "I felt the sore just now, when I was washing myself."

"All manner of things can cause a lump upon the body. Mayhap it will go away of its own accord." I tried to sound as if I believed that, for it would do no good for her to know what ailed her. It was enough that I knew.

I reckon that if you are born beautiful, then the outside of your head is so important that you don't have to worry overmuch about what there is on the inside. Leastways, I never could see any sign that Ann ever wasted any time trying to think out anything. While she was brushing her black hair into a glossy sheen, or when she rubbed lampblack on her eyelids to make her dark eyes big and calf-like, those eyes would go soft and vacant, like two puddles of spilled ink, and she rarely spoke when she was tending to her rites of beauty. Those things ought not to take up so much space in your head as to crowd out other thoughts altogether, but she never seemed bored, though she did little enough of anything. Whereas, me—why, it seems like I cannot stop myself from thinking, even when I want to. Even when I am bone-weary and trying to drift off to sleep, notions keep buzzing around behind my eyes until I wish I could swat them away like gnats. Sometimes in the back of my imaginings there is that shadow of my bodily sickness and an ugly picture of what the end will be like for me, but mostly I am able to keep away from that abyss by playing a never-ending game of draughts with everybody who crosses my path.

*Do I need to repay anybody for some slight or injury, and, if so, how can I safely do them a bad turn? — Is there someone standing in the way of something I want, and, if so, what lie can I tell to push them aside? — Who is vexing me by being too rich, or too smug, or too happy? How can I put a damper on that?*

I never ran out of scores to settle, and little seedlings of mischief to tend to. But Ann and Tom just seemed to roll along through life on a cart of new-mown hay and cabbage roses—never worrying about slights or rivals, never trying to come out ahead or fearing being left behind. They just . . . *lived*. Why, calves walk into the butchering shed with as much forethought as those two had about where life would lead them.—It must be restful to be able to live like that, floating, instead of fighting back against the current, but I take no pleasure in idleness.

I am always trying to win a game that no one else knows we are playing.

I figured that Ann's habit of not bothering to think was the reason she had not worked out what was ailing her and how she had come to catch it. She knew full well that I had lain with Tom Dula, same as she had, and surely by now she knew that I had the pox. It stands to reason that I'd give it to him, and he would pass it right along to whoever he took a notion to bed down with. Funny that she didn't see it coming, that she didn't even recognize it when it caught up with her, while I had laid awake nights planning for just such a calamity to overtake her. Maybe for an instant or two it irked me that she could not see my cleverness behind the trap that had sprung on her, but then I remembered that I needed the Meltons' bed and board, so I held my peace, and went back to acting like a concerned and devoted cousin.

"I reckon you caught it from Tom," I said. "You said yourself that Laura Foster was the talk of the settlement for all her goings-on with men. I reckon poor Tom paid the price for her loose ways." I held my breath then, to keep from laughing at this bare-faced flimflam, but Ann was nodding her head like I was telling her something she already knew. It is easy enough to lead a mule in the direction it already wants to go, and Ann had the wind up something fierce over our drab little cousin Laura. She *would* believe that Tom might be stolen away by that little mud hen, as if that were anything worth worrying about.

If I hated anybody in the world more than I hated everybody in general, I believe I'd wish Tom Dula on them. But Ann thought that the sun rose over his left shoulder, and it suited her to blame her troubles on Laura Foster, for she was already dead set against her.

The next time Tom darkened the door, she lit into him like a scalded cat. He had come in smiling, probably hoping for a pleasant spell by the hearth, and a plate of corn muffins, if I had made any, for he'd wait until doomsday to get anything baked by the fair hands of Ann Melton. But he got more warmth than he bargained for that day: Ann's wrath could have melted an anvil.

She ran at him, same as she often did to fling herself into his embrace, but, though he stood open-armed to meet her, she pulled up short, and thrust her face up in to his, and screamed out her words as if he was still on the other side of the gate. "I am poxed, Tom Dula! Bound to die! And it is on account of *you*."

I stood off in the corner, watching this, and holding my breath so as not to laugh. But it was interesting to watch the pair of them. I spend a lot of time watching people, seeing when they smile or frown, and what they say to good news or bad tidings, and I try to remember to do the same, for if I did not make myself remember to smile or frown, all I would ever show the world is an empty stare. I was born past caring about anything.

When Ann flew at him, Tom Dula froze, and turned ashy pale, letting her wrath break over him like a bucket of cold water. If he could have turned and run, I believe he would have. "You have killed me, Tom!" she wailed, beating her little fists against his chest, and letting loose a storm of heavy weeping.

He held her close to him, with an empty stare upon his own face, but he stroked her hair and murmured soft words to her, the way I have seen people talk to a child that has fallen down and cut itself, or to a horse that is fixing to bolt. Finally, when the nerve storm looked to be about over, he tilted her chin up so that he could look into her face, which was blotched and streaky with her tears, but she didn't look as unsightly as she ought to have done after such a flood of temper. If I had let loose a tantrum such as that, I'd have looked like a withered winter apple dug out of the root cellar. But not Ann. She looked like a rose in a shower of warm rain. Ann had too much of everything, which was hard lines on the rest of us, and that set me to thinking again on what I might do to change that.

"What has sot you to wailing?" Tom asked her, with an edge to his voice, but he was smiling a little, too, for Ann's tempers are legion, and most of the time they are of no more consequence than a summer squall.

This time, though, she was not to be comforted with smiles and embraces, even from her beloved Tom. She glared up, cutting him with those dark eyes. "I am poxed, Tom," she said, not screaming any longer, but in a quiet, shaky voice that was holding back a flood of tears. "You give me the soldiers' ailment, and since you never had it when you come home from the War, I reckon I know where you came by it lately."

He was looking over her shoulder straight at me, but before he could say anything, Ann stamped her foot and said, "From Laura Foster! That's where!"

I was holding my breath then, wondering if Tom was sober enough to have worked out where he picked up the pox in the first place, before he went and passed it on to our drab cousin Laura, but I need not have worried. If Tom had sense enough to work it out, he didn't say so. He and James Melton were alike in that respect: right or wrong, they generally let Ann have her own way about things. All she had to do was weep and storm, and shout at whoever displeased her, and the men generally stepped aside and let her have her way.

I did, too, sometimes, but not on account of her carrying-on. I could watch her rave and scream from sun-up to midnight without batting an eye, but I thought it best not to let on that I was not afraid of her, nor that I cared so little for her contentment. I had my bed and board to think of, after all. I found the easiest way to deal with Miss Ann was to let her think she was getting her way, and if I could do that, and still go about my business on the sly, so much the better. I'll take peace and quiet, if it comes cheap enough.

I was watching her, though, all the time. Looking to see where that little spot of weakness lay within her. If you intend to hurt someone, it's best to find out where hitting them will do the most good. I studied her posture, checking for a sign of tautness in her neck that would show she was fixing to set at Tom again, once she got her second wind, but she was slumped against him with her face pressed against his chest, making little kitten noises, while he stroked her hair.

They didn't take any more notice of me after that, so I went away to see to the chickens.

Later on I heard that Tom had gone off to see Dr. Carter to get treatment for his ailment, same as Ann did. R.D. Hall said that Tom was in a bate about his affliction, and claiming he would "put through" whoever gave it to him. But he never did any more than just complain about it. As far as I could tell, Tom's tempers were like summer storms: quick and hard, but gone in a flash, leaving no trace they'd ever been. Women's anger is different. We burn long and slow, and you may never see the flames, but that doesn't mean it's over.

Wilson Foster's place is a five-mile walk from the Melton farm, over in German's Hill, just past the Caldwell County line. Ann swears that Tom Dula makes the journey every few nights, leastways she's afraid he does, so I reckon all that marching in the infantry got him used to the exercise. Or maybe he's just like a sorry old dog that will travel clear across the county to find a bitch in heat. Making that five-mile walk afforded me a deal less pleasure than it would Tom, but I set my mind on doing it every week or so anyhow, taking care to arrive in the early evening so as to be gone by the time Tom made his rounds.

It's a good thing that James Melton is an able shoemaker as well as a farmer, for I must have worn out half a deer hide in shoe leather, walking those muddy paths in the April mists to reach German's Hill before full dark. The damp cold seeped all the way to my bones, and plastered my hair against my cheeks, but I was set on going, not for the joy I'd find at journey's end, but for another kind of joy altogether.

When I could get my chores done, I'd set out at earliest twilight, and count on reaching the Fosters' place in time to help Cousin Laura get supper on the table, which meant, of course, that I would be asked to help them eat it. I didn't mind peeling potatoes and frying up apples, because if I had stayed to eat with the Meltons, I would have had to do all the cooking, instead of just helping out by doing half of it. Besides, I judged that Cousin Laura was more apt to talk when she was too busy fixing supper to think overmuch about what she was saying to me. I hoped she would get to talking and all but forget that I was there, and then I would learn what secret it was she was fluffed up over, like a broody hen.

If I put my mind to it, I can gentle people the same as I've seen some drovers do to horses. Soft words, no quick movements, and never a hint of judging them or being riled. People in these parts are not, by and large, trusting souls, and the War has made them even more leery of strangers. When we came of age, Laura, Ann, and I, strangers—in uniform or not—meant trouble. We saw barns burned and livestock stolen. Ordinary farmers got bushwhacked and left on the road with their throats cut, murdered by one side or the other, as if which side had done it would have counted for anything. I reckon all of us learned to give as good as we got, and to take whatever we could from them that had more than we did. But the War was over now, and maybe some folks were letting themselves forget what they had learned about the danger of trusting people. Anyhow, I wasn't a stranger to Laura Foster, for all that we didn't grow up together. I was kin. And if you can't trust your kinfolks, who can you trust?

*Why, nobody.*

I wouldn't forget that lesson, and I figured I'd give her cause to remember it as well.

So I told her how lucky she was to be so thin and pretty. Scrawny passes for pretty while you are young, and it puts people in a good mood to be warmed with praise; though you would be wasting your time to try it on me, for I can always see the truth through the white-wash.

I let her talk by the hour, it seemed like, about how life was passing her by while she was stuck in her daddy's house, taking care of his young'uns like a hired girl.

I sat beside her at the table, peeling puckered winter apples, and nodding my head in agreement every time she stopped to draw breath. I remembered to pat her hand and pull a sorrowful face when her tears spilled over on to her sallow cheeks. Laura was making stew for dinner, same as she did most nights, because watery flour and potatoes is the best way to make a smidgeon of meat feed a slew of people. Two skinned rabbits lay on the table beside the flour bowl, looking to me like stillborn babies, but that was a comment I kept to myself.

"T'ain't fair." Laura's voice was shaking, and I saw tears plop in to the stew pot.

"It is hard lines on you, Laura," I told her, for it was plain what she wanted to hear. "You have put in enough of your youth taking your mama's place in this house, and it's only right that you should have a chance to make a family of your own."

"Well, it is," she said, wiping her wet face with the back of her hand. "And I mean to do just that before too long. You wait and see."

"I'm sure Mrs. Dula would welcome another daughter about the farm, though she already has one of her own. But Tom's sister is a grown girl now, and she'll be out and gone before too long, I'll warrant."

It had been a stab in the dark, and when Laura stopped stirring the stew and turned to stare at me, open-mouthed, I saw that I had guessed wrong, and I hastened to set it to rights before she remembered herself and stopped confiding. "Of course, I don't know what anybody would want with Tom Dula, for all that our cousin Ann sets such a store by him. I guess you could hope to live long enough for him to inherit that land, if the taxes don't claim it first, but if it's up to him to run the place, it will fall to ruin about his ears one of these days."

She tossed her head. "I ain't studying about Tom Dula, Pauline. He's all right to pass the time with, 'cause Lord knows there ain't nothin' else to do around here, but going over to the Dulas wouldn't hardly be a change from where I am now. Just swapping one dirt farm for another, and waiting for hard work and childbed to take me off, like it did my mama."

It seemed to me that she had just ruled out mankind in general with those true words, but I judged she was not bright enough to work this out for herself. It was only Tom she was set against, and not the male sex in general. Laura thought she was going somewhere, and I wanted to know where.

I tried again. "Anyone can see how good you are at taking care of young'uns. There's more than one widower in these parts with motherless babes to raise, and a tidy little farm in need of a helpmeet. Any of them would be glad to take you to wed."

Laura shook her head. "I have had enough of other people's children. And enough of hill farming, too. I want to get clean away from here."

I couldn't afford to make any more wrong guesses about what was in her mind. We were near to the secret now, and she would be like a broody hen a-guarding it. I cast my thoughts about, trying to light on some man who would be able take care of her without having a farm to rely on. The local gentry did not figure in my calculations. There were rich men enough, even in Wilkes County, but Laura's soiled reputation had spread in whispers about the settlement, and I knew that no doctor or landowner would bother with a penniless girl who was damaged goods. Even if she had been beautiful, they'd not have troubled to marry her, and beautiful she was not. But I doubt she had ever been five miles from home, so there was no use thinking of anybody farther afield than the settlement.

I don't know what made me light on an answer just then, unless it was thinking about fallen women, and remembering how folks had said that Ann had gone and lain with the drovers for a yard of cloth or a sack full of beans.

The drovers run cattle from over the mountains in Tennessee right through here on their way to the bigger Carolina cities farther east. If a girl wanted to get shut of her home county, that would be the way out, for they were only passing through. Like as not, Laura would have met them the same way Ann did, by bartering what she had beneath her skirts for whatever they would give her for a few minutes of pleasuring behind a tree somewhere. The wonder of it was that any of them would want more of her than that. I couldn't see why.

"You found you a drover," I said, soft as I could, for I knew she'd be in mortal fear of being overheard.

Laura got big-eyed and put one skinny finger to her lips, and shook her head.

I thought surely I had got to the truth at last, but I could tell by the way her cheeks turned red that there was more to it than that. "Well, whoever he may be, I am happy for you, Cousin," I said, pushing my mouth into a smile. "And you have my word that I will not breathe a word to your father." Which was true, as I had other plans for the news.

She nodded. "I know I can trust you, Pauline. You know how unhappy I am, and you know what it's like to be a servant. So does he."

I nodded, and squeezed her hand to give her encouragement, and I was careful not to show how she had riled me with those easy words. No, I did not know what it was like to be a servant, really. I never felt like those that took me in and paid me wages were my betters. I was getting room and board for my doctor visits, and working when I had to, so that I could keep the Meltons' roof over my head, but I never felt tied to anything or anybody.

What did either one of the Meltons have to make them better than me? A few acres of scrub land on a hill in the middle of nowhere? Why, they neither one of them could read or write any more than I could, and there wasn't one dish in that house that wasn't made of tin. And, as for being clever, I'd show them who outranked who before all was said and done. Whenever I took a notion, I could walk out on Cousin Ann, and, when I did, I'd pay her back for all the ordering I took from her, and all the times I worked while she laid around, queening it over me, because she had married a man with land. One of these days I would show the whole sorry bunch who was master here, and when I had done calling the tune, they would be a deal worse off than they ever thought I was.

Now, though, I was lacking in stones for my sling, so I had to take care to sweet-talk Cousin Laura so that she would confide in me. She had poured me a tin mug of chicory coffee, and I took a sip of it, wishing I had a dollop of honey to cover up the bitter taste, or, even better, a big slug of whiskey. Still, drinking it kept me warm, while I tried to think what women wanted to hear when they reckoned themselves in love.

"So he's not a drover, then? But a drover is a fine figure of a man. Strong, too."

Laura wasn't paying any mind to my prattle, which was just as well, for I had no idea how to praise nasty, smelly cow men, who hardly saw the indoors from one season to the next, and who looked to the rain for their bathing. I had been with drovers a time or two up home, and it was all I could do to hold my breath until they were done with me.

"He is no drover by trade, but he sure is a fine figure of a man." Laura leaned close and whispered to me, and her tears had stopped. "I've known him all my life, but of course we didn't see each other any more once we stopped being little children. We just lost track of each other, I reckon, for our paths would never cross in the ordinary way of things."

I was toting up all she said, trying to work out what she was getting at. "Surely you'd see him at church, Laura."

She shook her head. "Oh, no. If he went to church, he would go with his own people."

I had it now, but I was so thunderstruck by the news that I could not even speak to interrupt her.

She got all moony-eyed, remembering meeting up with him again. "I had gone to see Cousin Ann, and he was out on the road, chasing a brindled calf that had got loose from the pen, and it near took my breath away to look at him. I didn't even recognize him at first. His black hair was spilling out from underneath his hat, and his skin was the color of a buckeye nut, and, though it was September, I reckoned he had a touch of the sun."

"It sounds like *you* did," I said, but I remembered to smile to take the sting out of the words, and I went on without thinking, "Sounds like he's at least a half breed."

She nodded. "He says his granddaddy was a Shawnee. But of course, the coloreds mostly do say that around here. They seem to think it is shameful to be kin to the people that owned them, though I can't see why. It's no fault of theirs."

"And who were the people that owned him?"

She leaned even closer, barely whispering it to me, as well she might. "His people were slaves of Wash Anderson's family over on the Stony Fork Road. Johnny is free now, of course, but he still lives with the Andersons, and works on that farm of theirs, between the Meltons and the old Bates Place. But he says he's wanting to go west, where life is easier for such as him."

I sifted through this piece of news. *A freed slave.* Even if it were true, him claiming to be Indian would hardly have mattered alongside of that. It did make one thing clear, though: how it was that a handsome young man could want Laura Foster. I reckoned that no man but a colored one would think her worth having, for if my mud hen cousin outranked anybody in this world, it would be the likes of him.

She was too caught up to see the sneer on my face, and I took care to wipe it away quick, before she did spy it. "He's a-wanting to go west real soon, and he says he'll take me with him."

"How do you come to be with him?" I said quickly, to stop myself from asking why any man bent on heading west would want to be saddled with my drab and penniless little cousin.

"Well, when I met him a-chasing that calf in the road, I stood in front of the beast and flapped my apron to make it run back toward him. He put the rope around its neck, and stopped to thank me for my help. Then I took a more careful look at him, and I remembered who he was, so I smiled back. He asked me how I was, and said he was sorry to hear that my mama had died. I walked on back to the Andersons' barn with him while he put the calf back in its pen, and we talked about how we all used to play together as young'uns. I remember that he was always good to me in those days. He'd skin up a tree to bring me an apple, or pick berries for me, even in the briars, and when we all took cane poles down to the river to fish, he'd put the slimy old worm on the hook for me. Then we got to talking about how everything has changed since we were young, on account of the War and all."

I didn't suppose he was sorry that the War had changed things, for it had given him his freedom. I wondered what they found to talk about beyond that. They ought to have been worried about somebody seeing them passing the time of day together. Plenty of folks around would take exception to that, and if they had a mind to teach him a lesson, he'd be lucky to escape with his life. But Laura was too far gone to be reached with common sense. "After that, I started walking that way most every week on purpose, and we got to be friends again. His name is John, and he treats me better than Tom Dula ever thought about."

Well, he would, I thought, for one harsh word or a slap from him, and his fine white lady-love could let out a squawk that would get him strung up from the nearest tree. "So he is called John. What's his other name?"

She shrugged. "Still calling himself Anderson. As light as he is, I guess he may have more right to the family name than most slaves do."

"And the other—you know—his neighbors? Do they know?"

"There aren't many colored folks in Reedy Branch, and if there were, they wouldn't care what Johnny and me do together. We lost so many young men in the War that a woman is lucky to find any kind

of man at all. It's him or a fat old widower, I reckon, for Tom Dula
ain't the marrying kind. The freed slaves mind their own business,
same as we do. And maybe they think it serves the white folks right
for him to take up with one. Like winning a little battle for all of
them. But we don't care about that. We're the same as we were as
children—just . . . kind to each other."

I thought John Anderson was playing conkers with the devil to
be risking his neck for the likes of Laura, but that was his lookout. I
just wished he had picked Ann, is all. I wonder how that would have
set with Tom Dula. And I wondered if James Melton could be bothered to care if his wife took up with him instead of Tom.

I looked at Laura, trying to figure out what she was planning to
do. "So you have sworn off Tom now?"

She shrugged. "He comes by now and again, and I don't say no.
No point in it, is there? Locking the barn door on Tom after he's already had it? I can't undo that."

She would get no argument from me, because I never could see the
sense of what folks call "faithfulness," nor why they would want it. The
chicken don't care if you eat her egg or another hen's for your breakfast,
and I didn't see that there was much more to it than that, but I do
know that, for some reason, most people do mind about such things.

"And, anyway, people in the settlement know about me and Tom.
It keeps them from looking for anybody else taking up with me."

The stew would have boiled away if I had not got up to stir it, for
Laura was sitting at the table, twisting a plait of her rabbitty brown
hair, and looking calf-eyed into the fire. "I do miss Johnny something
fierce, but we can't meet too often, for fear we'll be seen together.
Once people got to talking, there'd be no shutting them up, so I keep
having to do with Tom, and seeing Johnny only now and then. I feel

like a bear in a cage. There ain't nothing else to do around here, except chores. If I didn't have something to do besides washing and cooking, I'd take leave of my senses. Tom is as good as anything else. Us being together is nothing to either one of us, but just a way to pass the time that don't feel like working."

It always felt like work to me, but I nodded like I understood her nonsense. "So your heart is set on your nut brown boy—if he keeps his word about taking you away with him?"

She slapped the table with her open hand, and the stirring spoon clattered off on to the floor. "Not if! When! He swore it. Johnny says he plans to light out of here when the weather gets warm—near the end of May. I've made up my mind that when he comes through here, I'm packing up my clothes, and going with him."

I laughed. "Well, you'd best not let word get around that you are fixing to run off with a freed slave, Cousin. Else he won't get any farther than the end of a rope."

She so far forgot herself as to shout at me. "Don't you think I know that? I ain't told nobody but you, Pauline. I'm counting on you not to give us away." Right away, she clapped her hand over her mouth, and looked around, fearful that somebody had come in and overheard her, but nobody was there except the baby, asleep in its pallet on the floor. It stirred and moaned at the sound of its big sister raising her voice, but Laura cast a fearful look at the baby and quieted down at once. It tossed a time or two, and rolled over so its back lay to the fire, and went on sleeping.

"Oh, please, Pauline," she said, whispering again, and grabbing at my sleeve with her fingers. "You have to keep my secret. Don't let on to nobody that I told you. It's only for a couple more weeks, and then I'll be shut of here for good."

I shrugged. "It's nothing to me, Laura. I just hope your man realizes the chance he is taking. If he gets killed for messing around with you, it'll be on your head, not mine."

"But you promise you won't give me away?"

"I will not tell anybody that you have any lover other than Tom Dula. I swear." It makes me smile when I can tell someone the absolute truth, and still be planning their destruction. None of them could see more than a yard in front of their noses. But I could. I had everything I needed now to bait my trap, and so long as it ensnared Ann Melton, I did not care a damn who else got hurt. That was their lookout.

# ZEBULON VANCE

How did I come to be mixed up in the trial of Tom Dula in the first place?

He was a stranger to me, and his part of the Carolina mountains lay a hundred miles from the part in which I grew up. In my explanation I will attempt to be truthful, but I am sure there are those among my opponents who will deem my honesty *arrogance*. Honesty has very little to recommend it. Mostly, it gets you into trouble, even faster than liquor; and, though I have no personal weakness for the latter, I do find the former well-nigh irresistible.

*"Tell the truth and shame the devil,"* people say. Well, I'm not entirely sure that it would. I think Old Scratch might positively delight in watching us engineer our own downfall by practicing a trait universally acclaimed to be a virtue.

So let me tempt fate with the truth: I needed the work, and those Wilkes County lawyers who asked the judge to appoint me to spearhead the defense wanted to be spared the local notoriety of having championed an unpopular defendant. It is required that lawyers accept a certain number of cases pro bono in order to keep their license to practice, and since I had been politicking for most of the previous decade, I had some catching up to do with my legal obligations. A paying case would have been an even greater kindness, but I cannot pretend that I did not need the pro bono credit even more. I also needed a much-talked-about trial to bring my name before the public—favorably I hoped. At least in Charlotte, where I had set up shop with Clement Dowd, public sentiment would not run so high against my client as in Wilkes County.

That's why the two local attorneys, Allison and Armfield, were willing to let me lead the defense. They were both able men, with more trial experience that I had, but Wilkes is a sparsely populated place, and practically everybody there was kin to either the accused killers or the victim. There can't be any joy for a local lawyer in bearing the brunt of the strong feelings such a case was bound to stir up. But since I lived far away, in Charlotte, they reasoned that I could represent an unpopular defendant and come out unscathed, because nobody where I'm from knew or cared about the particulars in this little backcountry case. I don't suppose anybody even much cared if I won or lost it, so long as the letter of the law had been carried out to the satisfaction of the court. And I needed the practice in front of a jury—how better to accomplish that than by taking an obscure case among strangers?

I don't suppose anybody gave much thought to the poor accused man when they were making these plans for their own convenience and for my professional advancement.

Hard lines on him.

Those fine upstanding gentlemen who had undertaken the defense of Thomas P. Dula were conscientious attorneys, and they made every effort to be cordial to me, but I do not think they were overly concerned about the outcome of the trial, which they seemed to think was a foregone conclusion anyhow, as they believed him to be guilty. The accused man could not afford to pay them to think otherwise, so their thoughts turned on observing the rituals of justice, rather than on justice itself. They kept meticulous records, with particular attention to their own expense forms, and they passed the time at trial courteously amongst their fellows in the law, and for both sides the defendant was simply a "situation," the reason for the ritual they all observed, but otherwise not a part of it. Such a procedural charade is easier to bear if the wretch is guilty. You tell yourself that a loss in court may be the means by which true justice will be served, and, if you should happen to win, why then it sweetens the victory to know that the credit is all yours and not owing to any virtue or merit on the part of the defendant.

I did not take capital cases in my youth, in the little stint in the circuit court up around Asheville. Always for me, the law was a means to an end, an apprenticeship through which I must pass in order to reach public office. It worked, too: Congressman, Governor . . . I had gone far in three short decades of life, but I was honest enough not to risk some poor devil's life while I was putting in my time as a practicing attorney. Let me get some horse thief acquitted or take sides in a land squabble—that was momentous enough for my blood.

Times had changed for me though. I had applied for parole from the United States government, for my part in the lately defeated Confederate government. They ought to have taken into consideration how long and hard I argued to dissuade my home state from seceding in the first place, but of course that carried no weight with them.

. . .

One of the attorneys assigned (just as well) to sit second chair to me
for the trial was Captain Richard M. Allison, who was a cavalry officer in the War before he was invalided out in '64, and then, like the
rest of us, he had gone back to the tamer business of fighting battles
with fine words and stacks of paper. I suppose that Allison will be
called "captain" for the rest of his life, even if he lives half a century
past that four-year madness of a war, but I aim to leave off the courtesy title of "governor," just as soon as I am allowed to get myself elected
to some new office again—"senator" would be favorite.

When the good captain told me of the incident in Wilkes County,
my first thought was how improvident it had been of this Dula fellow
to indulge in an act of private violence in such perilous times as
these. Surely we had troubles enough in the land, with bushwhackers
marauding the country roads, carpetbaggers infesting the new state
government, and all manner of profiteering and petty scoundrels at
work picking at the carcass of the Old North State for the spoils of
war, without some callow young veteran adding a senseless murder
to the burden of the populace.

The young woman's death occurred in May of 1866—we were
then only a year past that war that had brought enough carnage to
the states comprising the Confederacy to put one in mind of the End
of Days. And the accused is a veteran of the 42nd infantry—not one
of mine, thank heaven, though I have heard it said that I spent little
time with my regiment while I had it, so that I might not even recognize a staff officer, much less a humble private. Still, everywhere I go
I am beset by men who claim to have served with me in the War, and

I hear them out, smiling and clasping their hands, but mostly I am thinking that if all those who claimed to have fought with the 26th North Carolina had really done so, we could have beaten the Yankees and Napoleon besides.

Captain Allison interviewed the two prisoners when they were first brought in to custody, and so when I arrived in Wilkes County to take nominal charge of the case, I sat down with him on that fine October afternoon, savoring the sunshine and a basket of mountain apples that some well-wisher had bestowed upon me outside the courthouse. Another comrade in arms, no doubt.

I had seen the prisoner for a short while that day, just to introduce myself and to assure him that I would do what I could for him. *Do what I could for him.* How often that phrase has come to my lips these past five years! When I was Governor, every day's post brought a heart-rending letter from some poor wife or mother, pleading with the all-powerful Governor of North Carolina to release her only son from his regiment, or to let him come home to be tended until his wounds healed. I sent them back what sympathy I could, but the truth was that even governors cannot tell the army what to do, and they would have paid no attention to me had I tried.

Usually the appeals on behalf of soldiers came from poor people in the mountain counties, because they are proud to claim me as one of their own. I know what swallowing of pride it took for these stoic and self-reliant people to ask for help from a powerful stranger, and I shared in their shame—theirs for asking and mine for being powerless to help them. Save a poor enlisted man with no influential family connections? Why, that's exactly who does die in a war, and everybody knows it—except, I suppose, the friends and family of the poor boy trapped in the thick of it. I doubt that even an emperor could change that fact of life—much less a governor.

That feeling of helplessness in the face of a poor young soldier came back to me as I stood there in the jail in Wilkesboro, echoing that threadbare phrase for the thousandth time. I wonder how many of the grieving wives and mothers actually believed that I could perform a miracle on their behalf. Judging by the polite but wary look on the face of the prisoner, he had no such illusions about my ability to cheat death. I felt sorry for him. Illusions make life bearable.

He was polite to me, a little in awe perhaps of having the former governor come to see him, but he seemed to take no comfort from my empty phrases. Perhaps that would make it easier for both of us when the inevitable verdict came in.

"Why did he do it then?" I asked Captain Allison. I was paring the apple with my little silver knife, but I was no less attentive for that. If I cannot pace, then I think better when I focus on some small task at hand. I could tell by the expression on that careful lawyer face of his what reply was forthcoming, and I held up my hand to forestall it.

"Yes, Allison, I know. Dula is presumed innocent until those twelve scoundrels that comprise the jury say otherwise. We'll take that as read. But we are not in court now, and there is no one in earshot of this porch to make mischief with our conversation, so just tell me why he is thought to have done it—if that phrasing suits you better."

I do believe the captain blushed, either at my plain speaking or in contemplation of the answer he would be forced to give to my question. He hemmed and hawed for a bit, looked away, and finally mumbled, "It is woman trouble, Governor."

I sighed. "We have a new governor in Raleigh now. It might be best to leave off calling me that before the Federals take a notion to haul me back to Capitol Prison for presumptuousness." I wouldn't put it past them. "Woman trouble, is it?"

He nodded unhappily. "The accused has a sordid reputation for being unchaste."

I was glad that my mustache hid the smile I could not quite suppress. "Well, he was a soldier, Allison."

"So were we all, Gov—er, Mr. Vance. I hope that military service did not cause us to lose the honorable principles we were taught in church and in childhood."

"Perhaps our client did not acquire those same principles, and surely the women he associated with were not the gentle ladies we are accustomed to."

Allison shuddered. "I should say they are not. Some of the details of this case . . . we shall have to clear the court of all female spectators—though why they would wish to attend in the first place, I cannot imagine."

Well, I could. But I let that pass. "Now what exactly do you mean by woman troubles?"

Captain Allison leaned forward, hand cupped above his lips, and hissed at me, "He has the pox, sir!"

I have the honor to be married to a preacher's daughter, who was raised in the genteel society of the Morganton planter class, so perhaps he thought I would be as easily shocked as my Harriette by such news, but I grew up in the rough-and-tumble world of the Carolina backcountry, and, after my father died, my family ran a way station for the cattle drovers who passed through Madison County. Between my association with these colorful specimens of humanity, my early career as a country lawyer, and my later years in Congress, I was quite inured to the specter of human iniquity in all its many forms.

I cannot say that I understood the impulse, though.

You might think otherwise, for, as I said, I grew up in the mountains that form Carolina's border with Tennessee, and many of the frontier folk up there had little use for the social conventions, and I do confess that for a year or two I enjoyed the drinking and the dancing of rough-and-ready Asheville, and I'll even admit to brawling a time or two, before I came down with the fever of ambition and went to bettering myself through education and mingling in polite society. In those days I lived up to the light I had, but it wouldn't have been bright enough to read by.

Despite my youthful escapades, the one snare that I never got caught in was a dalliance with unsuitable women. I never let my youth and high spirits blind me to that extent to the road that lay ahead. I was intent on bettering myself, and the road to privilege is best traveled alone until you are almost there.

As pretty and winsome as a frontier girl might be at seventeen, she would have proven a millstone around my neck if I had tried to marry her and drag her, unlettered and unrefined, up to the seats of the mighty, where I was bound and determined to go. I knew better than to risk my future for the momentary pleasure of a youthful romance. I waited until I was accepted to read law with the Woodfin brothers, two prominent attorneys in Asheville, and then I began in earnest the hunt for a suitable bride.

Do not misunderstand me. I was no fortune hunter in search of an heiress, nor did I marry one. Birth and breeding were what mattered to me. My Harriette was the orphaned daughter of a Presbyterian preacher—but she was raised by a gilt-edged family of the plantation aristocracy in Morganton. It was not money that I was after. I needed a well-born young woman, cultured and socially acceptable to the frontier Brahmin. She would see my potential to make something of myself, and I would honor her for her gentility, and aspire to live up to her standards. She would be my guide and my mentor among those "quality folks," whose ranks I had been determined to join since my days as a clerk at the resort hotel in Warm Springs.

I came from a good family myself—it was only the poverty caused by father's early death that put me at a disadvantage. But my mother meant for her seven children to succeed in life, and so when I was nearly twenty, she sold our drovers' inn in Lapland, and moved us to a modest frame house in Asheville. The town of Asheville had been built upon land purchased from Mother's family, the Bairds, and from my paternal grandfather David Vance, who had fought in the Revolution. In Asheville, if nowhere else on earth, I could count myself a prince.

I think John Woodfin took me on as a pupil to read law on account of that pedigree. I do not know what else he could have seen in a raw-boned youth from the hills. In addition to the Bairds and Grandfather Vance, the war hero, I was kin to the Erwins of Morganton through my mother's mother Hannah Erwin. Woodfin set a store by that, because he and his brother Nicholas had married two McDowell sisters from Morganton, and kinship with the Erwins and the McDowells connected you to everybody who was anybody west of Raleigh. I knew that my association with the Woodfin family would give me an entrée into that frontier aristocracy, and it was there that I proposed to seek a wife. Morganton is forty miles east of Asheville and outside the mountains. Like water, money and power seem to flow downhill, so the closer one gets to the flatlands, the more of it there is.

Presentable young men with prospects are at a premium in the Carolina backcountry, and so a few months after I began my association with the Woodfins, I was invited to a formal party at Quaker Meadows, the McDowells' elegant home in Morganton. It was there that my fellow law student Augustus Merrimon introduced me to the McDowells' ward, Miss Harriette Espy, orphaned in infancy, and raised by the McDowells, so that, while she was not an heiress, her social connections were like threads of spun gold. The tiny young lady standing by the punch bowl, silver ladle in hand, was auburn-haired with earnest gray eyes and a kind face.

"You are reading the law?" she said, after the introductions had been effected. "Oh, what a noble calling!"

"Well, that doesn't relieve the tedium too awful much," I said, trying to balance a plate in one hand and a cup of punch in the other. I felt like a mule in a choir loft.

She ignored the jest. "I do so admire a learned man, sir. My own dear, departed father studied at the Princeton Theological Seminary. I shall pray for your success, Mr. Vance."

I had recently decided to leave the Woodfins' tutelage and attend the University of North Carolina, and so I played on the heartstrings of this pious young lady, telling her that I should soon be far from home and friendless, and assuring her that entering into a correspondence with my unworthy self would be an act of Christian charity.

The courtship wasn't all smooth sailing, for Miss Espy ran a tight ship when it came to piety, decorum, and, most especially, absolute fidelity. Why, before we had exchanged no more than a handshake and a sheaf of letters, I nearly lost her, when that infernal stick-insect

Merrimon told her that I had been paying addresses to another young lady—an incident that occurred months before I even met Miss Espy, mind you, but she wrote me a letter that would have frozen a bonfire, telling me that our association was at an end, but that she would pray for me. Well, I deserved a law degree just for being able to talk my way out of that one, for it was the hardest case for the defense I ever had. (At least until the matter of Thomas Dula.) But in the end I carried the day with Miss Harriette, and on August 2, 1853, in the Presbyterian Church in Morganton, Miss Espy became Mrs. Zebulon Baird Vance, before God and a host of frontier gentry, whose approval at last I had won.

Forever after, folks said that Harriette was the apple of my eye, and so she was, for like that apple in the Garden of Eden that imparted wisdom to our first parents, so my Harriette bestowed the wisdom of civilization upon me—the gift of powerful friends and the wit to use our connections to advance my career. Indeed I treasured her—but to return to the metaphor of Eden, I am mindful that *any* apple from that fabled tree would have conferred those self-same gifts.


So I sat there on a porch in Wilkesboro, peeling an unmetaphorical apple, and listening to Captain Allison stammer through an explanation of the behavior of our client. I was not shocked, though I would have never repeated a word of our conversation to my sainted wife. She would have been horrified beyond the power of speech. She'd have expected me to give up the case on the spot, I suppose, and since I was not being paid a red cent to conduct the defense, it would be hard to argue to the contrary. But, after all, somebody had to defend the poor boy.

I put down the apple. "So you are telling me that this Dula fellow had seduced the victim, Laura Foster, and promised to marry her, but that he was also in an adulterous relationship with his codefendant, Mrs. Ann Melton? And the state's witness, the servant girl, Pauline Foster . . . she also claims that the accused has had—"

Allison nodded unhappily. "Carnal knowledge. Yes. So she alleges."

I let out my breath in a long whistle. "I see what you mean about requiring that all ladies be barred from the court when all this testimony goes into the record."

I was thinking what a waste his life had been, if he had chosen only to spend it on idle pleasures that led nowhere. Life is a gold coin—but you can only spend it once. How sad that a likely-looking fellow should throw away his one chance for so little of lasting value. I hoped he enjoyed himself, though. How sad if it had all been for nothing.

"I spoke with him briefly, you know," I told Captain Allison. "He did not strike me as a dissolute fellow."

My colleague ventured a tight smile. "Well, sir, they keep him sober in the jail, you know."

"Even so . . ." I shook my head. "He is quite young. . . . I perceive weakness . . . laziness covered by a facile charm, perhaps. . . . He struck me as the sort of amiable fellow who would go along with anything a comrade suggested, provided the task was not too onerous, or if agreeing was less troublesome than saying no."

"That may be, sir, but it won't save him."

"No. I hadn't got to the point of thinking about ways to get him off, Allison. I was just indulging in a bit of speculation. I always want to know why people do things."

He shook his head. "You know, Mr. Vance, I'll bet you that some-times they wish *they* knew."

After a moment of companionable silence, I said, "Well, you know, I also met the other defendant today."

Perhaps it was a trick of the sunlight, but I could swear that Cap-tain Allison was blushing again. "Oh—er—did you?"

My mind was still on biblical metaphors. I remembered an apoc-ryphal story that—as the husband of a rock-ribbed Presbyterian—I was not encouraged to believe in: the tale of Lilith, Adam's "other woman." They say she wasn't human—a demon, perhaps, or one of the fairy folk they talk of in the old country. Dula's codefendant Ann Melton brought that old story to mind.

When I asked to see her at the jail, I was mindful of doing my bounden duty as her attorney, but I dreaded the encounter, for I imagined some poor weeping wretch, too frightened to speak, cling-ing to my coat sleeve and begging to be saved from the gallows.

But when the jailer brought her into the interview room, I found that I had done Mrs. Melton the grave injustice of underestimating her. My first impression—which I was careful not to show—was sheer admiration of her beauty, which affected me as I might stand back and appreciate a waterfall or a sunset, without having any desire to possess it. She was beautiful—not in the robust country way of an ordinary farm girl, for that is merely the bloom of youth and animal spirits, and it fades as fast as summer lightning. Ann Melton's face had the sculpted perfection of Pygmalion's marble goddess made mortal. Her alabaster skin was offset by smoldering dark eyes and a cloud of black hair that fell in waves about her shoulders. And she carried herself like a duchess, who had, by some error, fallen among ignorant rustics who had rudely imprisoned her. How extraordinary that such a rare creature should have come from an illiterate and shiftless family living in a primitive backwoods cabin in the middle of nowhere. Had she been more fortunate in her circumstances, she could have married a prince, I should think. All those thoughts passed through my mind in the time it took her to enter the room and sit in the chair opposite me across the little pine table in the interview room. No doubt she had been studying me, too, for her glance at me was one of cool appraisal. Here was no weeping wretch, in fear of her life, but rather a cool and disdainful beauty, who took men's admiration in stride, and who took it for granted that her perfection would spare her the indignities visited upon lesser beings.

"I am sure this is most bewildering to you," I said, attempting to put her at her ease.

She rolled her eyes and permitted herself a small mocking smile. "I understand it all right. People have been talking all summer, and they figure one of us killed Laura Foster."

"Or that you did it together."

"Well, we didn't."

"Do you know how Miss Foster met her death?"

She shrugged and looked away. "It's nothing to do with me—or Tom."

"Well, there's no percentage in trying the two of you together, in any case. I intend to request severance in this case. That means that you will each have your own trial."

She nodded. "Different juries?"

"Yes."

"And in his trial, you'll say I did it, and in my trial you'll say he did it, and we'll both walk free."

I blinked. I had expected her to demand that I discover the real killer. "Well, I hope that we may see both of you acquitted of this terrible deed, but I would be remiss in my duty as your lawyer if I did not warn you that if you are convicted, you would be hanged."

She gave me a pitying smile. "They'll never put a rope around this pretty neck."

# PAULINE FOSTER
## May 1866

Ever since I found out that I had got the pox, I had been keeping still and listening whenever folks talked about it. They said it takes people in different ways, some faster than others, so I could not know what is in store for me. They said, though, that sometimes the disease poisons the mind, driving the sufferer to madness, and causing him to thrash and rave in a world of delirium until he finally rots from the inside, and dies. That may be a mercy, to be deprived of thinking so that you don't realize what has become of you. But the future never troubles me overmuch. What I got to wondering about more and more was whether the madness of the pox had anything to equal the lunacy afflicting them that called themselves "in love."

By the beginning of May, Ann Melton was pacing the floor like a penned-up bull downwind of heifers, and imagining Tom at Laura Foster's place at any given hour of the day. It was tempting to think that the pox had got to her quick and gone to her head, and I can't say I would have minded much if it had, but she seemed the same as ever on any subject except Tom. I tried to reason with her a time or two, more to get some peace than to give her any, but she would not be comforted with common sense, so I gave it up, and let her rave.

It didn't sweeten my day any, though, to have to listen to her carping while I did the chores, sweeping around her feet like as not, and stepping over her to pick up an old bed quilt that had fallen on to the floor, while Ann wept and cursed Tom Dula for the faithless hound that he was.

"I don't see that he's changed," I said once, to shut her up. "He is the same rotter now that he was at fourteen, bedding a married woman, and anybody else who would let him. I don't see why it's bothering you now. You've had most of your life to get used to the way of him. And you ain't tied to him, so if he makes you as miserable as all that, you need never see him again. Just stick to your husband, who never gave you a minute of grief, and forget about Tom Dula."

Ann laughed. "That won't happen."

"Likely not. Well, then, if you're just fuming about his latest dalliance, why, you said yourself that such carryings-on don't signify nothing to Tom." Here I paused and pretended to be busy with my sweeping, but all the while watching her out of the corner of my eye. "Unless you think Cousin Laura means more to him than the rest."

She threw me a look. "'Course not!" she said, as if I had suggested that chickens could talk. "Tom ain't never loved nobody but me, and he never will. I know that as well as I know my own name. As if he could prefer a scrawny milksop like her over me! He's just trifling with Laura to pass the time, and to spite me for not dropping everything in my life for him. I reckon he thought I'd go off with him when he came back from the War, and I was so thankful to see him, I might have done it, but if I had, we'd have both starved. I have told him so often enough, but he won't see sense about that, and it hurt him that I refused to go. I think he minds about it still. That's how I know that 'tis more spite than devotion that takes Tom over to German's Hill."

I shrugged. "Bid him not to go then. If he is as set on you as you claim, he'll do what you tell him to, won't he?"

She laughed merrily at that. "What? Tom? Harken to me over a dalliance, when I up and married James Melton without a by-your-leave to him? Why it would just give him that much more joy in doing it, knowing he was paying me back as well."

I stopped straightening out the tangle of quilts on her bed, and turned to look at her. "Well, if it don't mean any more than that to him, then why do you care about it?"

She got all quiet then and put her face in her hands. Then she said, so softly that I barely heard her, "Because it wounds me to think about him being with her."

"You mean like you being with James Melton?"

"That's different."

"How?"

"I had to live, didn't I? Had to get shut of my mama before I ended up like her, with a passel of fatherless young'uns, and nothing to look forward to but the next bottle."

I shook my head. "Even so, it's funny to hear you harping on faithfulness, while you are still living with that husband of yours."

Ann shrugged and turned away. "It's different. Tom knows."

Spring had finally come to the valley, and I was glad of the warm weather, for I was mortally tired of wearing the same dirty, sweaty clothes all the time, and not getting a chance to wash them. The Melton cabin stank of sweat and chimney smoke and unwashed chamber pots, but now that the days were fine I could go out in the yard and boil the clothes in the kettle, and on warm afternoons, we could leave the doors open and air out the room for a while. I didn't feel much like giving the place the scrubbing it needed, and if Ann didn't insist upon it, why, I wouldn't, but I figured out how to get rid of most of the stench, just to make it livable in there.

I gloried in the sunshine, not even minding the chores so much as long as I could be outside, and I was feeling stronger with every passing day. I thought maybe Dr. George Carter's treatments had worked and made me well, but when I asked him about it, he said not. He thought it was only the mild spring weather that made me feel better, and that I still needed more treatments of bluestone and mercury. I hoped he was wrong about my sickness, but I did see how the sunshine could make me feel well, even if I wasn't. The farm work was still hard and never ending, but at least I didn't have to do it in bitter cold. There was less wood to tote, and soon we'd all be eating better as the gardens began to come up, and the game became more plentiful in the woods. There ain't much meat on a baby rabbit, but it's easy to kill, because it ain't got the sense to run from the hunter. And full-grown courting rabbits aren't much harder to pick off, because they seem to lose their minds come mating time, and forget to be careful.

My dim cousin Laura put me in mind of a courting rabbit herself these days, for she was so snake-charmed over that dark lover of hers that she'd walk into any snare you cared to lay in her path, so little did she notice anything going on outside her own head. All I had to do was nod and smile, and sit still and listen while she rattled on—and she'd have kept it up by the hour, if I could have stood it, but nothing she ever said interested me in the least, except that when I wasn't thinking about six other things, then I was sifting through all the babble, listening for something I could use. She wanted me to brush that long scraggly hair of hers until my arm ached, and all the while she'd be daydreaming out loud about that golden day when she'd get shut of her old life forever, and ride off into the west with her man. She hardly remembered I was there, for she was barely there herself. She had moved clear into the future, and she'd be sleepwalking until she caught up to it.

Tom Dula looked in at the Fosters now and again, but not nearly as often as Ann thought he did, for he loved the fields and woods, and the coming of spring meant that he could spend more time rambling in the sunshine, or—more likely—out napping under a tree where nobody could find him to put him to work. I reckon he did his share of hunting, too, though, because somebody had to put food on the Widow Dula's table, and with her other boys killed in the War, the job of supporting the family fell to Tom. He was happy enough to fish for his supper, or to snare some rabbits in the woods, but I never did see him behind a plow.

I never failed to ask Laura had she seen him since I last stopped in, and she'd give me a blank look as if it took her a moment even to recollect who he was. Then she'd shrug and tell me if he had or hadn't been by, as if it didn't matter to her one way or the other, and she couldn't be bothered to spare him a second's thought while she was busy dreaming about her sweetheart.

All of this news of their mutual indifference would have made Ann shout for joy, but I took care that she would learn none of it.

.  .  .

At least the walks I took for my visits to German's Hill were easier now, since the wind had stopped cutting through the valley like a skinning knife, and the lengthening spring days meant that I could near 'bout get there before nightfall now. Laura would be weaving in the evening after supper was done with, making cloth for a new dress for herself, and I always made a show of admiring it, hoping to put her in a good enough mood to make me one, too, for Dr. Carter's nostrums took all the money I made at the Meltons', and I couldn't even remember the last time I had anything new to wear. Everything I had was faded, or patched or threadbare, and I longed to throw the lot of it into the fire, but I had no way of getting anything better.

What the War didn't make impossible to get, it made too expensive to come by, so mostly we did without, and I was tired of it. If I could get a decent dress for the price of honeyed words and listening to a daydreaming fool, then I'd do it. I wish there had been a loom at the Meltons', for I'd even have been willing to learn weaving myself to get something clean and new to wear, but since Ann never did much of anything, there wasn't any use in James Melton buying one, for it would have been quilted with cobwebs before Ann ever got a yard of cloth out of it.

Anyhow, I suppose it was best that I kept going over to Wilson Foster's place to keep abreast of Cousin Laura's doings, while I kept on thinking what I could make of that secret. Meanwhile, I had each long walk back to think up new tales to tell Ann about how devoted Tom was to Laura, and how she doted on him. Of course, Ann could have gone over to German's Hill herself anytime she pleased and found out the truth of the matter, but I knew full well that she would do no such thing. Walking five miles up a muddy trace was not something Ann would willingly do, even for the best of reasons, and the Meltons had no horse, so she must go everywhere on foot. Her mother lived down the steep hill and across the Stony Fork Road, and she made that journey tolerably often, mostly to foist the children off on her, but there were few other destinations that she deemed worth the effort it would take to get there.

Ann never did care much for the society of other women, nor they for hers. She felt it was her right to be the center of attention, and she liked to be petted and made much of. Having to pass an evening sewing, or listening to the prattling talk of another woman on subjects that did not pertain to her, would have bored her to screaming fits. The thought of listening to other people's babies wailing, and having little children underfoot, putting their sticky hands on your dress, was enough to keep her from visiting most of the women on nearby farms, except when being stuck at home had made her miserable enough to endure a neighborly call.

Ann was never one to do anything out of duty or for the sake of other people's good opinion. Besides, she was so furious with Laura these days that she would never willingly go over there and face her rival. Ann was fond enough of shouting at folks and leaving her finger marks on them when they displeased her, but she dreaded looking the fool. I only had to hint a time or two that Laura would laugh at her jealousy and make sport of her misery, and when she got to believing that, it would have taken wild horses to get her over to Wilson Foster's place. It's funny how easy it is to make people believe what they want to believe or what they are most afraid of.

Ann hated every word I said about Tom Dula and Laura Foster, but never once did it cross her mind to doubt my word. One time she got so furious over what I had to tell that she went and kicked over a slop jar I had not yet emptied, and I had to get down on my knees with a rag and mop it up and then scrub the newly cleaned floor all over again, but it was worth it, just to see her weep.

You know how the Bible said that God called things into being just by saying the words of creation out loud? *Let . . . there . . . be . . . light.* Well, I reckon I know what that must have felt like, because in my own way I was doing much the same. It seemed like things I made up in my head turned into truth just because I spun tales about them and passed them off as gospel. The hardest part was to keep from laughing.

Ann practically pushed me out the door to go visiting in German's Hill, and when I got back, sometimes around sun-up, if I had stayed late and slept over, she'd be in a bate to get me off alone so she could hear what I had to tell. It wasn't easy, either. Sometimes I had been up drinking until the wee hours, and on that damp morning walk back, with my stomach queasy and my head pounding with every step I took, I'd be hard-pressed to get my thoughts together well enough to dissemble to Ann.

"Well, roll out the biscuit dough," I'd say, "while I catch my breath and get the eggs going in the skillet. It will take a while to tell you everything."

Most times Ann would be so crazed to know the worst of what was happening between Tom and Laura, that I could get her to do more than half the chores, while I spun out my tale, which I had worked up on the long walk back. It wasn't easy, neither, trying to think up sweet talk and what courting couples might say and do. All that syrupy nonsense always bored me so much that I never paid it any mind when folk were doing it around me for real. Now I was having to invent a romance out of whole cloth, and it was harder work than plowing with the milk cows.

One time Ann almost caught me, though, for I had just opened my mouth to tell her a new tale about Tom Dula's visit a-courting Laura, when Ann interrupted me to say that Tom had spent yester evening with her and James Melton. Hearing her out gave me time to think up a new piece of news, so when she drew breath, I told her that Laura had wept and raged for want of seeing her sweetheart last night. I got out of that predicament all right, but it was a near thing, and I thought to myself that in future I'd best wait and hear Ann's news before I delivered any more of mine.

It worried me that Tom had been here while I was gone. "Did he say anything about Laura?" I asked Ann, trying not to sound overly concerned about it.

She shook her head. "He never says two words about her. If I didn't know any better, I'd think he didn't give two hoots about her."

"He's trying to throw you off the scent, Ann. He knows there'll be trouble if you find out how things are between him and Laura."

She shrugged. "I don't like it, but I don't reckon it matters. Remember I told you about that Caroline Barnes what he courted a while back? That blew over, and this will, too. He'll always be at my beck and call. Always."

I went back to kneading biscuit dough then, and thinking on how I could use that.

Every now and again, Tom really would show up at Wilson Foster's place, and then I'd breathe a sigh of relief, because it meant I could have some real conversations to recite to Ann instead of having to conjure everything up out of my head on the cold walk back. Mostly, though, even when he did come, I'd have to improve on that, too, for there wasn't much between Tom and Laura that I could see. He didn't look calf's eyes at her or sweet-talk her like courting fellows generally do. Seemed to me like he'd as lief talk to her brothers as her.

Most times of an evening, when he did show up in German's Hill, Tom would slink in like a stray dog, flashing a smile to whoever caught his eye, and if he was invited to take supper, he'd pull up a chair between the boys, and tuck in with the rest of them, talking farming or hunting, or whatever anybody had a mind to run on about. Oh, he'd wink at Laura now and again, especially when he wanted biscuits or taters sent his way, but then Tom always winked at the ladies. I'd seen him do it to fat, gray widows twice his age at a social, and he didn't mean nothing at all by it. Maybe it made him feel important to watch old ladies giggle and blush when he showed them a penny's worth of his sunshine. He even tried it with me a time or two, but I just looked at him like he was something I'd have to scrape off my shoe, so he quit trying to dazzle me. Tom Dula didn't have one single thing that I wanted, except that it was in his power to hurt Ann Melton, and for that alone I tolerated his society.

He didn't seem to affect Laura much, either, with his smiles. Maybe her head was already too full of thoughts about her other lover, but truly I think that Tom's charm mostly worked on fat old ladies that he wouldn't have looked at twice, for real feelings. He was a handsome boy, and not much man about him, for all that he had been in the War. I think marrying-age women have to be more practical about who they take an interest in, but those dried-up old sticks who sat out the settlement socials gossiping in corners—why, they just beamed on Tom Dula as if he was a brand-new speckled pup. They didn't mean anything by it, either, I reckon. Maybe he was just a pretty child to the likes of them. But child-bearing women had too many real babies underfoot to bother about a handsome boy, who wouldn't work or settle down.

Once at a social when Tom's name came up in conversation, one of the younger women said, "Tom Dula? Why, he'd be like having a blood racehorse on a tenant farm—nice enough to show off, but useless for everyday." And all the other ladies around her nodded in agreement.

The exception to that was Ann. Ann never would hear a word against him, and for his part, no matter what other dalliances he might get up to, it seemed like he never changed toward her, either. I think if there is such a thing as love, which I don't altogether believe, then what Tom felt for Ann was real, and the rest was just a way of making his life easier by giving people what they wanted, as long as it didn't cost him nothing. He would take anything pleasant that was foisted upon him—sex with a likely young girl was the same as a piece of pie to him, as far as I could see—but it meant no more than that to him, either.

I had to be careful carrying tales to Ann about Tom Dula. I didn't want to make her so mad that she'd light in to Tom when next he came around. I wanted her simmering mad, but not aflame. Anger muddies up people's minds, so that they don't think clearly and they act too fast, without counting the cost of what they've done. I am blessed not to have that affliction. Nothing shakes me inside. When people pour their boiling anger over my head, I just get colder and slower inside, like a bear in a winter cave, and let them rage, while all the while I am thinking how I will hurt them down the road, when they have even forgotten how they treated me. I never forget anything.

So we lived through that first winter since the end of the War, and though folk said it was a mercy not to have to hear about any more men dying, and not having shortages from the blockades and the armies attacking the railroads, things still weren't altogether peaceful again. There were bushwhackers still at large, attacking travelers on the roads or robbing isolated farms. We didn't worry about them overmuch, since there wasn't anything any of us had for them to take, but it was a reminder that times were hard, and likely to stay that way for a good while yet.

Most of the time, even if the devil himself had been riding rough-shod through the Yadkin Valley, I would have been too tired to care, for me and James Melton and those two sorry milk cows had every foot of the farm to plow and seed, and at the end of the day in the fields, we all had other work to do, besides, even the cows. It was hard lines on all of us, I figured, to have to work two jobs—me in the fields and doing the house chores besides, and James Melton making shoes of an evening, when he was so tired, he'd fall asleep in his chair and pitch forward until he woke himself up, and then he would yawn and stretch, and go back to sewing leather again.

Ann didn't change with the seasons. She still lay abed as long as she could, swallowed in quilts, and she took no more notice of the farm in spring than she had in winter. Some of that might be to my credit, though, for I had given her other things to think about. If Laura Foster's dark lover was really going to carry her off, it would be soon.

I didn't think about the three of them all the time. I had my chores, and my doctor visits, and a jug of whiskey when I could get it, and the company of the fools in the settlement and now and then a man, when I felt the urge, but all the time in the back of my head, like crickets chirping in a nighttime field, my mind kept clicking along on ways to get back at Ann and Tom. I didn't always heed those thoughts, any more than you listen to the crickets, except when everything is still, and you are not busy with chores—but they are there whether you heed them or not. Always there. I thought May would drag on forever, and though the weather was fair, I itched with impatience for something to happen—and finally it did.

One afternoon, when James Melton had gone off to buy salt or nails—I forget which; doesn't matter—Tom had stopped over to the house, and he and Ann were making sheep's eyes at one another. I could tell they wanted to be alone, so I made myself look busy in the cabin so's I could spoil their dalliance.

Finally, bold as brass, Ann says to me, "Why don't you leave off sweeping, Pauline, and go over to the Fosters' for a spell?"

I smiled to myself. I wasn't to be got rid of as easy as that. "Why, I would. But coming home in the dark is a perilous journey."

She looked at Tom and they both smiled. "Why, Pauline, what would bushwhackers want with you?" asked Tom, giving me that wink, like he always does when he thinks he is charming some silly old biddy.

I shrugged. "It ain't that. It's the darkness. The brush and briars is awful grown up along the way, and the ground is so uneven, that I'm afraid I'll trip and fall in the night and break my neck."

I could tell it would be nothing to them if I did, but Ann could hardly force me to go unless she gave the problem a lick and a promise, to humor me. She turned to Tom. "She's right about the path. It could use some tending to, and it ain't like you got anything better to do, Tom. Why don't you go borrow my mama's mattock, and see can you smooth it out some?"

Tom yawned and stretch. "Maybe tomorrow," he said, only considering doing it at all to please Ann. I could fall down a well for all he cared.

By then I had decided that anything was better than standing around watching the two of them paw at one another, so I put away the broom in the corner, and said I would go anyhow, but that if I broke my neck coming back from German's Hill in the dark, it would be on their heads. They just laughed and told me to be off, and I reckon they forgot about me altogether two heartbeats after I shut the door behind me.

I didn't really have anything fancy worked out in my head. When it comes to making people do things, it's like chasing chickens in the barnyard—you never know which way they're going to run. Sometimes, though, I test folk in little ways to see if I can make them run the way I want them to. So most of what happened just happened. All I did was flap my apron at them to begin with, so to speak, and the rest just followed naturally.

I was a good half mile from Wilson Foster's place when Laura came running toward me, so I stopped, and when she got near enough for me to see the grin on her face, I knew she was big with news.

"He's wanting to go, Pauline!" she said, giving me a hug out of pure rapture, and I stood as still as I could and did not shudder.

Her sallow skin was pink with excitement and she must have brushed her hair a hundred times that afternoon, because it was shiny and smooth, tied up at the nape of her neck with a scrap of frayed pink ribbon. She had on her homemade calico under an apron, though, so I knew that whatever was going to happen wasn't happening now. She wasn't ready yet.

I mustered up a smile. "Well, of course he is, Laura. From the way you talked, there was never a doubt in my mind that he'd keep his word to you." Mostly it's easy to tell people what they want to hear. You just figure out what you really think and then say the opposite. "Just one thing though. . . ."

"What's that?"

"Well, Tom Dula has caught the pox, you know, and he is going around saying he got it from you. So I reckon either way, you are afflicted same as him. I wondered if you have told your intended about that?"

Laura's smile drained away, and she scuffed her shoe in the dirt. James Melton had made her those shoes, and I wondered what he would say about how she kept them. "Well, I have seen Dr. Carter for it, and he is giving me physic. But as for Johnny . . . I ain't been able to bring myself to tell him yet, Pauline. I don't know how he'd take it. And of course I don't reckon he knows about me and Tom, neither. I just want to get gone from here so bad, that I dare not take a chance on scaring him off." She clutched at my sleeve. "You won't tell him, will you, Pauline? Swear?"

I laughed and jerked my sleeve free of her bony fingers. "Why, laws, Cousin, I never even set eyes on the man except from a distance when he's working outside. What would I go telling him for? I told you I was happy to see you get away from tending to all those young'uns. You can trust me."

At that she hugged me again, and I stood it as best I could. "Oh, Pauline, you are the best friend I have! I knew you'd not let me down." Those muddy eyes of hers were fair dancing with excitement. "I'm just going off now to see my Johnny. I can't let him come to the house, of course. Daddy seen me talking to him one time, and I thought he was going to take a switch to me, but I swore to him there warn't nothing in it. But you could come with me and meet him, Pauline.

Then I could say I'd been off with you. Maybe we could bring back wild onions or a mess of salad greens for supper, and say that's why we went."

I nodded, and kept my smile plastered on. That was the first sensible thing I had ever heard said about Wilson Foster. But to go and see John Anderson would take me right back to the Meltons' place, and I had no mind to walk an extra ten miles just to accommodate her, so I said, "I'll keep my eyes skinned for wild greens as we go along then, but I'll not come back with you once we get back to Reedy Branch, I'll just go back up to Ann's place and start supper there."

I was kinda anxious to meet Laura's nut brown boy. I reckoned he'd be more interesting than the sorry old farmers around Elkville, but we never did get all the way to the Andersons' farm. Maybe he knew she was coming, though she had not said so. For all of Laura's hugs and honeyed words about what a boon companion I was to her, I knew that she had got in the habit of lying to keep folks from finding out about her lover. And she had not told him about having the pox, which is a silent lie. So I had no cause to think that she would be entirely truthful with me, for all her fine sentiments of friendship. Perhaps she was not such a fool as I took her for, which was just as well for her lover, for she could get him killed quick enough. I might have told on the pair of them just to see the fur fly amongst those dull farmers in Elkville, but for the fact that I had other mischief in mind.

Anyhow we never reached Reedy Branch together, for before we had gone more than three miles, at a place where the road was bounded on either side by woods, a voice called out to us, and Laura clutched my arm and motioned for me to stop. I peered into the woods, trying to catch sight of a figure among the trees, but it was late in the day and the shadows lay deep in the pines.

A moment or so later, I heard a whistle from the woods, and before I could utter a word of caution, Laura had left the trace, and was hurrying toward the thicket, with her skirt hitched up to her shins, the better to run. I muttered a foul word under my breath, and set off after her.

I had resolved to be cheerful and welcoming no matter how awful the fellow was, but when I reached the edge of the woods, she was in his arms, and, when I caught sight of his face, I had to admit that he looked a durn sight better than I thought he would. You can't put any stock in the descriptions a besotted woman gives you; they can't see straight. But Laura's part-Shawnee—or whatever he was—had a lean face with dark eyes over sharp cheekbones, and his skin had a copper cast to it that did put me in mind of the Indians. He was dressed shabby, like any old farmhand, but I had known better than to expect anything else. I couldn't see what he'd want with drab little poxy Laura, but maybe her pale skin made up for the rest of it. I reckon it must have. He acted right glad to see her.

I caught up to them then, threading my way through the tall weeds of that overgrown field and into the woods, mostly keeping my eyes cast down looking for snakes.

"This here's my cousin Pauline Foster. She knows about us," Laura told him.

He met my stare with one of his own, and he nodded slightly, just to show he had heard her, but he looked none too pleased to see me standing there. I guess his dealings with people hadn't given him any reason to trust strangers, especially white ones.

I smiled anyhow, because I choose my enemies with care. This man didn't matter to me one way or the other, so I had nothing to lose by being civil. Sometimes, if people are fools, friendliness makes them think you're on their side. "You'll get no hindrance from me," I told him, which was true enough.

He looked down at Laura and back at me, and then he said, "Well, all right then. I'll take her word on that. She'd never do me any harm if she could help it."

We walked on a few feet farther into the woods, so that passersby on the road wouldn't spot us. We settled ourselves down on the pine straw, Laura nestled up against John, who was careful to keep his distance from me, and we kept our voices low as we talked. I kept quiet at first, not knowing what he might take offense at, and half hoping he'd forget about me altogether, so that I could listen to their plans, but I made him too jumpy for that. He watched me the way I had kept an eye out for snakes in the untilled field.

"My cousin tells me you are wanting to go west," I said, watching his face when I said it.

He nodded. "I'm tired of being a farmhand around here. I'll take what work I can get over the mountain."

"Were you free before the War, or just lately?"

He gave me a hard look. "I'm free now, and that's all that matters. The rest is over and done with."

"Well, I hope you get your new start then."

Laura kept saying, "I'll be so glad to get shut of this place!" and then she'd reach up and stroke his cheek, or lay her head on his shoulder.

Finally, because the boredom of watching the two of them was making me sweat, I said, "So you mean to make a run for it, you and her, do you?"

He glanced left and right, as if he thought I had salted away a regiment of soldiers in the bushes. But there was nobody around but just us three. "I'm moving on west to Tennessee, maybe farther. Miss Laura here, she has a mind to go with me."

I almost laughed at the "Miss Laura," but he was right to be careful. Best not even to drop the "miss" in private, lest you make a habit of it, and slip up one day in public. "How are you planning on going?" I asked him. "On foot? You'd better not let her daddy catch you, else he'll beat her like a tin drum, and I reckon they'd just hang you."

He didn't flinch when I said that. But that didn't surprise me. He would have to be more crazy than brave to have taken up with a white woman in the first place, so I knew he was what folks would call uppity and dangerous. Well, so was I, but mostly I had enough sense to keep anybody from finding out about it. Maybe he did, too, but I doubted it. You could read his feelings on his face like watching clouds scud across a March sky. He'd live longer if he went west. And longer still if he went alone, but I could see that he meant to take her with him.

"We would have a horse," he said at last.

"Just the one?" I inclined my head toward Laura, who wasn't paying our talk any mind. She was leaning up against him, and plaiting blades of grass into a ring, while she hummed to herself.

"Just the one."

"You'll not get far enough fast enough with two of you on one horse."

He smiled at that, but his eyes stayed cold. "They'd hang me quicker for a horse thief than for taking off with her, don't you figure?"

"Best not to get caught at all. You know, her daddy has a horse." I don't know how he came by it, him being a sharecropper and all, but he sure enough had a little white mare that was about as drab and scrawny as his daughter was.

Laura looked up when I said that. "Yes, that's the one. We mean to take Daddy's horse. They couldn't do much to me, could they? If it was me that took it?"

"Of course they couldn't," I said, not because I believed it, but just to speed things along. "I reckon you'd stand a better chance of getting clean away if you each had a horse, though. Else they might catch up with you on the road before you reached Tennessee."

They looked at each other then, like the horse was already taken and they were galloping away to the west—they was seeing it happening in one another's eyes. I kept still, to let the thought take hold in their heads. I was watching a mayfly buzzing around in the field, looking for cow dung. Mayflies flit above the ground on fairy wings, but they don't live long.

"We will make do with one," John Anderson said.

"Do you think we could?" said Laura, catching both his hands in hers, her eyes shining like mayfly wings. "Just take Daddy's old mare, and light out of here before anybody misses us?"

He hesitated, and glanced over at me again.

"You ought to start early," I said. "As near as you can to sun-up, before too many people are about. Just meet somewhere and go. They'll not hear about your plans from me, now or ever."

That decided him. "Let's go tomorrow. First light."

"You don't want to go to her house," I told him. "Somebody might see you, and then they'd hunt you down for sure. Best to meet up someplace where you won't be seen."

"She's right, John. I'll pack my clothes and take the horse come sun-up. Where can I meet you?"

"At the Bates' place. It's only a stone's throw from the Andersons', so no one will see us together on the road. We'll meet there and head straight for the mountains."

Laura hesitated. "What if somebody was to see me on the road before I get there? They'll know I'm running away."

"Why, tell them you're running off with Tom. Nobody would mind about that, and by the time they find out any different, the two of you will be long gone. You mustn't tell anybody—anybody—who you're really going with. If you do, you'll get John hanged for sure."

John Anderson nodded, liking the plan. Then he turned back to me. "Swear that you won't tell about us running off. On your life. Swear it."

And I swore, hand on heart, and eyes awash with tears. I meant it, too. Oaths are nothing to me. Some fool who can't keep a secret is trying to make sure that somebody else will, that's all. So I always tell people what they want to hear. But this time I meant it.

An hour or so later I hurried back to the Meltons' place to tell Ann that Laura Foster was eloping—*with Tom Dula.*

# PAULINE FOSTER

## May 24, 1866

<hr/>

For once I didn't mind the long, muddy walk back from German's Hill, for I needed every mile of the journey to think out what to do next. It was like trying to piece together squares on a quilt to make a pattern, only sewing is stupid and tedious work, and I had always hated it—but this cutting and piecing together of people's lives makes my heart quicken with excitement.

I walked back along the trace, following the fading sun, which was just about to sink below the blue mountains in the distance, where I'd come from back in March. Sometimes it was hard to tell where the clouds stopped and the mountains began; they had that same blue hazy look against the sky, as if one was no more solid than the other.

I didn't meet anybody on the road, and I'd scarcely have taken note of it if I had, for my mind was running faster than a snow-melt creek, thinking on what I would say and who I needed to talk to before morning.

I could have ended Laura's fine plans for an elopement then and there, I think, if I'd told her secrets in the right ears. If I'd warned her daddy that he was about to lose both his mare and his daughter, I reckon he'd have put a stop to it. Or if I'd told some of the neighbors—or that high and mighty Colonel Isbell, who thinks he is the lord and master of everybody in the valley—that Laura Foster was fixing to run away with a colored man, they'd have stepped in. And if I had just told that nut brown boy of hers that Laura was afflicted with the pox—I doubt if even her white skin would have made her a prize to him then. Being hanged for running off with her or catching the deadly pox from her—it was all the same in the end. Death. And more than she was worth.

But I had no particular score to settle with Laura Foster, except for the fact that somebody loved her. She was making foolish choices, and she would bring about her own ruin without any help from me. I reckoned that I had more wrongs to repay in other quarters, and I meant to see those debts of cruelty paid in kind, hurt for hurt. It would take a careful piecing together, though, this blood quilt in my head. One dropped stitch and all would come undone.

When I neared the Melton place that evening, it was already gathering dark and the wind had picked up some, making a tedious journey of the last mile, but I would have walked barefoot in the snow to deliver the news I brought back with me.

I was almost to the house when out of the dark, a white hand grabbed my arm and jerked it hard. "What are you doing back so late? James will be wanting his supper!"

I could just make out Ann's pale face in the moonlight, but I had known it was her already. I could smell the whiskey on her breath, as I squirmed to get free of the grip of her claws on my arm. "Why don't you fix his supper your own self then? You're his wife, aren't you?"

She tossed her head. "Don't you sass me, Pauline. I am going over to my mama's tonight. I told you that this morning."

I saw that she had a little bundle of clothes with her, and then I remembered that she had declared that she would be gone to Lot Foster's place by evening. I laughed. "Why are you going there, Ann? Can't you sleep with Tom here like you always do?"

She tightened her grip on my arm and shook me once or twice for good measure. She would have slapped me, but she was near drunk, and I kept twisting this way and that to avoid her.

"I have seen Tom already," she said. "Though not for long. I said I would get him some whiskey tonight. If he don't come for it, I'll send one of the girls to fetch him at the Dulas' place. Though she mustn't say it straight out if that cat of a sister of his is in earshot. I don't mind his mama knowing, but his sister is a devil about trying to keep us apart."

I choked back a laugh. I wanted to say, "Some people are funny about adultery, I guess," but that would only have set her off again, so I swallowed my bitter words, and asked instead, "How did he seem to you tonight?"

She shrugged. "Tom? Same as always. Restless. Why?"

When she said that, I closed my eyes for two heartbeats and decided to take a stab in the dark. Chances were that my words would come to naught, but if they struck home, I would have done what I set out to do, and what I had planned on that cold walk back from German's Hill. "Well, I don't think you will see Tom anymore tonight at all," I told her. "I don't doubt that he'll be afraid to face you. You know how Tom Dula is. Always easy and smiling, saying whatever he thinks folk want to hear, and not to be trusted an inch toward keeping his word. Or perhaps he has told you already?"

"Told me what? Why should he be afraid to face me?" Ann's voice quavered, and she forgot to tighten her hold, so I wriggled out of her grasp, with marks of her fingernails stinging my arm, and glad for yet another injury to pay her back for.

"You mean he didn't let on to you?" I shook my head. "Well, if he didn't say nothing, I don't reckon I should. Anyhow, I have sworn to keep it a secret."

Ann dropped her bundle of clothes into the weeds, and took me by both shoulders, but I stood my ground, and she thought better of shaking me again. The wind whipped that black hair of hers into clouds around her face, and she shook her head to get it clear of her eyes. "We put you up, Pauline," she said, with tears of rage in her voice. "We let you stay with us out of Christian charity. . . ."

I had to bite the inside of my lip to keep from laughing at that. Oh, yes, Christian charity, indeed—to work me like a field hand, do-ing the kitchen chores and cleaning the cabin, tending her babies and the animals, and helping out in the fields—while she lay around like a farrowing sow, not doing a hand's turn of work. Yes, they were the souls of kindness, all right. But I pretended to see the sense in what she said, and after a moment's pause, I said, "All right, Cousin, if you think it is my duty to confide in you, then I will break my oath and tell you. You might as well know now as later, so that it won't be such a shock to you when it is over and done with."

She let me go again, and took a step back, clapping her hand across her mouth. She gulped down a few deep draughts of the night air before she said, "Is it Tom? What about him?"

I shook my head. "You may have seen the last of him."

"Why?" She looked about her, wild-eyed in the moonlight, and in an instant she would have gone running to the Dulas' place, so I said quickly, "He means to run away with Laura Foster, first thing in the morning. Come sun-up."

She stared at me for a moment as though the sense of my words couldn't quite sink in to her head, and then she threw back her head and laughed, ending with a sob of relief. "Tom run off with that mud hen? Has the pox addled your brain, Pauline? What would he want with her?'"

"He means to marry her."

"And what use is a wife to Tom Dula? Like teats on a bull, that's what—no use at all." She laughed again. "No job. No land. No money. Oh, he'd make a fine bridegroom indeed."

"Well, it would make his sister Eliza happy, wouldn't it? And maybe his mother as well, just to see him settle down with somebody and quit pining after you."

"He never would, though. He loves me. He's told me so often enough."

"Maybe he said the same thing to Laura Foster. And to Caroline Barnes before her. Anyhow, they are eloping in the morning. She told me herself. She says they are heading west to start fresh."

Ann put her fist up to her mouth, and stood stock-still, for all the world as if she had forgotten I was standing there. I thought she might faint, and if she had, I'd have left her where she lay, but after a moment or two, she just whispered, "I don't believe it," in a watery voice that ended in a sob.

I shrugged and said nothing. The less you argue with people the more they believe you.

She peered at me, willing me to speak, but I kept still. "I'll ask him myself then! I'll march straight over to his mama's, and make him tell me face to face like a man."

I shook my head and let my shoulders sag, trying to look like I pitied her.

She got very still then, taking deep breaths and twisting her hands together, and I reckon she realized that screaming at a man is no way to get him back. "Do you swear this is true, Pauline?"

One of my favorite things in the world is to lie by telling the strict truth. I said, "I swear that Laura Foster told me she was eloping come sun-up tomorrow."

She looked doubtful again. "How? It's a long walk to Tennessee."

"She's taking her daddy's mare. I reckon it'll carry the two of them, as little as she is. 'Course, there may be a child on the way, but it won't weigh anything yet. She's not showing that I could see."

"Did she tell you that?"

"Not in so many words, but why else would he be in such a hurry to marry her?"

"What would that matter? That baby could be anybody's."

"Well, she's a pretty little thing, isn't she? So meek and frail. Maybe he wants to think it's his."

Ann flung herself away from me, and started up the road. "I'll scratch his eyes out!"

Now I grabbed hold of her arm. "You need to simmer down, Cousin. Do you think that's likely to do any good? If he is fixing to run off with her, then having you tell him he can't will just make him bound and determined to go. At least, that's how it looks to me."

Ann stopped, took a deep breath, and looked up at the stars instead of at me. "But I can't let him go. He's all I ever cared about, Pauline."

"I know," I said softly, hoping that she would hear sympathy and understanding in my voice, even though it wasn't there.

"I could tell Uncle Wilson. He could stop Laura from running off."

I nodded. "For a day maybe. Or even a week. But if they mean to do it, they will. Besides, Uncle Wilson might be relieved to see somebody make an honest woman of Laura. Why should he care how you feel about it?"

We stood in silence for a moment in the cold night air, Ann staring up at the stars and me thinking furiously, trying to stay one step ahead of her threats. It was too early for lightning bugs, and even the crickets were silent that night. I waited, letting her turn the whole problem over in her mind. I thought I heard her choke back a sob.

"He doesn't care nothing about her, Pauline!"

"Well, he wouldn't be the first man to marry to get a housekeeper, would he? Maybe he just wants to settle down—like you did. And you may think Laura cares little enough about him, too, but you must know how bad she wants to get away from that house, tending all those young'uns. For all she knows, this may be her one chance. A lot of good men died in the War. There aren't enough of them left to go around."

Ann had been drinking already that evening, and that was a stroke of fortune for me, for it dulled her thinking even more than usual. She didn't think to wonder why two unmarried people of legal age would bother to run away to Tennessee to get married, when they could have invited the whole of Elkville to a wedding if they'd a mind to wed. I'm glad she didn't think of that, for I had no answer ready there. And she didn't seem to think it strange that an idle fellow like Tom would leave a comfortable home where he did precious little work to go and shift for himself in a strange place. It's hard for people to think straight when you have hit them with the thing they fear most in the world. She went right past wondering if it was true and straight into wondering how to stop it.

"Where is she meeting him, Pauline?"

"Why, at the Bates' place around daybreak," I said. "I think if you were to watch the road from your mama's house, you'd likely see her go by, if you wanted to go over there and talk to her. You'd want to get her alone, though—before anybody else comes."

I could tell by her breathing that she was mad enough to spit nails. That and the drink is likely why she didn't ask me a sensible question, like why Tom and Laura would meet up at the Bates' place. Laura lived five miles away, and Tom's house was a mile east, down the Reedy Branch Road, and from the Bates' place they'd have to backtrack to get on the road that led up the mountain to Tennessee. Why would they meet there when there were miles of woods between Laura's house and the mountain road? Why the Bates' place? *Because it was a stone's throw from John Anderson's quarters.* But if my luck held, Ann would not know that—at least not until it was too late to save her.

# PAULINE FOSTER
## May 26, 1866

O n the last Friday night in May, old Wilson Foster was stumping all over the settlement complaining loud and long about Laura running away from home. The weather was fine that evening, and after supper, instead of staying home, people congregated up at the Meltons' house, passing the pleasant evening with one another and enjoying the fresh air after a long winter of being cooped up in smoky little cabins. We had a houseful, and hardly enough likker to go around. Ann's brother Thomas Foster had come over, along with Will Holder. Jonathan Gilbert, who some-times worked for James Melton, was still there, helping him cut leather for shoe making. Washington Anderson turned up, of course, hunting Tom, but he wasn't around, for once.

Foster hadn't been asked to the party, but he showed up in the yard outside just as the light was fading, dressed in his usual raggedy farming clothes, and he shuffled into the cabin, looking forlorn.

"Have any of you'uns seen my Laura?" Wilson Foster asked them, after he'd downed a few swigs from the jug to take the chill off his bones.

177

Nobody had.

"Well, I reckon she might have took off with Tom Dula. I've caught them in bed together a time or two. Has he been around?"

Tom Foster spoke up. "I seen him just a while ago this evening. But he was by hisself. I never did see Laura."

The men looked peeved to be put off their drinking by an old man bearing troubles, but at first they were polite enough, saying it was a shame that Laura had gone missing. Nobody reckoned there was much to it—maybe she had gone off visiting kinfolks up in Watauga. Will Holder said he hoped he'd find her soon, then they'd turned their backs on him and went back to what they were saying before, not giving him another thought. Well-brought-up people will be civil to anybody, but you shouldn't make the mistake of thinking you matter to them. I wondered if old Foster had figured that out, or if he even cared.

He didn't seem to heed their indifference, but just went on moaning about how ungrateful Laura was to have gone off and left him, and how he didn't know what he was going to do with all those young'uns to take care of, in addition to all the extra chores. I wondered if I was the only one wondering who was looking after his children while he was out and about, visiting with all and sundry, but nobody spoke up, and I never heard that anybody in the settlement offered to do any cooking or laundry for him, either.

While he went around, asking if anybody had seen his daughter, I kept still in the doorway, watching Ann to see how she was taking this news, but her face was as blank and innocent as a barn cat's. I wished I'd had more turns at the jug. It's easier to put up with fools when you have a tot of likker warming up your insides to deaden the noise. Good thing I'd had a drop or two to drink before he came, but it was wearing off now, and I could have used reinforcements.

Somebody handed old Foster a gourd of whiskey, and I hoped that would shut him up, but between gulps, he went on and on about how hard it was on him with Laura gone, and then he started in again, bewailing the loss of that infernal horse, and saying that he reckoned he could do without Laura well enough, but he wanted that mare back.

"She ought to be easy to track," he said. "She's got a sharp pointy place on one hoof where I had started to file it down, but had to leave off afore it was done. You look for that pointed hoof print in the dirt, and you'll find my Belle. I know which way she was a-going. I tracked her past the Scotts' place and down the river road. Picked her up again on the Stony Fork Road, and found tracks all the way to the old Bates' place. She went off the road then. Started through an overgrown field, and I lost the trail. Don't reckon she can have gone far, though." He looked around, hat in hand, eyebrows raised, waiting in certainty for someone to offer to help in the hunt.

I'd had a bellyful of hearing about that horse, and I was tired of listening to the old man whine about his young'uns, as if nobody else in the world had a hard row to hoe in life. As if nobody here ever lost somebody to the War, or got a sickness they'd never get well from, or worked every day sun-up to dark and still stayed poor and hungry. I was tired of hearing it. So I stood up, and called to him over the heads of half a dozen folks, "I'll get your horse back for you, Uncle Wilson. Just gimme a quart of whiskey, and I'll bring her right on back to you."

The men had been talking and laughing amongst themselves, so loud you could hardly hear yourself think, but when I said that, it was as if I'd dropped a hornet's nest into their midst. All the talking stopped at once, and they all stared at me and him, waiting to see what was going to happen next. I thought they'd take it as a joke, but

I had misjudged, because nobody laughed. And everybody remembered.

Uncle Wilson stood there for a minute, staring at me with his mouth open, and then he just shrugged and turned away. I guess he figured I was making fun of him, which was true enough, I suppose, though I did want that whiskey awful bad. It was no secret that I was powerful fond of hard likker, and they must have thought that was all there was to it: me trying any way I could to get another jug. I didn't say anything else after that. Maybe I had said too much already.

Thomas Foster, who had not been brought up well, and who had taken more than his share of the whiskey, must have been as tired as I was of the old man's lamentations, and he began to make sport of his uncle. He set a twig alight in the fireplace and began to stagger around with it. He stumbled against Wilson Foster, and set the old man's beard afire. They scotched the sparks in a moment, and Wash gave him a dipper of water to soak it in, but even then he didn't take the hint and leave.

Finally, James Melton, who always had a kind word for everybody, if he spoke at all, patted his arm a trifle gingerly, and said, "Surely Will is right. Your Laura has gone to visit relatives. I reckon we could pray for her safe return if it would ease your mind any."

This was too much for Foster's temper, for he had come in search of information, not threadbare homilies. He leaned in close to James Melton, though he was too short to reach his face, and he breathed out fumes of bad breath and whiskey. "Why, man, I don't care if I was to never see the little hussy again, but the thing is, she went and stole my mare. And I damn sure want that horse back."

His salty language put James off almost as much as his breath did, and with a sigh of disgust, he turned away from the old man, and sat down near the fire with a bit of shoe leather he was working on. A couple of the men who overheard him just nodded, not at all surprised at his words or his attitude. Most everybody hereabouts knew that there was no love lost between Laura and her father, and horses did not come cheap. Wilson Foster didn't even own his own land. It was a wonder he had a horse at all, and he certainly wouldn't part with it without a fight.

I was standing in the doorway, next to Ann Melton, well away from the smoke and the fumes in the little cabin. Ann was watching the road like she was expecting Tom to turn up any minute. The men didn't much want us in there anyhow. Nobody ever had much good to say about Ann, for her carrying on with Tom Dula was common knowledge in the settlement, and, as for me, I was just the hired help, so I counted for nothing.

After Wilson Foster had sat down next to Will Holder, waiting for another turn with the jug, I heard Wash Anderson tell him, "My older sister saw your daughter this morning, Mr. Foster, just after sun-up. She said Laura was riding east along the road past her place, and that she stopped and spoke to her for a moment or two. I don't reckon my sister would want me to tell you that, but it's so. She said that Laura meant to get away from home, and she wished her well. Said she wouldn't say anything that might help you find her and drag her back."

Wilson Foster looked like he wanted to argue about this, and I reckon I could have told him a few home truths about his daughter, but I kept my resolve to be quiet and let people jump to their own conclusions.

Jonathan Gilbert nodded. "It is all well and good for Laura to take care of her brothers and sisters and keep house for her father, but she's past twenty-one now, ain't she? I reckon she's entitled to a man of her own—if she can find one."

There was a pause before Thomas Foster said, "Of course, she has never lacked for companionship, has she?" The way he said it, you knew he didn't mean Sunday-school chums. You don't have to spend too long in a group of respectable people before one of them bares poison fangs. The only difference between them and a rattlesnake is that a rattler has the decency to warn you before it strikes. People never do.

They had heard about Laura's goings-on, all right. I wondered if any of these fellows knew firsthand about her dalliances with men, and whether they knew she had the pox, but nobody spoke up about that.

Then when the talking died down for a minute, I heard James Melton say to old Foster, "You must be worried something fierce, Mr. Foster. Even if she has gone off to see some kinfolk, these are perilous times, especially for an innocent young girl. There are still bushwhackers about, and I do not yet trust the roads. I hope nothing has happened to her on her journey."

I was beginning to get a little irritated, listening to all this soft soap about poor Wilson Foster and his beloved missing daughter. He had spent a good half hour lapping up sympathy and making himself important over the disappearance of Laura, whom he didn't care two pins for. I thought it time to take him down a peg or two, in front of all these mealymouthed fools.

I walked up to him, like I was going to give him another helping of sympathy, and then I said, loud enough for everybody to hear, "I know you must be worried, Uncle Wilson, seeing as how Laura may have run away with a colored man."

He glowered at me, not at all happy to have that brick dropped in front of half the settlement, but, as he turned to leave, all he said was, "I am afraid of that, too."

That shut everybody up for a good half minute, and then of one accord, they all turned away and began talking about ten different things at once to cover the sound of all that plain-speaking. Ann gave me a look when I said that, but she kept silent. Laura Foster might have been forgotten then and there, but I was not prepared to leave well enough alone.

The day after Laura went missing, Tom Dula came early to the Meltons' house, wanting James to fix his fiddle and to get his shoes mended. Ann was not at home, but he did not ask after her, and it would have been no use if he had, for I didn't know where she'd gone. Will Holder stopped by again, and they all commenced to drinking and swapping lies, same as always.

We sat up most of the night, till the fire burned low, and then we all drifted off to sleep any old how. I ended up sharing a bed with Tom Foster.

An hour or so before sun-up, Ann came dragging in. I woke up when I felt the cold air when the door opened, and I saw her standing over by the fireplace, taking off her wet shoes. The hem of her dress was wet, too, as if she had walked a ways through wet grass. She got undressed and slid into the bed alongside me.

I didn't have long to loll abed, though, for with daybreak, my chores commenced. I had milked the cows, and gathered the eggs, and came back in to cook the breakfast, and Ann never stirred.

Later, when Tom came in with that fiddle of his, wanting James to mend the bridge for him, I said, "Well, here you are bright and early. We all figured you had run off with Laura Foster. Her daddy was here last night, trying to trace her, on account of her making off with his mare. He said he reckoned that you and her had run off and got married."

Tom stopped in his tracks and looked at me like I was foaming at the mouth. Then he laughed, and helped himself to a dipper of milk out of the pail. "What use do you suppose I have for Laura Foster?"

I shrugged. "You've been sniffing around Wilson Foster's place for weeks now, so everybody reckoned you'd gone away with her."

He finished the milk, and wiped his mouth on his sleeve. "Well, I'm here and she ain't, so that settles that, doesn't it?" He gave me a hard stare as he said it, daring me to say one more word on the subject.

I just nodded, and tried to look like I was scared of him. Maybe he didn't know where Laura Foster had gone, but I was certain that she wasn't coming back.


The settlement talked about Laura Foster and precious little else all the way until Sunday. After all, Laura was a young, unmarried girl, and nobody knew what had become of her. Her disappearance was a nine days' wonder. There isn't much to talk about in a little farming settlement, especially with the War being over. For nigh onto a year, *no news* certainly had meant *good* news—no more death rosters sent back from the battlefields to break people's hearts; no more bad news about shortages or rationing to drive folks to the brink of starvation; no more terrifying reports of armies headed this way to steal the food or requisition the livestock or burn the barn. The War had given everybody enough excitement to last a lifetime, and they weren't sorry to see it end.

Now, though, human nature being what it is, people were beginning to tire of the sameness of peacetime in the backwoods. They craved a little excitement again. Not more war and death, to be sure, but just a tidbit of scandalous news to spice up the endless talk about crops and weather.

All the people I met at the store and on the way there—well, the women, anyhow; I don't know what the men talked about—ruminated over Laura's disappearance like so many cows chewing cud. A few of the timid old ladies would have it that she had been set upon by bushwhackers and carried away, but most of the rest, who knew about Laura's soiled reputation, figured that she had gone off of her own accord, probably run off with some man fool enough to want her. I did more than my share of visiting the neighbors that week, but mostly I just listened to the talk, and held my peace.

There was a group of ladies at the store on Saturday, eager to swap stories about Laura's disappearance. Mrs. Betsy Scott was chief among those who held that she had run away on purpose. Now the other Mrs. Scott was adding her pennyworth of information about seeing Laura on the morning she left—the last time anybody ever saw her. Maybe Mrs. Scott figured that enough time had passed now for Laura to get clean away from here, and over into Tennessee if that's where she was headed. If that was so, then it wouldn't do any harm if she told what she knew. Anyhow, she gave herself airs about it until I wanted to shake her like a terrier with a rat. When you know something for a fact, and other people act like they know it all when they are just guessing, it is hard not to shout at them. My smile felt like it was tacked on with ten-penny nails, but nobody seemed to notice.

"I know for certain that she was leaving for good," Miz Scott said to anyone who would listen. "When I saw her on Friday morning, she had a bundle of clothes slung over the saddle, and she said she was going to meet somebody at the Bates' place. Well, it must have been Tom Dula she was meeting. Everybody knows that Laura and Tom were . . . sweethearts."

When she said that, not a one of us could look at anybody else for fear we'd bust out laughing. *Sweethearts.* Well, then, I reckon every hen in the barnyard is *sweethearts* with the rooster. But in a little settlement, nearly everybody is kin to everybody else, so you don't go slinging mud at anybody if you can help it, or else you'll start a kinfolk squabble that would last longer than the War.

I was tempted to tell her the truth just to see the look on her face, but that would have run contrary to my purposes. I bit my lip, and kept still, letting her run on.

"When I saw Laura that morning, I even asked her had Tom come to her place—for I was surprised at hearing that Tom Dula was willing to run away with any girl at all, especially if it would end with him having a wife to support. . . ."

There were murmurs of agreement all around at this point. Nobody could quite picture Tom Dula choosing to work for a living, and he never seemed overly fond of Laura—not enough to make the sacrifice of his freedom, anyhow. Nobody came out and said, "You don't buy a cow when the milk is free," but I'll wager I wasn't the only one thinking it.

"She said that they were going to run away to Tennessee."

I bit back a smile. So Laura had told the nosey biddy that she was running off with Tom. That might buy the pair of them some time, because nobody would have cared if she eloped with Tom. Let them worry that trifling scandal to death while she made away with her nut brown boy. That's what I would have done. Let Miz Scott think that, then.

A stout old widow woman, who was no fool, spoke up. "The Bates' place is north of you, ain't it, Miz Scott? Why, I reckon it would take that Laura Foster the rest of her life to reach Tennessee if she was a-riding *north* instead of west."

There used to be a blacksmith's forge at the Bates' place, but it was long gone now, and the place had fallen to ruin and the yard was choked with weeds. The only reason that anybody would go there would be to meet somebody they didn't want to be seen with.

Miz Scott pursed her lips. "I am only repeating what I was told. Maybe the two of them met somewhere, and then turned around and headed west from there. There's more than one road that will get you over the mountain to Tennessee. But I recall that I did tell her that if it were me, I'd have been farther along on the road by that time of morning. She said she had started as soon as she could, and that they were meeting at the Bates' place." She kept nodding her head, like she was daring any of us to contradict her. Nobody wanted to argue with her, for she looked on the verge of a temper, and that would have broken up the gossip party. Somebody said they hoped that Laura made it to wherever she was going.

"But it seems strange, all the same," one of the younger wives said thoughtfully. "If Tom came to her place at sun-up, like she said, why didn't she just go off with him then? Why would she wait and meet him a couple of hours later at the Bates' place?"

"And Tom Dula doesn't have a horse. Were the two of them fixing to try to get to Tennessee on that one mare?"

"But she did not go off with Tom Dula," the stout old widow reminded them, nodding hard to drive home her point. "Because Laura Foster may be gone, but *he's* still here."

Mrs. James Scott touched her arm to show she agreed with her. "I thought of that myself." She leaned forward and dropped her voice to just above a whisper. "Now I saw *him* on that Friday morning. I had finished breakfast by then, and I spied him walking up the road. I asked him did he want to come in, but he said he wanted to meet up with my brother."

Washington Anderson, that would be. And I knew where Wash had been the night before: at the Meltons' place. There was a whole crowd of us in that little cabin—but not Ann and not Tom, for she had gone to her mother's, and he was off somewhere—his mother's house, for all I know. But that Thursday night, Wash Anderson was with me at the Meltons'. And he still would have been there Friday morning, like as not, as much as we all had to drink the night before.

Everybody looked interested in the other Mrs. Scott's news about Tom. She said, "My neighbor Hezekiah Kendall says he saw Tom on Friday morning, too, just before I did. Around eight o'clock. Mr. Kendall asked Tom if he had been '*after the women*,' and Tom answered, 'No. I have quit that.' When he stopped at my place, I didn't ask his business, and he didn't tell me. But he was headed toward the Meltons' place."

They all looked at me then, so I said, "Well, he got there, all right. I was just bringing in the milk pail Friday morning when Tom showed up."

They looked at one another then and got all quiet for a minute. Then they all started talking at once about something else.

.   .   .

Anyhow, a day or so later, I heard that Wilson Foster had got his mare back on Saturday evening, although it wasn't on account of me, and I never did collect that quart of whiskey from him, which is all I cared about the matter. The day after Laura stole the mare, it just showed up back in the yard outside the barn, still bridled, but with the lead rein snapped in two, as if it had been tied to a tree branch, and broke the rein, pulling itself loose when being tied up had made it hungry and scared enough to break free. The mare may have wandered around for a while, but it wasn't far enough from home to be lost, so after a couple of hours it went on back to German's Hill where it belonged. When I heard that, I thought: *Wilson Foster got his wish. He got his horse back, but not his daughter.* And it looked as if I had got my wish, too.

I was down at Cowle's store when I heard about that, a day or so afterward, and at the time I had made no effort to join in the conversation, but later on, back at the farm when I was alone with Ann, I had plenty to say about it. "Did you hear Wilson Foster has got his horse back?" I asked her, that evening, as I was making the chicken and dumplings for supper.

Ann nodded, but she wouldn't look at me. She had been mighty quiet herself those past few days. She didn't seem to care if she ate or not, and she had spent most of last Friday in bed. Now, Ann was bone lazy at the best of times, but that was unusual, even for her.

"Well, I reckon they'll be sending out the searchers by tomorrow, then."

"Searchers?" She froze. "Why would you say that?"

"Stands to reason, don't it? Last week Laura ran away on her daddy's mare, and now she has not been seen for days. Then the horse shows up with a broken lead rein, and there's still no sign of its rider. Since the mare found its way home, people will figure that where it was tethered couldn't have been very far from home. Seems to me like Wilson Foster ought to be hollering for men and hunting dogs to start combing the woods to see if they can find Laura. She can't be far off, not now that she's on foot. The horse proved that." I said all this as calmly as I could, but I was watching Ann's every move while I was saying it, and it was all I could do not to laugh. She looked scared to death and her hands were trembling. ·

Ann glanced at me, and then she looked toward the cabin door, as if she expected a search party to break in on us at any moment, but all was quiet. James Melton was outside somewhere, still tending to his chores, and we'd had no visitors all day. Still she spoke so softly I had to strain to hear. "They'll not find her."

I shook my head. "The dogs might."

I was wrong about the searchers, though. They didn't use dogs, so it took them a lot longer to find her than it ought to have. In fact the whole thing began to look like a nine days' wonder that would die down in a few more weeks until people completely forgot that a girl had gone missing.

Not that I cared one whit about her, but if I could help it, people wouldn't forget she was gone.

The week after Laura Foster disappeared, the month of June began, and every time folks got together they were still making guesses about what happened to her.

I couldn't let on that I had a good idea about what had happened to Laura, and who she had been going to meet. I was saving all that. I was looking forward to watching Ann fall apart, waiting for the trap to be sprung. I planned to say as little as possible, and let the rumors take their course, unless people showed signs of losing interest in the story, and then I might chivvy them along a little to keep it going. I thought I would do more than my share of visiting in the days to come, just so I could listen to the tongues wagging.

It turns out that I needn't have bothered, though. All it takes is for one person to keep worrying away at something, like a dog with a marrow bone, and then you can rest assured that sooner or later something will come to light. I thought I would have to be the person to keep prodding everyone to wonder about the fate of Laura Foster, but I reckoned without J.W. Winkler. He's a young fellow with a farm near Elkville, and I don't know what any of it had to do with him, for he wasn't a magistrate or a lawman, or any kin to the Fosters that I knew about, but he took it into his head to take charge of the hunt for Laura, and he for one did not believe that she had gotten away to Tennessee.

At Cowle's store I heard some of the neighbors talking about how groups of men had gone out in search of some sign of Laura. Most of them gave up after a day or two, for it was the busy time of year for farmers, and they had enough to do to take care of their livestock and their fields, but J.W. Winkler would not let the matter rest. After the others went home, he kept on combing the woods alone, starting at the old Bates' place, where Laura had told Mrs. Scott she was headed, and he walked every path he could think of to get from there to the Dulas' place.

"He is bound and determined to find her," said the storekeeper, handing me the candy I had bought with the two pennies I had to spare.

"Why?" I asked her. "He wasn't sweet on her, was he?"

"No, that's not it. He said she deserves a Christian burial. And he said there'd be no peace for her family until she was found."

Well, strictly speaking, I was part of Laura Foster's family myself, and it didn't make any difference to me whether he dug her up or not, but I simply nodded to the storekeeper, big-eyed and solemn, and told her what she expected to hear: what a fine and determined man Mr. Winkler was, and how I hoped there was nothing out there in the woods for him to find.

I think he gave up for a little while, because, after all, he had a farm to run same as the rest of them. The month of June dragged on, and we went ahead with the planting and the weeding, and the rest of the weary round of chores on a farm in summer. The searching may have eased up for a while, but the talking didn't.

On Saturday the 23rd of June, after we had finished a long day's work, Tom Dula stopped by the house, as he did most days. I was stewing up a mess of soup beans and corn pone for supper, and James was working on sewing the sole of a shoe, sitting on his bench in the doorway to catch the fading light. Ann was somewhere about the place, using the outhouse or taking a stroll to cool off likely as not. She wasn't doing anything useful, that's for certain.

Tom came up to the door, smiling and sniffing at the smell of supper cooking, but I didn't speak to him, for whether or not he stayed to eat with us was not on my say-so. As he stood there on the threshold, James Melton put down his needle and looked up at him. I watched them there side by side in a shaft of sunlight—one blond and tall, with sharp features and hands never still, even in the evenings, as he worked his other trades to shore up his efforts at farming; the other dark-haired and handsome, as gracefully lazy as a cat on a hearth rug. I didn't feel much of anything for either one of them, except maybe a little respect for Melton, because he earned his keep, and disgust at Dula, for lazing about, living off his mother and doing not a hand's turn if he could help it. I always did like dogs better than cats. I wondered how those two felt about each other. They had been neighbors all their lives, even in that Union prison camp, and they shared a woman—whether one of them knew that or not. I wondered about that, too.

James Melton set down the shoe he was holding and looked up at Tom. "I didn't expect to see you back here anytime soon."

Tom squinted down at him—maybe from the glare of the sun. "Why is that?"

"Well, people are going around saying that you killed Laura Foster, so I thought you'd have lit out of here by now."

Tom stood very still then, but his expression did not change. "Who has been saying that?"

"The Hendrickses, for one."

There was such a long, taut silence between them that I was sure Tom wasn't going to answer. I even thought he might haul off and hit James Melton without even letting him get up. But then Tom laughed and said, "Well, I reckon the Hendrickses will just have to prove that, and perhaps take a beating besides."

Melton nodded, and I don't know if that nod meant that he believed Tom or that he hadn't expected him to say anything else. Anyhow, he picked up his shoe again and went back to work without saying another word. Tom came in and sat for a minute. He nibbled at a piece of corn pone, but then he got up and started pacing, and before too long he had barged back out the door and was gone.

# ZEBULON VANCE

Tom Dula and Ann Melton . . . what a long time ago that was. A brief interlude in my life, really, when I practiced law in order to feed my family while I waited to be let back into politics. As soon as the government permitted Confederate officials to reenter the political fray, I went back into the election business, and ended up in the Senate, where I mean to die in harness. I have not represented a defendant in court in decades, and I never will again, but from time to time my memory summons up those two star-crossed clients of mine, and I see them as they were in 1866—young, handsome, and indifferent to the opinion of the world in general. I did not understand them at the time, and I believe I thought that when I had attained age and wisdom, I would come to know what it was that motivated them, what was in their hearts. But as I sit drowsing by this fire in a Washington parlor, I know that I am as far from comprehending them as ever.

We are bound for different heavens, those two rustic souls and I.

They loved each other, I suppose, or what passes for love with young and passionate people, whose impulses are not tempered by education or moral guidance. Their lives were without purpose or direction, and so perhaps they became each other's purpose.

But Ann Melton was married to another. I recall that well enough, for that is the one thing in this matter that I do understand. She was born to a drunken slut of a mother, and by some wondrous chance she grew up to be a beauty—that was her one chance to escape the squalor of her mother's life, and it is no wonder that she took it. A prosperous man with a house and land and the means to put food on the table offered her a home and marriage, and at the age of fifteen she took it. I find no wonder in that. It is the best thing I know of Ann Melton.

I would have done the same. Perhaps I did, in fact. I would like instead to think that in marrying my Harriette I was fortunate to have fallen in love with a gentlewoman whose breeding and social connections were so perfectly suited to advance my own ambitions. I hope I made her a good husband. I meant to, and she never uttered a word of complaint, bless her, but she was worth her weight in gold for a man with political and social aspirations well beyond his personal means. So in my youth I let my head rule my heart, so that my choice of a partner should further my ends, for I had much to accomplish.

How then to explain my second marriage? My dear Harriette, delicate soul that she was, passed away in 1878, and by then I was forty-eight years old, well past the giddiness of youth, and serving in the United States Senate. Having established myself as a respected and prosperous statesman, I no longer had need of anyone's assistance to make my way in the world. I was never a ladies' man, nor one who had any interest in dalliances with the fair sex. Like a plow horse with blinders on, I saw only the furrow that I must plod along, and no amiable distractions ever kept me from my duty.

I suppose when I became a widower, I could have indulged myself in sensuality at last: married some fair-haired beauty, and eased into my dotage with a pretty doll to amuse me as the fires of ambition burned low. Or I could have dispensed with matrimony altogether, and immersed myself in the neverending duties of a serving senator.

But I did neither of those things.

*Ah, Flossie Martin. What will they say of you in the sonorous biographies that are sure to be written when I finally take leave of this world?*

Precious little, I'll warrant. My Harriette was beloved in my home state, for its aristocrats counted her as one of their own, and she stood by me through all the tribulations of the early years, braving the dangers of war in the Governor's Palace, never leaving my side until I sent her away in those last frenzied weeks of the conflict. To the North Carolinians who elected me Governor twice over, and sent me back to Congress to represent them before the nation, Harriette Espy will forever be Mrs. Vance.

But in 1880 I married again.

Mrs. Florence Steele Martin was a prosperous widow from Kentucky, well past the bloom of youth, just as I was. There would be no second family of young Vances from this union—and the grown sons I already had were scrupulously polite to her, but they plainly thought the family would be better off without her. In their calculations, though, they reckoned without the War.

When I was hauled away to prison on my birthday, three weeks after Appomattox, Federal soldiers swarmed through our little house in Statesville and took all our belongings. We never got them back. After that, I earned little enough as a lawyer, because in those days of Reconstruction, no one had much money to spend on litigation. And the pay of a Senator is modest, because it is supposed that those who hold the office come from rich and powerful families, which, by and large, they do. But I did not. I was looking at the declining years of my life with precious little fortune to shore up the cares and vicissitudes of old age. Florence Martin was wealthy, and I was democracy's answer to an earl: a United States Senator. It was a sensible and satisfactory alliance, and we were neither the poorer for it.

We summered in the mountains near Asheville in our stately mansion Gombroon—named for the Persian pottery of that name, for I was a cultured man of the world by that time, still close to Asheville in my heart, but in other ways very far from it indeed, and my last home was proof of my success. Gombroon was the most modern style of estate, three stories high, with a turret and sprawling porches, and all the accoutrements of a fiefdom: an orchard, a vineyard, a dairy, and formal gardens. I felt that I had earned such prosperity, but it was the wealth of Florence Martin that made it happen, and I was grateful for that.

But would I have died for her? Assuredly not. I never felt such reckless passion for any human being, and it was the thought of that devotion that brought Tom Dula and Ann Melton to my mind, even after so much time had passed. I tell myself that they were still caught up in the madness of youth—just past twenty, both of them, though war and hardship had made them old beyond their years. Whatever they felt for one another, that lust that made everything else in the world fade to insignificance: I never felt that. Never did. And I could never quite figure out whether I envied them their transports of sentiment or whether I pitied them, as one would a madman whose delusions blind him to the realities of life.

But they died young, and I lived on for decades, ending up revered and prosperous in a mountain mansion, safe from the riptides of emotion that sweep lesser men away to their deaths.

# PAULINE FOSTER

## June 26, 1866

◄-✦═══◎═══✦-►

The next day, J.W. Winkler and a host of his neighbors went out combing the woods again. They all spread out, one right next to the other, and walked forward in a straight line, same as people say the Redcoats used to do when they marched in to battle during the Revolution. Spread out like that, the searchers were sure not to miss a single foot of ground as they went along. They kept up that battle formation, walking in circles outward from the Bates' place. Sure enough, when they got to a clearing just north of the abandoned farmstead, one of the searches noticed a broken bit of flax rope tied to a dogwood. They reckoned it matched the broken lead rein on the halter of Wilson Foster's wayward mare.

That discovery fixed their attention on the clearing, and they all fanned out now within that small area, practically bumping into one another in their eagerness to examine every inch of ground. I wasn't there, but afterward they would tell anybody who would listen about what happened out in that clearing. Before too long, one of the searchers, who had his eyes fixed upon the ground, spied a patch of red on the bare earth about a hundred yards from where the rope was found, and they reckoned it was a bloodstain, and that the killing had been done there.

When I heard about that a day or so later, I caught my breath, and scarcely dared to let it out again, for I thought that surely after finding blood and rope, they'd keep combing over the underbrush in that clearing until they discovered the burial. But I need not have worried about it, for I was wrong about Laura's resting place. After the excitement of their discoveries had worn off, they all went back to the general store to boast of their adventures, and I suppose they might have had a few drinks to celebrate their success.

After that it would have been getting on toward suppertime, and the search party began to come apart. Before long they had all gone their separate ways, and with all the farm chores that needed doing this time of year, none of them could spare the time to come back another day to continue the hunt for more signs of Laura Foster. I was disgusted with them for quitting the hunt when I reckoned they were close enough to spit on the grave, but of course I had to keep quiet about it, and just as well that I did, for I had guessed wrong. When they didn't stumble upon the grave, I resolved to find out the truth of the matter.

It was the end of June by then, and they had no real proof that Laura was dead, but the rope and the bloodstain gave folks in the settlement plenty to talk about, and, in the evenings and on Sundays after preaching, they yammered loud and long over what they reckoned the rights of the case to be. By now nobody really doubted that Wilson Foster's daughter was dead. The horse had found its way home, and its rider could not have got far without it, not without being seen, anyhow, for all of Wilkes County and Watauga County besides were looking out for her.

The lack of a corpse did not stop the settlement from declaring that murder was done, and generating a lot of hot air trying to get to the bottom of it. Most of the speculating centered on Tom Dula, because he was known to be carrying on with her, and most people thought she had been intending to elope with him. You wouldn't catch me disputing their conclusions. Tom Dula was not the marrying kind; he did not care a fig for Laura Foster; and he had no reason to elope with her if he did want to marry her—but if the citizens of Elkville were too slow to work that out for themselves, they'd get no help from me. I just wish they had pitched on Ann as the culprit.

She heard all the scandal mongering, though, and it gave her fits. She wept and stormed and told anybody who would listen that Tom was innocent—which was true enough, but not a soul believed her. When he came to the house now, they huddled in corners and talked in whispers. I contrived to listen, when I could.

Finally, when the whispers grew louder than a swarm of bees, Tom made up his mind, and all Ann's tears could not deter him.

It was the last Monday in June, two days after Winkler and his searchers had found the flaxen rope and the bloodstain in the clearing, that Tom called on the Hendricks family, trying to convince them to stop telling all and sundry that he was guilty. He got no joy from that meeting, though.

"We won't quit till we've found her and hanged her killer," they told him. "The farmers may have to quit searching and go back to tending their fields, but Colonel Isbell vows that he won't stop searching until he finds that poor girl, and a prosperous gentleman like him has all the time in the world."

Tom laughed at that. "*Colonel* Isbell! Why he wasn't nothing but a captain in the 22nd North Carolina. I reckon these days a colonel is just a captain with money."

Since Colonel Isbell is about the richest man there is in Happy Valley, that remark of Tom's probably shocked the Hendrickses about as much as the thought of murder. Anyhow, Tom said he could see it was no use trying to talk sense into them, so at last he came away, and that evening he showed up at the Meltons', as downcast as I've ever seen anybody.

Even before that Ann must have known that the situation was grim. That afternoon while James was out in the field, and I was supposed to be weeding the garden, I went inside to rest awhile with a cup of water, and I found Ann kneeling on her bed, and tearing a piece of clapboard off the log wall behind it, so that the logs and mud chinking showed through. Then she took a long nail and poked a hole through the chinking between the logs, and she was trying to pass a piece of string through the hole.

I had seldom seen her so industrious, and I stood there in the doorway for a minute or two watching her go at it. Finally I wearied of seeing her wrangling that string, and I spoke up. "What are you doing now, Ann?"

The nail clattered to the floor, and she turned on me with stricken eyes. "Don't you never sneak up on me like that, Pauline!"

I shrugged. "Wasn't trying to catch you at anything. It's hot outside. I just came in for water."

She sneered, "Any excuse not to work!"—which was rich coming from someone who never did anything herself.

She eased down off the bed and picked up a knife that had been lying in the folds of the quilt. I caught my breath, thinking she might mean to make a run at me with it, but she simply turned away and pushed the knife between the head of the bed and the wall. I said nothing about it, and neither did she.

I got my water, and sat down on a stool, sipping it, while she went back to coaxing the string through the hole. When at last it went all the way through, she gave a little cry of satisfaction, picked up the nail and one of James's shoe-making mallets from his workbench, and she swept past me and out into the yard. I didn't follow her, but presently I heard a tapping on the wall outside, so I went out to see what she was doing, taking care not to let her catch sight of me again, for she was agitated. I saw that she had found the bit of string that she'd poked through the hole in the cabin wall, and now she was tying the end of it around the nail she had just driven into the outside wall.

*Now that is meant for a signaling device,* I thought to myself, and there could be but one person that she would want to summon her in such a way. I reckoned she planned to tie the other end of the string around her wrist when she went to bed. *She means to slip out tonight and talk in private.* This was a strange twist of events, because they had never resorted to sneaking around before. Tom always came in, bold as brass, and saw her at any hour he pleased. So why were they fixing up a signal string now? I resolved to keep off the whiskey tonight, so that I could stay awake and see what transpired.

I slipped away around the back of the house before she could catch sight of me, and I went back to weeding the garden. We never said a word to each other for the rest of the afternoon. Ann paced the yard like a caged bear, and I think I could have shouted at her and she'd not have heard me.

It was gathering dark when Tom Dula finally showed up, but, although James was sound asleep in his bed, Ann was yet awake, and I reckoned that all her trouble over the nail and string had been for naught, for Tom opened the cabin door and came in without a word to either of us. He sat down on a stool next to the empty hearth and stared into its blackness as if there were flames there that only he could see. Ann touched his arm a time or two, and he looked up at her, and tried to smile, but it weren't no use, and an instant later he would fall back to gazing at nothing again.

"You must be tired," I said to him. "You want me to fix you a bed?"

He barely glanced at me. "I can't stay," he said, talking more to Ann than to me. "I'm off home directly."

Ann started to say something, but he had turned away again, so she got out her wooden comb and began to brush her black hair down over her shoulders. I couldn't see any sense in holding off on my drinking now, for there would be no secret meetings between them tonight, so I reached under Ann's bed for the jug she kept there, and took a long pull of whiskey to make me drowsy. Ann looked like she wanted to talk, but she could see that Tom was in no mood even to hear chatter, much less try to join in.

After a few more minutes of silence, broken only by the peaceful snores of James Melton, Tom got up and stumbled past us to the bed. He threw himself across it, like he was going to sleep, and he buried his face in the covers, but after a moment or two, I heard him bawling like a new-weaned calf.

I looked over at Ann, and she looked more scared than sorry, but she didn't go near Tom. She blew out the candle, and we sat there for a minute or so in darkness, listening to Tom's sobbing.

We had made a pallet of quilts on the floor in case Tom wanted to stay, and Ann crawled into it, and lay down like she meant to go to sleep, and as it was cold and dark now in the cabin, I crawled in after her, figuring I might as well sleep, too. I was hoping that the likker I'd drunk would ease me into oblivion, despite the snores and the weeping, but as I stretched out there, waiting for the darkness to drag me under, the pallet started to shake, and I realized that Ann was crying, too.

I figured something was bound to happen soon, for there was no use in the two of them laying there three feet apart in their separate miseries. I was glad neither of them expected me to comfort them, for I never could understand what made people cry. I know that some people weep when they cut a finger or get a bellyache, but pain never takes me that way. It just makes me angry that I cannot stop the hurt. Grief and regret are things people talk about, but I do not see the point in dwelling on things that are over and done with and cannot be changed. I wondered why Tom and Ann were weeping, and all I could figure was that they were afraid of what was going to happen to them. If they had turned to me for consolation, I would have told them what fools they were to waste time on tears. If they were afraid of what was coming, they'd be better off planning to fight back with clear heads, instead of bewailing their fate. But they didn't ask me for anything, so I lay there trying to muffle the noise so I could sleep.

Presently, Ann's shoulders stopped heaving, and she turned back the covers, and slid out, making straight for the door and slipping outside without a word to me or Tom. He heard her leave, though, for a moment later he had got up and followed her out. They were gone for a couple of minutes, and then Tom came back in alone and in the light from the open doorway, I could see him go straight past me and over to the head of Ann's bedstead. He slid his hand underneath it and pulled out that knife I'd seen her hide there. He stuck it into his belt, and I saw that he meant to take it away with him.

"I'm bound for Tennessee, then," he told her.

She shook her head, too stricken to speak, and after a moment she reached up and stroked his cheek with her hand.

It was a mild summer evening, and, after Ann had stolen out of the house, Tom caught up with her under the trees in the side yard. I knew she didn't want her husband overhearing too much of their talk, for they reckoned that he knew nothing of what had happened to Laura, but also because they had private things to say to each other as lovers. I wondered why they bothered to be so secretive. I never saw any sign at all that James Melton cared one way or the other what they did.

I had a jug of whiskey I'd got from Wash Anderson two days before, and since I'd finished Ann's, I took it out of the shed where I'd hid it, and I went around to the front of the house where some weed cedars grew close to the house, and I crawled up underneath one of them with my whiskey, close enough to hear most of what Tom and Ann were saying, and to get a glimpse of them through the cedar branches, but I reckon I could have stood right out in the open and waved my arms and they'd not have seen me, so intent were they on each other.

*That is just what is wrong with them,* I thought. *They never see anything but each other.* If James Melton was made a prisoner in his own house by his wife's indifference; if Laura Foster became a plaything for one of them to make the other one jealous; and if Wilson Foster lost his daughter and half the community wasted many days in planting season hunting for her corpse—why, none of that made a bit of difference to Ann or Tom. Just as long as they had each other, the rest of the world could go hang.

But they wouldn't have each other for long. I sat still under the cedar branches, and listened to the lovers' farewell.

"I can't lose you," said Ann, and I think she'd have screamed it to the sky if she hadn't been afraid of being overheard.

Tom held her for a while and then he pulled away, and said, "I'll come back for you. Let me get away to Tennessee and get myself situated there, and along about Christmastime, I'll slip back over the line and come back to fetch you. You can wait that long. And then I reckon we'll be together for good."

His voice broke as he said those last words, and then they didn't say anything for a long while, but they just clung together like little children, crying like their hearts were breaking. *Tom Dula crying.* I never thought I'd see the day. He had lived through that god-awful war and seen all the horrors of a Yankee prison, and here he was sobbing like a child at the thought of leaving my vain and empty-headed cousin. I listened to her pleading with him not to leave her, and there in the darkness I was grinning like a possum, for if she had really wanted to spare him that journey, she could have. A dozen words to any upstanding man in the community would have seen Tom out of trouble—but of course such an act would have put Ann herself in peril, and whatever she thought she felt, I knew that she would not risk her own precious neck for anybody. Not she!

Even if Ann loved Tom more than she ever loved anybody else, she still wouldn't bestir herself to keep him from harm. Or perhaps she thought that they were safe enough if they did nothing to provoke any more suspicion. I don't suppose Tom would have let her sacrifice herself for him, anyhow. They wanted to be together, which required that both of them be free.

I took a silent pull on my jug of whiskey, and wished they'd have done with their touching farewells, for I was tired of listening to them.

After a moment, she put her hand on his arm and said, "You don't have to go, Tom. They'll not prove anything against you. It's only talk, is all."

"They've hanged men for less. I'd be better off away from here. Once I'm gone, it will all blow over. Let them think I did it, as long as they don't come after me. I've been a prisoner once, thanks to the Yankees. I don't ever mean to let it happen again."

Tom Dula left that night, taking one of the westward trails up the mountain, through Watauga County, the same direction I'd come from, and his leaving was the very thing that Ann had tried so hard to prevent. Her despair was no secret to anybody, for she never could conceal her thoughts, such as they were, nor her feelings. She moped about the cabin, giving way to floods of tears, and she ate so little that it was a shame to waste the food by putting it on her plate. Since she could not read or sew, and she would not seek solace in the society of her neighbors nor in prayer, she honed her misery on her husband and me, nagging about the least little thing, or shouting, or giving way to another storm of weeping, as the spirit moved her. I mostly ignored her sallies, but every now and again, when my patience wore thin, I would flare back.

James Melton never did, though. He bore her grief and her tempers with the same calm forbearance with which he had endured everything else. I wondered how he stood it, for as beautiful as she was, one can get used to beauty the same as anything else, and what was left wasn't worth a tinker's dam, as far as I could see. So once when James and me had the place to ourselves, Ann having gone down the hill and across the road to mope at her mama's house, I put the question to him. "How do you stand it?" I said. "If she were my wife, I believe I'd beat her like a drum."

He allowed himself a faint smile. "I watched her grow up, there over the road. She was like a flower back then . . . so perfect. But so skinny and shabby, too. They didn't have anything. I couldn't even be sure she got enough to eat. And one day I made her a pair of shoes, for it saddened me to see her go barefoot so far into the fall of the year. She looked at me then like I had given her a golden crown, and she smiled up at me, looking so shy and grateful. Well, I would have given her the world right then. All I wanted then was to protect her, to keep her from ending up like that no-account mother of hers." He sighed and turned away for a moment, but not before I saw the glistening in his eyes. "I reckon all the shoes and fresh meat in the world can't make an angel out of a sow's spawn. Though I did try. Maybe if the War had not come. She was still so young, then. Sixteen, when I went away in '61. And when I came back, I found a cold-eyed woman with no more generosity of spirit than a barn cat. I knew then that I had made a bad bargain, but we had our babies by then, and I was honor bound to stay and do what I could. I'd not leave them to her."

"But you know then . . . about her and Tom?"

He nodded. "Yes. Sometimes I think he is the only thing that ever touched her heart. They were together when they were little more than children. I would blame him for that, except that I know how willful she is. And she's older than Tom, so like as not, it was her idea. I can't fault him for being so taken with her. I wish I could feel that way, even now."

I didn't know what to say, for all that was in my mind was the thought that he was a graven fool, and I knew better than to say that.

"She married me for a home and enough to eat, I reckon. And maybe she'd have been glad if the War had taken me and set her free. The War made so many widows—what would one more have mattered? Lord knows, I tried hard enough to die. I carried the colors of the 26th at Gettysburg, and I thought, surely, with men dying by the hundred there, stacked on the field like cordwood . . . surely, one man armed only with a flag would never live through it. But I did. I took bullets in an arm and a leg, and I was a year recuperating from those wounds, but I lived to go back to the army. They shot me again at Hatcher's Run in '65, and I ended up in the prison camp."

"I know. I heard what it was like up there at Point Lookout. Seems to me it would have been easy for you to die then. There's plenty that did."

He nodded. "But, you see, *Tom* was there. And men were dying like mayflies, so I thought, 'Well, the both of us will never make it out of here, so let the survivor go home and take care of Ann.' It is a jest of Providence that we should both be spared, while better men, less willing to die, were taken."

I nodded. "It was Ann's luck, not yours. She never loses anything, as far as I can tell."

"Now I can only hope that she will run away with Tom Dula, if that will make her happy. It would make *me* happy to get shut of her without costing me my honor."

"What would you do then?" I asked him.

He thought for a moment. "My young'uns need a mother. I

believe I'd find me a plain-faced, good-hearted, hardworking woman, and I'd count myself mighty lucky to have her. Ann was like a shooting star in my life, so beautiful it takes your breath away, but I reckon what you really need to find your way in the dark is just a good steady lantern. I am cured of hankering after beauty."

I noticed that he wasn't so cured of chasing beauty as to show any interest in me, but I let that pass, and we got on with the business at hand. I had nothing against James Melton, and no particular yen for him, either. I thought he might soon get his chance to be rid of Ann, and I wished him joy of it.

"He'll be back come Christmas," Ann would declare, saying it over and over the way granny women speak a charm to stop a nosebleed or take out fire from a burn.

I never answered back, but I thought to myself that Tom Dula would be a fool if he did come back for her. If once he got himself safely over the mountains, he had best stay gone if he wanted to outrun the rope.

He might have had sense enough to see that if he'd had months to think on it, but he didn't. The very fact that Tom had lit out for the hills just fanned the flames of suspicion in the settlement. On the Thursday after Tom left, Wilson Foster went to the Elkville Justice of the Peace, and told him that his daughter Laura was missing, and that he reckoned she had been done to death by "certain persons under suspicion." Then the old man reeled off the names of the folk that he suspected, and he got Mr. Carter to draw up a warrant, ordering the county sheriff to round them up for a hearing the next day at Cowle's store.

Tom Dula topped the list, of course, and then came Ann, but after that he listed Tom's first cousins Granville and Ann Pauline Dula. I don't know what they had to do with anything, for we didn't have much truck with them, but I wondered if the fact that Miss Dula is named "Ann Pauline" had something to do with it, as that is Ann's given name, too. Well, it is also my name, if it comes to that. There are a few too many "Ann Paulines" for a place as small as this, if you ask me.

Well, I'll bet Granville Dula and his sister were mighty surprised to find themselves in custody and bound over for a hearing on a charge of murder. They were close in age to Tom, and their daddy was Tom's uncle Bennett, on his father's side. They had more land and social standing than Tom and his widowed mother, and they were probably mortified to be dragged into the troubles of their no-account cousin Tom.

The next day, Friday the 29th of June, the lawmen and the local busybodies commenced a hearing at Cowle's store, and Mr. Pickens Carter heard evidence in the matter of Laura's disappearance. It didn't take him long to realize that Granville and Ann Dula had been scooped up by mistake, on account of their names, and he turned them loose in short order. They hurried out of there without a backward glance, looking both scared and horrified, as if they thought we all had cholera.

Next off, the justice of the peace let Ann Melton go, perhaps because she is small and beautiful, and men seem to think that women who look like angels act like them as well. They are usually wrong about that, but it never seems to teach them anything.

It looked bad for Tom Dula that he was the only accused person not present at the hearing. Mr. Pickens Carter asked a constable where he was, and, with a good bit of throat clearing and foot shuffling, the lawman allowed as how Tom could not be found, and that he was believed to have lit out for Tennessee.

The justice of the peace was uncommonly annoyed by that information, and he remarked that things certainly did look black for Tom, given the facts of the matter. With a look of sour displeasure on his face, Mr. Carter made out a warrant for Tom's arrest on suspicion of murder. He ordered copies of that warrant to be sent to the towns up the mountain, even over into Tennessee, where everybody figured Tom had gone.

The quickest way to leave Wilkes County from Reedy Branch is to follow the old buffalo trace that goes alongside of Elk Creek westward and up the mountain into Watauga County. If Tom followed the trail until it met up with the wagon road to Zionville, he could cross over the Tennessee line without delay. There were a lot of murmurs of place-names and speculation about where he might have run off to, and who he might know in Watauga County that he could hole up with.

The meeting was adjourned then, and everybody who didn't know any better went away thinking that Tom Dula had murdered Laura Foster; the trial would be delayed until they caught him, but the verdict was already in. Nobody seemed interested in trying to figure out why he would have bothered to do such a thing. As far as they were concerned, his absence was proof of his guilt. I wasn't about to tell them any different, neither.

"It won't do no good to send warrants after him," said Ann, when we got away from there. "He'll be in Arkansas before long, or at least out west in Kentucky."

He wasn't, though. If he had any sense he would have been, but I think he was bound to Ann by some invisible thread—his heart strings, maybe—and he could not get far from her to save his life.

# PAULINE FOSTER

## *Mid-July 1866*

*If it hadn't been for Grayson, I'd a been in Tennessee.*

Tom's disappearance was a nine days' wonder in Happy Valley. People hardly talked about anything else, and it pretty much settled the matter of his guilt as far as the settlement was concerned. Ann was wretched, listening to the talk about Tom, and worrying over what had become of him. I thought that if she ate any less she would waste away to a shadow long before Christmas, whether he came back for her or not, and if it would put an end to her moping and complaining, I'd be glad to see it happen.

As it was, though, he didn't stay gone until Christmas. Just past mid-July, he was brought back hog-tied by two local lawmen. We were able to piece together where he went and what he did from the tales told by Jack Adkins and Ben Ferguson, the two busybody deputies that Pickens Carter sent to search for Tom and bring him back to Wilkes County. Once they had fetched him back, and seen him safely locked in the stout brick jail in Wilkesboro, the two of them high-tailed it back to Elkville to regale folks with the story of the capture of that dangerous fugitive, Tom Dula. Oh, they were full of themselves about their exploits, but the truth is that Tom's capture had nothing to do with them. They just went and collected him as if he had been a parcel.

I heard the tale the day after Adkins and Ferguson got back. They were ensconced on the porch of Cowle's store, surrounded by curiosity seekers, eager to hear about their apprehending the bloodthirsty criminal. It was as if the neighbors had that soon forgotten that Tom Dula was a lazy, amiable young man they'd known all his life. Now suddenly they would believe he was a monster. I slipped in amongst the onlookers, to hear the story.

"He went right where we figured he'd go," Jack Adkins said, pointing westward toward the blue haze of mountains. "He took that Elk Creek Road to Zionville, and we reckon he laid out somewhere in Watauga County for a couple of days."

"Where'd he stay?" somebody in the crowd called out.

Ben Ferguson shook his head. "We never did find that out, and he wouldn't say. We're only going by when he showed up over the line in Tennessee."

"That was about two weeks ago," said Jack Adkins, taking up the tale again. "He turned up, near as dammit to barefoot, and calling himself by the name of Hall, on the farm of Colonel James Grayson in the community of Trade."

I put my hand over my mouth to cover my smile, for I was remembering what Tom had said about a colonel being a captain with money. When I thought to listen again, Ben Ferguson was telling how this Colonel Grayson had hired Tom as a field hand, and said he'd worked long enough to buy himself some new boots with his wages.

"We reckoned he'd go up the mountain to Watauga, and over the line into Tennessee, so we just rode up through Deep Gap, and started asking around up there if anybody had seen the fugitive."

Jack Adkins took up the tale. "It took us a couple of days to work our way up to Trade, but when we finally did, we talked to Colonel Grayson, who told us right off that he had engaged a new farmhand that sounded like the man we were looking for."

"He must have seen us coming," said Ben. "For when the colonel went to look for him, he was gone. So he set off with us, tracking Tom Dula along the road that leads to Johnson City. He didn't get that far, though. We ran him to earth in Pandora. He was on foot, so we were able to overtake him without too much trouble. We caught him soaking his feet in a creek there, and before he could get up, Colonel Grayson hefted a rock and ordered him to surrender."

"What did he do then?" asked one of the onlookers in an awestruck whisper.

"Well, he give up," said Jack, shrugging. "He wasn't armed, y'see, but the colonel had a big old .32 Deermore on his hip, so I reckon it was not so much the rock as the pistol that made him decide to surrender. Besides it was three of us against one of him, so he let us take him, and he came along peaceable. I'll give him that."

"He came along peaceable right then," said Jack. "But not the whole way back he didn't."

"Well, no," Ben allowed. "We took him straight on back to Grayson's farm, and they barricaded him in the corncrib for the night, with all of us taking turns standing guard outside. When we started back to Wilkes County the next morning, we put Tom up behind Colonel Grayson on his horse, and we tied Tom's feet underneath the horse's belly, so's he couldn't jump off and run away."

"He tried, though," said Jack. "Every now and again, we'd stop to give the horses a rest, and one time, Tom managed to loosen the ropes some. If the colonel hadn't noticed it, I reckon he'd have been off in to the woods before we knew what hit us."

"We watched him like a hawk after that, but he didn't give us no more trouble. We delivered him to Sheriff Hix yesterday evening, and they've got him locked upstairs in the Wilkesboro jail. They'd better keep a good watch on him, though, 'cause if they give him half a chance, he'll run."

"Did you ask him what he done with Laura Foster?" somebody called out.

Ben and Jack looked at each other and hesitated. Finally Jack said, "We didn't like to ask him anything about that. Our orders were just to bring him back on a fugitive warrant. I reckon it's up to the lawyers and judges to decide what happens next."

They all started talking at once then, but I stopped listening. If Tom was in jail and in fear of his life, there's no telling what he might say to whoever questioned him. I reckon he'd try to pin Laura's murder on anybody he could think of. Except, of course, his precious Ann. That's what I would do, if it was me in jail. Muddy the waters all I could. There was no love lost between me and Tom, so I figured it might not be long before he started trying to make people believe that I had something to do with it.

I decided it was high time I left Wilkes County.


Remember that.

*I left Wilkes County.* All I cared about then was keeping myself out of harm's way.

That night I stuffed my three faded dresses, some cold biscuits left over from supper, and what little else I had in to an old blanket, and stashed them under my bed. Then I lay down and closed my eyes, waiting for morning. I didn't bother to tell the Meltons I was leaving. They might have tried to argue about it, and there was no point in us having words over it, for nothing they could say would change my mind. Or else they might not even care at all that I was going, and if that was how it was, there would be no point in bothering to let them know. Anyhow, it's not like they owned me or that I owed them anything. I could come and go as I pleased.

The next morning before sun-up, I got up same as I always did, and I eased my tied-up blanket of belongings out from under the bed and slipped outside. James would think I had gone to the privy, and Ann wouldn't bother to wake up for hours. By the time they missed me, I'd have a good head start.

As I stepped outside in to the chill of the morning mist, I took a last look around the valley, as places seemed to float in and out of clouds moving across the ground. I looked over at Aunt Lotty's little place, straight down the hill and across the road, then below the north ridge at the Reedy Branch Road that led to the Dulas' land, and over at the Bates' place, deserted again now, since the searchers had given up and gone back to the business of farming. Wherever Laura was, she was resting in peace.

My gaze came last to rest on the Anderson farm, situated in the low ground between us and the Bates' place. I wondered if Laura's nut brown boy was astir there yet, but I didn't catch sight of him. I thought about warning him to keep his mouth shut about what he knew, but then I thought better of it. John Anderson had said nothing so far, and I think he knew well enough that it would mean the rope for him if he did speak up. All was quiet in the gray morning. Nobody saw me go.

I headed south down the Stony Fork Road until I reached the trace that runs along by Elk Creek. I was taking the same westward path to Watauga County that Tom took when he went to outrun the law. The self-same one that brought me here back at the first of March.

After the morning chill burned off, it was a tolerable walk—better than it had been in the bitter cold of late winter. It would be cooler once I got up on the mountain, but in high summer, that is a blessed thing, and I was looking forward to feeling the cool air on the mountaintop, instead of the blazing sun of a Wilkes County cornfield.

I passed nobody on the road, and I didn't tarry, either. I didn't care to look at the little purple flowers tucked in among the weeds along the path, nor did I stop to admire the mountains floating in front of me in a blue haze. I put one foot in front of the other, and I kept my eyes on the ground in case a snake should slither across my path. All the while I was listening for the sound of voices behind me or the thud of a horse's hooves, but nothing broke the stillness except now and then a snippet of birdsong. For my breakfast, I took one of the cold biscuits out of my blanket-sack, and ate it dry whilst I walked.

I hoped Wilkes County would forget about me just as fast as I meant to forget about them. I didn't care if they hanged Tom or Ann or half the county for the death of Laura Foster, as long as they left me out of it. I meant to get back to the top of the mountain, and to keep myself out of the way of the lawmen.

I can't say that anybody was glad to see me when I finally got back. Folk there never had much use for me, nor I for them, and absence had not made any hearts grow fonder. Still I had other kinfolk there, from my mother's family, and though they were not overjoyed to see me trudging up the path to their door, they saw their bounden duty as kinsmen, and they let me stay awhile, provided of course that I didn't eat too much and that I did my share of the chores, and more. They would not think to tell anyone that I was there, for my coming and going interested them not at all, and news of Wilkes County never reached the holler where their cabin stood. The outside world could go hang for all they cared. I figured to settle in until the trouble blew over down in Happy Valley, and then I would see what I wanted to do next.

I had not been there more than a week before Ann turned up at the door, escorted by Cousin Sam Foster. It is easy enough to track somebody in these parts, I suppose, for there are few enough people, and not much else to do besides take note of their comings and goings. One of the young'uns let her in—Ann does not take no for an answer—and then they sent him to fetch me from out the garden, where I was hoeing weeds in the hot sun. I might have thought it was a rest to leave off working in the heat, but being around Ann was never restful. Either she was ordering me about to tend her babes or cook and wash up, being too lazy to do it herself, or else she was in a bate about something or other, and everyone within earshot must listen to her moaning and bewailing about whatever it was. I had been about as glad to escape one as the other, but it wouldn't do to let her know that. I am particular about letting anybody know what I think about anything, because knowing such things might give a body power over me. When I came inside and saw her standing there beside the hearth, I wiped my hands on my aprons, tore off my poke bonnet, and went and embraced her as if seeing her had been my dearest wish in the world, but I took note of the fact that Ann did not come alone. I had walked all the way to Wilkes County in the dead of winter right by myself, and nobody spared a thought to my safety or comfort, but here in the middle of high summer Ann Melton must have a gentleman escort to ease her journey up the mountain. I added that to my stock of grievances against her.

Either the journey had taken the shine off her perfection, or else all the worry over Tom was taking its toll, for you'd have thought her well over twenty-one to look at her. Dark hollows shadowed her eyes and cheekbones, and her dress hung on her bony frame as if it were a hand-me-down from a woman twice her size. I did not remark upon the change in her, but I was pleased to see that she had got acquainted with suffering.

She did not mince words. "You have to come back with me, Pauline," she said, in a voice like flint.

I never tell people what I want. I just make sure that what I want sounds as if I am doing them a favor, so I said, "I cannot impose on your kindness any longer, Cousin. You and James were good to take me in when I was sick, but I have trespassed on your hospitality long enough." What I meant was that with the Wilkes County justice of the peace sending out warrants to arrest people right and left, I wanted to get well away from there, before I got caught in the snare myself.

That ought to have been plain enough for anybody to see, but most people cannot look past their own desires, and, since Ann was one of that sort, she believed my words instead of her own common sense.

She waved aside my protests of sparing her my presence. "It doesn't matter, Pauline. You have to come back. Tom is still in jail, and I hear they may be looking to arrest you next. If you stay here, it will look like you've run away."

Well, I had. Moreover, I couldn't see any percentage in going back into the thick of a legal tangle. Ann made it sound as if she was worried about me, but I'd never be foolish enough to believe that. Ann Melton would not walk forty miles up a steep mountain to save me from being torn apart by wild hogs, much less just to keep me from being arrested. In fact the only thing I could think of that would make her put forth that much effort was *him*: Tom Dula. I can believe that she'd walk barefoot through a briar patch for his sake—and not for much else.

Sam Foster stayed silent in all of this, looking as embarrassed as a man watching childbirth. He had done his duty to see his kinswoman safely up the mountain, but it was plain enough that he wished himself elsewhere now. James Melton had not come with her. He would have said that the farm, the children, and his shoe making kept him too busy for such an excursion, but I think the truth was that he did not much care what happened to her, and he was tired of dancing to her tune.

I studied her gaunt face, trying to work out what she had really come about. How would my coming back help Tom? Did she want me to tell some lie on his behalf? But perhaps there was no subtle scheme for me to divine. Ann's only gift from fortune was her perfect face; being able to think clearly and make a plan were not skills she possessed. I thought it most likely that she missed having someone to talk to, especially now. Hardly a word ever passed between Ann and James Melton, and she could hardly expect him to care that Tom had been put in jail. To Ann, it was no use fretting unless there was someone to hear you out, and she had no woman friends, for not a soul in the settlement could abide her. She thought of no one but herself, and she cared nothing for the womanly concerns of home and children. Who among them would hear her out if she wanted to weep and wail about her lover being imprisoned? Why, nobody. But she paid me eleven cents a day to cater to her whims, and I suppose that in the end she forgot that my friendship was boughten. All along she had thought she was doing me a favor by taking me in, and now she was here asking me for the favor of coming back.

"I never bargained on being mixed up with the law, Cousin. Eleven cents a day won't buy that."

She frowned a little, for she wasn't used to being denied anything. "But we're kin, Pauline. Couldn't you come back for my sake?"

Why do handsome folk always think you ought to be honored to do them a kindness? I didn't owe her nothing. I just stared at her, wondering if she would ever realize that.

"Pauline, there ain't nobody to talk to. I can't tell James about any of this, and like as not he'd be glad to get shut of Tom anyhow. You know that none of those sanctimonious biddies in the settlement will give me the time of day. And with Tom gone . . ."

Ann began to weep, though she might flood the room with tears for all I cared.

"Ain't we friends, Pauline, as well as kin? Didn't I take you in when you was sick? And now I am most sick to death with worry over all this, and I miss you. I miss having you around."

"I'll come with you," I said. "Let me get my things." I did not agree to go because I wanted to help either Ann or Tom, or because I cared one whit for her tears and her tribulations. I went because I wanted to watch what was going to happen. I also thought that I might need to be there in order to make sure that it happened.

I went back with them, leaving the cool shade of the mountain groves for the blistering sun on the cornfields of Happy Valley, and many's the time I cursed myself for a fool for doing it. I settled back in to doing the chores on the farm, tending the Meltons' girls, and milking the cows, and listening to Ann fret about what would become of them.

Once she said, "Poor Dula. I wonder if he will be hung. Are you a friend of Dula? I am. Are you a friend of mine?"

I thought that worry and eating next to nothing had addled her brain, but I forced myself to smile. "Why we are of the same blood, Ann. I am more than your friend. Did I not come back with you in your time of need?"

She sprang up from her chair, and grabbed my arm. "Come with me now then. I need to see that it's all right."

I hung back, knowing what was in her mind. "Come on where?"

She gave me a sullen glare. "Just out to the woods. Not far from here."

I knew what she meant, but I wouldn't say it out loud any more than she would. Finally, I said, "You mean . . . to where the horse was tied up?"

She shook her head, as pale as I've ever seen her. "Not there. Just down the Reedy Branch Road a ways and up the ridge."

I was tempted to ask her how she knew exactly where the horse had been, but she looked in no mood to be trifled with, so I kept on pretending I didn't know what had happened. She strode to the door and held it open, nodding for me to come with her, but I just blinked at her, like I was slow to understand, and finally she said, "Come on! I need to make sure that the grave has not been disturbed. Animals might have dug her up."

"But what if one of the neighbors was to see us going there and tell the searchers, Ann? What then?"

"What neighbors? My mama? Wash Anderson and his sister?

They won't think anything is amiss. They haven't yet, have they? We're just going out for an afternoon walk." She tried to laugh and show that she wasn't a bit afraid. "T'ain't far. Come on."

She shooed me out the door like a stray cat, without even giving me time to stir the stew pot or put on a shawl, and a minute later, we were making our way down that steep hill that leads down to the Stony Fork Road just opposite Lotty Foster's cabin. She wasn't out in the yard, though—*drunk already*, I thought as we passed her door— and I saw no one about at the Andersons', either. The Bates' place was as deserted as ever. I had thought we might be heading there, for the searchers had been milling around it for weeks now, and I knew they had found the horse's rein there, but Ann did not spare a glance for the west side of the road. She trudged ahead another quarter mile or so, directing her steps toward the wooded ridge that ran alongside the Reedy Branch trace. It was down that road near a mile that the Dulas lived, and I expected her to set off following the creek down to the Dulas' woods, but she just kept forging straight on through the field and threading her way through the weeds, heading up the ridge. She didn't hesitate, either. She knew exactly where she was headed.

About two hundred yards past the creek and up the ridge, we had left the open fields of the valley, and now we were stumping along through the woods along the southern slope of the ridge, with Ann forging so purposefully ahead that it was plain she knew the way by heart. I was trailing along after her, dodging briars, trying to keep up with her, and hoping that if one of us trod on a rattlesnake, it would be her.

I stepped on a dead branch once, and the crack it made when it broke under my foot made my heart jump clear up to my throat. I don't get scared the way other people do, but I can be startled, by sudden moves or loud noises, same as anybody. I was more careful after that, and not so intent on keeping up with Ann. If she wanted to show me something, she could wait for me.

We went a good ways up that ridge. I think that if it had not been high summer, I might have had a good view of the valley below, but the trees hemmed us in, making it as dark as twilight in midafternoon. The scrub oaks and pines made a canopy over the clearing, shading it from the sun. There was a bare patch underneath one of the trees, and around it the grass had been trampled down. The rest of the clearing was covered with grass or leaves, so this one bare patch caught my eye at once.

Ann stood in the middle of the clearing and looked all around her, and I could tell that she was trying to see the woods through somebody else's eyes—the searchers, like as not. Was there anything out of place that might make them take a closer look?

"There's newly spaded earth yonder by that bush," I said, pointing to a bare patch of ground. "Anybody could spot that."

She gave me a hard, unbroken stare. "What do you know about it, Pauline?"

I shrugged. "More than I care to know. Just that this is as far as our poor cousin Laura got that day. I reckon you'd know the rest, though."

She turned away without a word, and walked over to the bare patch, which was next to a big bush at the edge of the clearing. Then she knelt down and crawled partway underneath it. I went over there, too, and I got down so I could see what she was looking at. I was more interested in watching Ann than I was in what she was investigating. After all these months of watching her laze in her bed whilst James Melton and I did all the work about the place, it was strange to see her so energetic and determined. Seeing her hunched under that bush in her brown calico dress put me in mind of a fox, trying to dig out a nest of rabbits. I reckoned Ann had already got her prey, though, though I wouldn't have said so out loud just then. She has a fearsome temper, does Ann.

She crawled back out, dusting her hands on her skirt, and I peered down through the leaves, but there wasn't much to see: only a line of newly spaded earth, as if someone had dug a four-foot trench and then filled it back in. The lower branches of the bush covered it well enough, if you didn't know where to look, but we both knew that hunting dogs don't go by the look of things. I decided not to point this out to Ann, though, for she was in a high-strung state as it was, and if I'd told her that trench might be discovered, I'll be bound that she'd have tried to make me dig it up with my bare hands. *Ann Melton never dug that grave*, I thought. She may have stood by and watched the damp earth being spaded, but I could not imagine her soiling her tiny white hands with a shovel handle, nor putting forth the effort to dig a hole in the ground big enough to receive a human body. Oh, I could see her killing somebody quick enough. That fearsome temper of hers would carry her through that enterprise, but the arduous task of hauling a corpse up the ridge and concealing it under the soil—no, she would leave the spadework to someone else, and since I had not been pressed in to service to do it for her, I knew who had.

As it was, she contented herself with picking up a few handfuls of leaves and putting them down over the bare spot. She made me do the same, so I scooped up a pile of wet oak leaves that had been there all winter, and I let them fall on top of the spaded earth.

It seemed funny to think of somebody I knew and was kin to being down there, just a few inches below my fingertips. I reckon if I was to claw at the earth instead of dropping leaves on the spot, I could uncover her face and see her looking up at me.

I would like to have seen what her face looked like, after two months dead, but I had Ann to reckon with, and I knew that if I tried to dig, Ann would either collapse in a screaming heap or else pick up the nearest rock and lay me out where I stood to keep me from telling what I knew. So I contented myself with dumping another handful of leaves on the grave.

We didn't stay much longer after that. Ann walked twice around the clearing, studying that bush from every possible angle, but she made no move to do anything more. I figured she wouldn't. Moving the body was not to be thought of, even if her nerves could have stood it, which I doubted. We had brought no tools with us. Besides, I had yet to see Ann lift a finger to do anything.

Finally she sighed and wiped her muddy hands on her skirt. "They won't see anything. Let's go back."

As I followed her out of the clearing, she turned and caught my arm, digging her nails in to my skin. "You know what's down there, don't you, Pauline?"

I could see there was no point in lying to her, so I just nodded.

She dug her nails deeper in to my arm. "Well, if you don't keep your mouth shut about this, you'll be out here, too."

I believed her, and I resolved to be more careful of her in future. I wasn't afraid of her—just wary, same as you'd be if you saw a snake on the path in front of you. I knew she had a temper and she was too selfish ever to be trusted, but now she had told me something she ought to have kept to herself. Now she had cause to be afraid of me, and Ann always struck out at what made her fearful. So I must be watchful.

They say that once a dog has killed chickens, you might as well shoot it, for it has got the taste of blood and will never stop killing. I didn't think it would come to that with Ann, but I reckoned it would be easier for her if she took a notion to do it again.

# PAULINE FOSTER

## Late August 1866

⟡

I took to visiting the little general store in Elkville every chance I got, just to hear what people were saying about Laura Foster. Mostly, I'd just listen, but if the story looked like it was dying down, I'd blow a little on the embers to get it going again. No more than Ann talked to most of our neighbors, I didn't figure any of it would get back to her, but she must have had her ear to the ground from worry about news of Laura, because it did.

One time I ran into Jack Adkins and Ben Ferguson there at Cowle's store, and they were still talking about the disappearance. Ever since they went and fetched Tom Dula out of Tennessee a few weeks back, they had fancied themselves lawmen and thought it was up to them to set everything to rights—or else they were just nosier than six old ladies.

It is more than a mile from the Meltons' place on Stony Fork Road down to Cowle's store, and by the time I had walked it in the summer heat I was so hot and tired that I was in no mood to suffer fools gladly.

Jack hailed me as I came up the path. "Pauline—here—stop a minute. You're a cousin of Laura Foster, ain't ye?"

I nodded, trying to edge past him and into the store, out of the burning sunshine. "We don't much bother about the *begets* in the Foster family," I told him, "but I reckon I'm kin to her right enough, through my daddy and hers. Why?"

"We're trying to work out what happened to her," said Ben Ferguson. "Tom Dula's not talking, so we'll have to figure it out for ourselves."

I set my face into polite blankness and heard him out. People thought that we Fosters should care more than other people about what happened to our cousin, being blood kin, but if anything, I think we cared less, for we knew her better, and she wasn't much use to anybody.

Ben said, "She took her daddy's horse and went off on her own, so we know she wasn't kidnapped. And when she saw Miz Scott on the road that morning, she said that she was going off—with Tom Dula, some say. Only *she's* gone and *he's* still around, so you've got to wonder what became of her."

It was all I could do not to laugh. The two of them looked like puppies smelling guts at a hog killing. I think Ben could read, and he must have been filling his head with pirate tales or some such folderol out of a book. Or maybe they had missed the War, and were trying to scare up a little excitement now to make up for it.

"We're going to go on searching for her," Jack told me. "She's dead. We're certain of that. And Tom done it, but we don't know what he did with the corpse. But we reckon we'll find it."

I didn't think the two of them could find their bottoms with both hands, and for all my vows to hold my peace about the matter, I could not stop myself from twisting the tails of those two fool hounds. "Why, you may be sure she is dead," I said, just as solemn as a burying preacher. "Why, I killed her myself. Me and Tom Dula did. Can't tell you where we put her, though. But you all keep looking. You're sure to find her sooner or later."

With that, I pushed my way past them and on in to the store, while they were still standing there, rooted to the ground, speechless with shock. I made it all the way inside before I fell to laughing so hard I could not speak my order, but it is dangerous to jest with fools, for they are liable to believe anything.

After I had finished passing the time of day at the store, I figured I would give the Meltons the slip a while longer, as long as I was out. I could always claim later that I had been feeling poorly. I left the store and went south along the river road to the house of Mrs. Alexander don't-you-never-call-her-Celia Scott. I had been there once that day already, early that morning, but somehow Ann had tracked me there, and she boxed my ears for leaving the house without her say-so. The government had put an end to slavery three years back, but I swear you would think the Meltons hadn't heard about it, for they sure as hell acted like they owned me.

"What are you doing out visiting when your chores ain't done?" Ann Melton had barged in to Miz Scott's house so soon after I got there that she must have caught sight of me on the road. She grabbed hold of my arm, and shouted right in my face. "Nobody gave you leave to go off a-visiting! The cows want milking, and there is breakfast to be got, so you can just march yourself back home with me and get started on it."

Having a witness to this coarse treatment emboldened me. "Why must I do both, Cousin Ann? Milk the cow and cook the breakfast? I've not seen you do a hand's turn in many a day."

She slapped me hard then, and, putting one hand on my arm and winding the other one around a hank of my hair, she half dragged me out the door and down the road. Treating me like a slave afore company just made me all the more determined to give her the slip, so after I'd been to the store, I headed back to the Scotts' to finish my visit, and maybe to cadge a biscuit and honey, for before Ann hauled me away that morning, Miz Scott had told me she would be baking.

As soon as I had knocked, Miz Scott met me at the door, pale-faced, and peeking over my shoulder to see if Ann was following along behind me. Seeing nobody else in the road, she pulled me in-side, barring the door behind me. Then she sat me down at the table and she poured me a dipper of cold water into a tin cup. Before I could even take a sip, she had put the plate of new-baked biscuits on the table next to a pot of honey, and she bade me help myself. She didn't have to tell me twice, so I reached for a biscuit, and contrived to look like I had come a-visiting for the pleasure of her company.

"I was sorry to see that unpleasant scene that passed between you and Mrs. Melton this morning," she said, pulling up the other chair, and pouring water for herself into a chipped china teacup. "Your cousin is quite a high-strung woman."

I nodded, taking care to look sorrowful and a little afraid. "She has the temper of a penned-up bull, does Cousin Ann. You wouldn't want to cross her, Miz Scott. It's as much as your life is worth to make her angry." I said that last bit slow and soft to give her time to catch my meaning.

Miz Scott turned pale, and she clapped her hand to her mouth.

After a moment she whispered, "Have you ever known anybody to make her angry?"

"Besides me, you mean?" I took a sip of water and pretended to think on it. "There wasn't any love lost between her and our other cousin, Laura Foster over to German's Hill. I reckon you'd know the whys of that, same as everybody else around here. Ann and Tom Dula have been lovers ever since they were young'uns and figured out what sex was, and, even though she is married herself, Ann pitched a fit when he took up with Laura Foster. I heard her threaten Laura's life."

Miz Scott gasped and her eyes bugged out, froglike. "What are you saying, Pauline?"

I shook my head. "You must judge for yourself, Miz Scott. I must live with the Meltons, and it's not my place to say anything."

"But Laura has been gone these many weeks. And you say that Ann threatened her. Can you possibly mean . . . that Ann?"

I shook my head. "It's as much as my life is worth to say any more, ma'am. You've seen her in a temper. Can you blame me for not speaking out?"

Miz Scott opened her mouth to argue with me, but then she shut it again, and I reckon she was remembering Ann pitching a fit in her house that very morning, and she saw the sense in what I said. After that, she tried to talk about the weather, and to tell me about a new dress she was fixing to make with a bolt of blue calico she had got from the store, but her eyes kept straying around the room, and she kept on repeating herself and losing the thread of her story, and I think her mind must have been somewhere else. I just kept smearing dollops of honey on those biscuits, and swallowing them as fast as I could, while I let her talk.

She was on her third cup of water, and she had just about run out of things to say, when a pounding on the door made her spill the contents of the cup all over the table. She tried to sop it up with her apron, while the pounding went on, louder and faster. She gave me a big-eyed stare, and whispered, "Is it her?"

I tried to remember what people do when they are afraid. I opened my eyes as wide as I could, and made as if to bite down on the side of my fist. The pounding shook the door, and Miz Scott kept glancing toward it, while she tried to mop up the water with the tail of her apron. At first I thought she was just going to sit there and hope the visitor would go away, but the knocking never let up, and finally a voice said, "Open this door or I'll break it in!" and she had to get up and unbar it.

Ann Melton pushed past Miz Scott without so much as a how-de-do, and made straight for me with a look on her face that bespoke murder. "What are you doing here again?" She put her face up close to mine and screamed at me.

I didn't bother to answer her, but just sat there, taking note of the way her eyes got all squinty when she shouted, and seeing little flecks of spit on her lower lip. I judged that Miz Scott would be too upset by Ann's carrying on to notice whether or not I was cowering in fear.

"Pauline, you have no business to be out gossiping. You have got to come home!" Without waiting for me to speak, she grabbed my arm and jerked me up out of my chair. Then she gave me a great push in the small of my back and sent me stumbling toward the still-open door.

I grabbed on to the doorjamb and looked back at Miz Scott with pleading eyes, hoping she'd remember this scene if ever the time came. It is easy to get the better of high-tempered people like Ann. They get so caught up in their moment of rage that they lose sight of the consequences. But I don't.

Ann turned me loose, but only so she could shake her fist in my face. "I heard what you told Jack Adkins and Ben Ferguson, about how you and Tom killed Laura Foster. The story is all over the settlement by now. You have said enough to Jack Adkins and Ben Ferguson to hang you and Tom Dula, if it was ever looked into."

I shrugged. "You're as deep in the mud as I am in the mire."

She made as if to slap me, but she stayed her hand, and hissed in my face, "How could you tell such a lie as that?"

I hung my head and made my voice quaver. "I said it in jest, Cousin. I reckon I lose my head when I've been drinking."

"If you don't learn to hold your tongue, I will see to it that you lose the rest of your head as well. And if I catch you gossiping and telling lies again, Pauline, you'll end up the same as Laura Foster."

Miz Scott let out a little squeak when she heard that, and Ann, still blazing with wrath, rounded on her, and said, "You had better never tell what you heard here today, Celia Scott. Do you hear me?"

Miz Scott just stared at Ann open-mouthed, the way I often see people do when someone screams at them. It seems to freeze them in their tracks, the way deer turn to stone when they hear a noise in the woods. I could see the sense of it for deer, but not for people. When someone shouts at me, I know that they are too het up to think straight, and I find myself looking down on the scene as if I were watching from outside myself, while I try to find a weakness that I can use against them. I was cold and watchful now, but Ann had forgotten me for the moment.

She hustled me out the door, and as we stood on the path, I said, mild as milk, "Do you really think she'll keep quiet about this?"

Ann's eyes narrowed, and she glanced back at the still-open door. "Wait here, Pauline, else I'll thrash you within an inch of your life."

Without waiting for an answer, she stormed back up the walk to the front door, where Miz Scott stood twisting the tail of her apron, and watching us, to make sure we were leaving. When she saw Ann coming, she took a step back and made to slam the door, but Ann was too quick for her. She blocked it with her body, leaning against the door, and changing her tone to a near whisper, as cold as the March wind. I could still hear her, though.

She said, "Miz Scott, that there Pauline Foster is a liar and a troublemaker. You'd best not be repeating what you heard her say today in your house. For, so help me, if you get me or Tom in trouble by spreading Pauline's lies, I will follow you to hell to make you wish you'd held your tongue. Do you understand?"

Miz Scott looked at her for a long moment, like she wanted to answer back, but finally she just said, "I hear you. Now get off my land," and she slammed the door in Ann's face.

Ann stood there for a moment, still whey-faced with rage, and then she came back and grabbed my elbow again. "Come on, Pauline. We're going back home, and by god you'll keep your mouth shut from here on out, or I will kill you myself. You hear me?"

I did. And, what's more, I believed her.

She was right about what I said to Jack Adkins and Ben Ferguson, though. One ought never to jest with a lawman, for they have a grim view of the world. By the end of August, the pair of them had mulled over my remark for a couple of weeks, and no other evidence had turned up to lead them to Laura Foster, so they came to Reedy Branch and arrested me.

I didn't mind. I don't get affrighted like other people, and besides, it was only those two prize fools Jack Adkins and Ben Ferguson who came to collect me, and I reckon they were more uneasy about it than I was. Ben Ferguson blushed and stammered as he read out the warrant calling for my arrest, and Jack Adkins said, "Now, Pauline, don't take on, but we are bound and sworn to bring you in to answer on a charge of murder, but we reckon they'll let you go once you tell them the truth about what you know."

"We won't tie your hands or nothin'," Ben added. "But you must give us your word you'll come along peaceable. You can ride up in front of me on my horse, for it's a long way to Wilkesboro."

I nodded and gave them my word that I would go along willingly, which I would have promised them regardless, because to my mind saying something is not the same as meaning it. I believe I could have got away from them if I'd had half a mind to. They had sidearms, but I didn't think either one of them had the sand to shoot an unarmed female. They were both so embarrassed at having to arrest a woman of their acquaintance that they could hardly keep their minds on what they were doing, and they kept telling me that all would be well—as if their word was any good on that point. I nodded and tried to look grateful for their concern, but I thought that going to jail would be a fair bit of adventure, and maybe a chance to do some mischief as well. Anyhow, it would be better than doing all the farm chores and still having to cook three meals a day for the Meltons. Since I was a woman, I'd get a cell to myself, and I could use the rest.

It was a fine afternoon, and we took our time following the river road toward Wilkesboro so as not to overtax Ben's horse. Horses are dearer than people in Carolina these days, since the Confederate army put them through battles like meat through a sausage grinder. I leaned back and washed my face with sunshine, eyes closed, and smelled the fresh-cut hay as we ambled past the fields and woods on the way to town. I was glad I didn't have the cast of mind to be a worrier, so that I could enjoy the ride, instead of dwelling on what would happen once I got there.

Wilkesboro is a fair-sized town, sitting on a little rise above the plain, with a line of wooden storefronts facing the town square: a towering red brick courthouse with pitched roofs and a white columned porch atop a flight of white stone steps. Behind the courthouse, just before the town ends in fields again, stood the squat two-story brick jail with barred windows on the right-hand side, both upstairs and down, where the prisoners were kept. I wondered where Tom was.

On the ground floor of the building sat two white painted doors: a small and ordinary looking one on the left side, where the windows weren't barred, and a wide oak door squarely in the middle of the building. Ben Ferguson swung off the horse and caught its reins. "That there is the jailer's quarters," he said pointing left, as if I couldn't figure that out for myself.

He helped me down out of the saddle, and steered me by the elbow toward that wide center door. I looked back toward the courthouse, the way we had come, and from where I stood I could look straight down the dirt street, past the trees, to a wall of blue mountains hazy in the distance, mingling with the clouds. Watauga County lay that way, and beyond it Tennessee. I wondered if Tom Dula could see the mountains from the window of his cell.

I thought about calling out to him, to see could he hear me, but they hustled me in past that stout oak door, which was banded with iron on the inside, in case anyone tried to help a prisoner break out of jail. We stood in a wide hallway that ran the width of the building, and off to the right a flight of wooden stairs went up to the next floor. Through the open door on the left, I could see the jailer's parlor, a tidy little room with a rag rug over a plank floor and a dark heavy china cupboard set against the wall by the fireplace. I was hoping that they'd take me in there for questioning, but they started up the stairs, and ushered me in to a whitewashed room at the back of the building, with nothing in it but a cot and a bucket. It was cleaner than the Meltons' place, but too sparse for comfort. I didn't plan to stay long.

Jack Adkins turned to leave. "You stay with her, Ben. I'll go get Sheriff Hix."

With that, he was gone. I walked over to the window, and peered out through the iron bars, making sure that I could see the mountains on the horizon. Sure enough, they were there, and I thought to myself that if I ever got out of here—and I meant to—then I'd head back to those hills and never come down again.

Ben was fidgeting over by the doorway. "It's no business of mine what you do, Pauline, but if you want my advice, I think you'd better tell the sheriff everything you know. Ever since Laura Foster disappeared, you've been dropping hints right and left, and the word has got around. First you offered to get Wilson Foster's horse back in exchange for a jug of whiskey. Then you told Ben and me that you and Tom had done the killing. Now, I can't see any reason for you to have done this murder, if in fact that's what it was, but I warn you that they will not let you out of here until they are satisfied that you have told them whatever you know."

I hung my head and tried to look shame-faced. "I get to joking when I've been drinking, Ben. That's all it was."

He just stood there looking at me, as blank-faced as a sheep, and then he turned away without saying a word, and shut the door behind him. I heard the key turn in the lock, and then the sound of his boots clattering down the stairs. I figured they'd be back soon enough with the high sheriff, but until then I was on my own. I started wondering where Tom was. There was a downstairs cell across the hall from the jailer's quarters, but the door had been open, so I knew he wasn't in there. The upstairs room they had put me in was at the back of the building, and I knew that on the other side of that back wall, there'd be another room beside this one, facing the front. I walked over next to the empty fireplace and tapped on the wall.

"Tom?"

I put my ear to the wall, but I couldn't hear anything. I tried again: "Tom, it's Pauline!"

Maybe the walls were too thick for him to hear me, for all I got back was silence.

The sun was making long shadows on the lawn out my window before I heard footsteps on the stairs again. I had sat down on the cot to wait, but now I got up and stood in the middle of the room and waited for them to open the door.

The first man through the door was a lean middle-aged man in a black suit coat with a stern expression that told you he was the one in charge. Jack Adkins and Ben Ferguson flanked him like lap dogs. The sheriff sized me up through narrowed eyes. "So you are Perline Foster." He fairly spat the words, and I decided to let him say my name any way he felt like.

I hoped he was one of those older men who looked at any young girl as a daughter, because then if I stayed all polite and big-eyed he might think me an innocent fool and let me go. I wished I knew how to cry, because that would really make him pity me, but I never did learn how to do it. The best I could do was to take deep breaths and make my voice all quavery, and dab at my eyes as if there were tears about to fall.

"I didn't do nothing, sir. I was just joshing with Ben and Jack here so's they would take notice of me."

"Oh, they noticed, all right. We have Tom Dula locked up here for the murder of Miss Laura Foster, and you claimed that you helped him. When these peace officers testify to that in a court of law, I reckon you'll hang right alongside Dula."

I saw then that there was room for only one big-eyed, innocent girl in this matter, and that was Laura Foster, who garnered all the pity by being dead. What's more I was mindful that when the sheriff talked about hanging me, it was no empty threat. When President Lincoln was shot at the end of the War last year, folk said they rounded up everybody who was anywhere near the actor that did the shooting and strung them all up together in Washington. One of them was a woman—the landlady who ran the boardinghouse where the actor stayed, and they hung her same as the others. I wasn't scared, but I saw that I might have stepped in to more of a trap than I had bargained for. These lawmen were hell-bent to make somebody pay for the killing of Laura, and they didn't much care who, as long as it was solved quick. I thought I had better get myself out of trouble, before they decided to make me the scapegoat alongside of Tom Dula.

I hung my head. "All right," I said. "I'll tell you what I know."

They ended up keeping me in that cell all night, but I didn't mind, because after everything I told them, I knew I could never go back to the Meltons' house anyhow. Leastways, not while Ann was still there—but after all I had told them, I didn't think that would be much longer. They kept asking me the same things over and over, until the light faded from that barred window, and they had to light the oil lamp to keep going. Right around full dark, the jailer brought me some beans and corn bread, and they waited while I wolfed it down, and then they went right back to peppering me with questions.

I told them why I had come down the mountain in the first place, and what I was ailing from. Sheriff Hix got even more squinty-eyed then, and looked like he had stepped in something, but it ain't a crime to be sick, and he didn't have to like me, as long as he believed me.

So I told about how it was at the Meltons' farm, with Ann doing no work and not even sharing a bed with James. I allowed as how many's the night I had seen Tom Dula and Ann Melton rutting together in her bed with James asleep an arm's length away. I said that Ann had made me have to do with Tom Dula out in the barn one time, so that people would think he was coming to the farm to see me instead of her. And when Tom took up with our cousin Laura Foster? Yes, Ann surely did mind that Tom was going over there. They had set-tos over it more than once. And the night that Tom ran off to Tennessee, I saw her take a knife out from underneath her bed and give it to him.

The Sheriff leaned in close and stared me in the eyes. "Do you think the pair of them killed Laura Foster together?"

"I don't know, sir," I said. "I never seen it happen. But Ann showed me the grave."

You'd have thought they'd been struck by lightning when I said that. They looked at one another and then back at me, but I met their gaze as steady as a rock to show I wasn't lying. Finally Mr. Hix said, "Where is it?"

"On the ridge beside the Stony Fork Road. Across from the Bates' place."

He nodded. "We'll ride out to Reedy Branch in the morning, and you can take us there. Is there anything else you care to say?"

I thought about it for a minute or two before I shook my head. They would never hear one word about John Anderson's part in the story if I could prevent it. Not that I cared one whit about saving Cousin Laura's nut brown boy, but if the lawmen were to find out about him, they'd hang him for sure and seek no further for culprits. That would let Ann off the hook, which was no part of my plans.

"That's all I can tell you," I said.

I thought it was just as well that Tom Dula couldn't hear through that wall between our cells, for if he had known what I was telling the law-men about Ann, I think he would have torn that wall apart with his bare hands to get to me. As it was, I slept well, with the cool night breeze blowing in from the window, and no snores or thrashing bedfellows to disturb my rest. I could sleep past daybreak, and whatever they gave me for breakfast, I would not be the one who had to cook it. Then when the sun had burned the mist away from the hills, I'd go back to Reedy Branch, but not walking and begging favors, like I had back in March. This time I would ride like a queen down Stony Fork Road, and they would all be sorry that they had treated me with scorn.

I hoped it would be a pale horse. That would be fittin'.

# PAULINE FOSTER

## *September 1, 1866*

---

I thought it would be just me and a couple of lawmen going back
to Reedy Branch, but word had got out that I was fixing to tell
them where to find the body of Laura Foster, so that by the time
we rode out from Wilkesboro to the Stony Fork Road, we must have
looked like Stoneman's Cavalry paying a return visit to the county.

I was in exalted company, though they took little enough notice
of me, except to follow my directions. Colonel Isbell himself was
there on a fine blood horse. He had vowed to see the matter through
to its grim conclusion, and he was true to his word. There was an older
man with him—another one of the gentry, I judged, from the look of
his mount and the cut of his clothes. J.W. Winkler, who had spent
weeks searching the area and had found the mare's broken rein back
in June, met us as we proceeded up the Reedy Branch Road. I waved
to him, but he looked right through me as if he didn't know me at all.
They all thought I should have gone running to the law a few weeks
back, as soon as Ann led me to that clearing, but I had to think it
over. What was to stop them from thinking that I had lied about
Ann's taking me to the grave site? It seemed to me that if I showed

anyone where it was, that proved only that *I* knew its whereabouts—
not that anyone else did. And I thought that the more unwilling I
was to tell what I knew, the more likely they would be to believe me.
So it proved, anyhow, for no one ever doubted my story—and, indeed, it was true as I told it, but the lawmen had no way of knowing
that for sure. I was lucky that they took my word for it, but then
people will often believe what you say if you are calm in the telling of
it. They seem to think that people who are tearful or het up are telling lies, but sometimes it's the other way around. I can lie till the
cock crows and never turn a hair, while a truthful fool will weep and
storm while he tells his tale, in an effort to be believed. I hoped Ann
would wail and shout when they arrested her. That would seal her
fate, for sure.

When we got to the spine of the ridge, well past the Dulas' farm,
heading toward Stony Fork Road, where the Meltons', Lotty Foster's,
and the Bates' place all sat within sight of one another, I signaled for
the procession to stop, and, with my back to the creek, I pointed them
toward the steep slope in front of us that led to the wooded crest
of the ridge.

"She led me up there," I said, stabbing with my finger upward toward the tall trees. "I waited on a fallen log, while she went and
looked at the grave. But it lies up there on the ridge somewhere."

They turned their horses toward the field, and picked their way
along, studying the ground as they went, but they were well below
where me and Ann went, so it weren't no use, but I didn't bother to
say so. One of the riders stayed close to my mount as we climbed. All
the way from town they had taken care that somebody stayed near
me all the time, in case I took a notion to run, but I was staying put

to see what happened. I sang out when we reached the dead log, and I climbed off that horse, and settled back down on it. As I watched, the men spread out, working in pairs, slipping this way and that, through the bushes and past the trees, always searching for broken branches and clabbered ground. One of the Wilkesboro men stood next to me with a pistol on his hip, watching the searchers go across the clearing and head farther up the slope, but he wasn't interested in passing the time of day with me.

It was cool in the shade up there on the ridge, and I leaned back in a shaft of sunlight, smelling dead leaves and damp earth, and watching three gray pigeons flit about in the treetops. I could have done with a dipper of water and a hunk of bread and meat, because it had been a long time since my jailhouse breakfast, such as it was, but none of the searchers stopped to eat. I suppose that hunting for a body three months dead had put them off their feed.

They kept circling higher and higher up the ridge, going slow, and peering down at the ground as they went. Then a good ways above where I sat, I heard shouts, and the men came back out of the thickets and from the lower woods, and they all headed up at once in the direction of the yelling.

I reckoned they had found her.

Nobody bothered to tell me what was going on, but a few minutes later, someone ran back down and called out to my minder, "Mr. Horton's horse shied like it smelled something foul, and the colonel got down and saw that new sod had been put on the ground there. We think it's her down there. You can take the prisoner on up to the thicket to identify the remains. I'm off to fetch the doctor."

With that, he nudged his mount, and began to pick his way around the logs and underbrush, heading down the slope toward the Reedy Branch Road. It was a good two miles from here to Cowle's store and from the river road, two miles in the other direction to Elkville, so I judged it would be more than an hour before Dr. Carter would arrive to have his say about whatever the searchers unearthed.

I had seen dead folks before. They died often enough from want and wounds back in the War, and a time or two I had to help with the laying out, but I had never seen what was left of a corpse after three months underground. I wondered if they would be able to tell who it was if they did find anything.

When we reached the thicket where the searchers were gathered, I edged my way past a couple of men until I could see what they were doing at the grave site. Colonel Isbell and Mr. Horton had dismounted now, and they had scraped away the sod covering from the dug-out trench, and I could see that there was a cloth-covered lump lying there, not even two feet below the level of the ground: a shallow grave, indeed, but still deeper than I could picture Ann digging with her fine white hands.

The Colonel knelt beside the trench, and pointed to a mark on the side where the covering sod had been removed. "Look at that cut. The blade of a mattock made that, I'll be bound."

The other men looked at one another. Word had got around with the rest of the gossip that Martha Gilbert had seen Tom out skelping with a mattock near Lotty Foster's place on the day before Laura went missing. But nobody said anything.

Then, with everybody still watching, he reached down and lifted the bundle of clothes out of the hole so that we could see what was underneath. *What*, not *who*. It didn't look like a "who" anymore. What was left was a cloth-covered pile of skin and bones that put me in mind of a slaughtered hog—a skinny one that had run wild on the mountain and then died at the end of a harsh winter.

One of the lawmen motioned for me to come closer, and I stepped up to the very edge of the hole. "Is that Laura Foster?" he asked me.

The body was set in on its side, but faceup, and, although the hole was nearly two feet deep, it had been dug too short to accommodate even a body as small as that one. The legs were tucked up under the corpse, to make them fit. It was no proper grave. Just a place to dump a hunk of rotting meat.

I glanced around at the faces of the searchers. Some of them looked green around the gills, and the rest were ashen with anger and muttering amongst themselves. I looked back at the decaying lump of flesh that used to be my cousin. I knew her better than any of them did. But what was the use of taking on over her being dead? She was past hearing us now.

The skin on the face was mostly gone, but there was a hank of light brown hair still attached to the scalp. I knew that color. I could just see her feet, where they were tucked up behind her. She was wearing little leather shoes that I had seen James Melton making for her. They had held up better than the dress material in the damp earth.

I knew the dress, too: it was a checkered one, homemade. I had seen her cutting the cloth and stitching it. Over top of it she had put on a dark wool cape that was maybe too warm to wear on a May morning, but it was too good for her to leave behind, so she'd put it on anyhow. It was fastened around her shoulders with a pinchbeck brooch pin, the only finery she had. I wondered what would become of that with her dead.

It was her, all right.

The lips were drawn back in that skinless face, and I could get a clear look at her teeth. They were big teeth for her little face, and there was a space between the two front ones. Anybody who knew her would recognize those teeth.

"It is Laura Foster," I said. "I'd know her by her teeth—that space in-between the front ones. And I was with her when she sewed that there dress she is wearing."

Several of the others muttered in agreement. Most of them were acquainted with her—and it crossed my mind that some of them knew her maybe too well, though they'd never own up to that now. But even with the face mostly eaten away by the damp and the worms, we all could tell it was her.

One of the searchers said, "How did she die?" He wasn't talking to me, though, so I didn't answer.

"Doctor's on his way," the Colonel told him. "We ought not to touch the body overmuch till he can examine it."

"You reckon she was carrying a child?"

I had to put my hand across my mouth to hide a grin. What would that have mattered—to Tom or anybody else? Why, Lotty Foster had five young'uns by as many fathers, and nobody had bothered to marry her. If Laura Foster had been the Colonel's girl or the daughter of a lawyer or a doctor, then there'd have been a hue and cry if she fell pregnant, and the poor fellow courting her would have been hauled before the justice of the peace at the business end of a shotgun for a hasty wedding. But Laura's good name was in the mud long before Tom Dula ever took up with her. She had no more notion of chastity than any of the other Foster women, which is to say: none at all. Were these graven fools really thinking that Tom had killed her to keep from having to marry her? Why if she had put such a notion to him, he'd have laughed in her face—or else told her to saddle that baby on one of her many other lovers.

I didn't say any of that out loud, though. I could see that the sight of that bony little corpse was already making the searchers forget the real girl they had known all her life. By the time they had given her a proper funeral and commenced to heaping cabbage roses on her grave, every one of them would be remembering Laura Foster as a pure and beautiful maiden, a princess right out of a fairy story. T'would be no use trying to remind them what she was really like. She had been replaced by a changeling, and they had already forgotten the real girl.

"Wait for the doctor," somebody said. "He'll know."

They left her there right where they found her, so as not to disturb her before Dr. Carter got to see her. One of the deputies untied the bundle of clothes, though. On the morning Laura went missing, Mrs. Scott had seen it slung over the bare back of that mare, and that was how she had come to ask where Laura was heading. Considering that the bundle was all that Laura Foster had in the world, it was a sorry little parcel, indeed. A few scraps of raggedy underclothes, a wooden fine-tooth comb, a yellowed cotton nightdress . . . it wasn't much to show for twenty years of living on this earth, but I wasn't sorry for her, for I had no more possessions to my name than she did, and maybe she had all that she deserved, at that.

The men stood around smoking or talking quietly to one another, and they all turned away from the sight of Laura's body lying there in the hole. I suppose it seemed uncivil to them to be carrying on with the small pleasures of living in the presence of one who could no longer enjoy them. It wouldn't have put me off my feed to look at her, but there were pleasanter sights in the wildwood, and nobody had anything to eat, so I walked a little ways away from the grave, and sat down in a patch of sunlight, thinking I might close my eyes and rest until the doctor came. It was only then that I remembered that I had not screamed when they showed me the corpse. I cannot weep, but I wished I had remembered to scream or make like I was going to faint. Somebody might remember that I did not act affrighted enough and hold it against me.

Finally we heard shouts from the field below that told us the lawman was back, bringing Dr. George Carter in tow. When they finally reached the laurel thicket where we were congregated, the doctor stood there alone for a moment, looking like a lord, sleek in his black cloth suit and string tie, and his shiny black boots, while the rest of the men were in ordinary work clothes, and muddy from a morning spent combing the woods. I raised my hand and gave the doctor a little wave, because, after all, I was his patient, and I had been seeing him regular these six months or so, but he looked right on past me as if I had been one of the hounds. Maybe he thought I was mixed up in the killing, or maybe he thought my pox made me not fitten to associate with, or maybe he just didn't see me. I didn't care much; he had other things on his mind.

Colonel Isbell went forward and shook Dr. Carter's hand, and the rest of the crowd parted as if he was Moses, and he walked over to the open grave and knelt down beside it. He stared down at the sorry little heap of flesh for a minute or more, but all he said was, "Well, now . . . ," and he blinked his eyes a time or two real fast. I don't reckon doctors cry, either.

Gently, without another word, he began to examine the body, and the rest of us edged forward again so we could watch what he was doing, but not so close as to be noticed and told to step back. I couldn't see much, on account of the hole the body was in being so deep, and the doctor's back being in my line of sight, but at least I could tell he had peeled back the material of that rotting checkered dress, and he was probing her chest with his fingers, trying to find some sign of what had killed her.

At last he stood up, drew a white linen handkerchief out of the pocket of his coat, swabbed his forehead, and then wiped his hands again and again on it. He addressed his remarks to the Colonel, but loud enough for the rest of us to hear. "Well, the body is that of Laura Foster, as I am sure you know already."

They nodded, and somebody muttered, "Didn't need a doctor to tell us that."

Colonel Isbell's expression didn't change. "How long has she been dead?"

"Oh, since the last morning she was seen, I have no doubt. That body has been in the ground there a good three months."

"Can you tell what killed her, then?"

The doctor nodded, and motioned for Colonel Isbell to kneel beside him at the grave. Then he reached down, and lifted a bit of the rotting cloth on the bodice of that checkered dress. "There's a slit here. Do you see it?"

Those closest to the grave leaned over to get a look, and the rest of us hung back, listening. The smell from the open trench hung over us like a thundercloud, and few cared to get any closer to the source of the stench. Back in June when the laurels bloomed, the scent of their pink flowers might have covered the smell of decay, but now at summer's end the odor of death had no rivals. I had seen all I wanted to, and smelled more than that, but I still wanted to hear what the doctor made of the matter.

"This cut was deliberately made. You can just see the corresponding wound in the flesh beneath it. Here, someone help me to remove these clothes so that I can get a better look."

The Colonel stepped away, and let one of the farmers in the search party assist the doctor in his grim task. A few men looked away, from modesty, I suppose, but though there might have been a few among them that would have liked to see Laura Foster naked while she was living, the sight of her now roused in them nothing but disgust, or perhaps, in the weakest ones, a stirring of pity. One or two sodden old fools even wiped away a tear.

I had got accustomed to the smell now, so I edged past the squeamish ones for another look.

When her naked breast lay open to the air, the doctor put two fingers into the hole in her flesh, and poked around a bit. Then he put his face down close to the wound to peer inside. Nobody moved or spoke. We just waited to hear what he would say.

Finally he motioned for Colonel Isbell to take a look, and we heard him say quietly, "Something sharp—I should say a short-bladed knife—was thrust up through her breast, here between the third and fourth ribs."

"Into her heart?" said the Colonel.

"Well . . . I cannot be sure. If the blade was thrust straight in, it would have missed her heart entirely. But if the knife had been held in a slightly elevated position, it would certainly have cut the heart. The body is so badly decomposed that I cannot tell which."

"But that's what killed her, then?"

"If the knife missed the heart, it need not have been a mortal wound, but if the heart were punctured, then it would have necessarily been fatal."

"I hope she did not suffer."

The doctor made no answer to this, which made me think that he knew very well that she had. Before anyone could ask again, someone called out, "Was she with child?"

Dr. Carter sighed, and shook his head. "Again, I cannot know for certain. If she was less than ten weeks into her term, then there would be no trace. You see the state of the body." He shrugged. "If she were more than ten weeks gone, and if I opened her up, I might find foetal bones in her womb, but I cannot see that it matters, as we could not tell who the father was. And unless the sheriff or a judge instructs me to do this, I am inclined to leave her be. She was put through enough, poor child."

Some of the searchers murmured agreement. They led me away then, as they were making preparations to bring the body up out of the hole and take her down the ridge to a more sanctified resting place. I thought she'd end up buried back in German's Hill, probably on the land her father was sharecropping, and half the county would attend the funeral. That would be no tribute to Laura Foster, though. Most of the crowd would be curiosity seekers, and they'd go just to say they had been, without caring one whit more for Laura dead than they had for her when she was alive. She was a nine days' wonder, nothing more.

They took me back to Cowle's store then, where there'd be a

meeting about what had transpired, and I was glad to go, because it had been a long, wearing day, and I was so hungry that I could feel my backbone against my belly button. I spent the whole ride there thinking about food, and hoping they'd offer me something stronger than water to wash it down with, but they didn't seem much interested in me anymore, now that I had told what I knew. Here and there along the river road that went along to the store, people stood outside their houses or on the edge of their fields and stared at us as went past. I felt like a queen in a parade, and I raised my hand a time or two to wave at them, but they just stood stock-still and stared back with stony expressions. But I didn't care. It was my day in the sun.

It took most of the afternoon, and there was a great to-do when the searchers brought the body in and laid it out on a counter in the store, with everybody outshouting everybody else to tell what happened, but finally they let me go, and I was glad to leave all the tale telling and the gawking to that horde of folks who crowded into the store so they could say they were part of the story.

The crowd was buzzing with tales about the case, with most of them telling more than they knew. I kept still and listened to what they were saying, and one time I heard the storekeeper's wife telling one of the women that Ann Melton had been to the store a week or so back, and she asked her if she was afraid that the lawmen were going to arrest her over the death of Laura Foster. The storekeeper's wife dropped her voice to a hoarse whisper, but I had edged close enough to hear her say, "And when I asked her that, Mrs. Melton just laughed at me—*laughed*, mind you!—and then she said, 'They'll not put a rope around this pretty little neck.'" Her listeners gasped at the brass of that remark, and the storekeeper's wife nodded with grim satisfaction, but hearing it caused me to shiver, for Ann Melton is a beautiful woman. When people say that beautiful women get away with murder, maybe it is more true than they mean it to be.

Mr. Pickens Carter, the justice of the peace, heard everybody out, as if it were a court, except that no lawyers were present. The searchers told how I had helped them find the burial place, and that I had cooperated with them by telling all I knew.

He said to me, "You are free to go, Pauline Foster, but you may not leave this jurisdiction, for you will be called as the state's chief witness in a few weeks' time at court in Wilkesboro. You must swear an oath that you will testify."

I don't know why people set such a store by the swearing of oaths, for they don't cost anybody a red cent, but I could see that the justice of the peace believed in them, so I stood up before him, big-eyed and solemn, and I faithfully promised that I would appear in court when they called me. I probably would, too, because I had started it all, and I wanted to see it end.

I waited around on the edge of the crowd at Cowle's store until I heard Mr. Justice Carter say to the constables, "Go and arrest Ann Melton."

I wasn't there when they took her away, though I was sorely tempted to go and watch in case she fought and cried, and had to be dragged screaming from the house. I went back at dusk, though, to see about getting my clothes and what they owed me for my last days of work. James Melton was there alone, sitting at the table, making a pair of boots.

I stood there in the doorway, watching him work in the fading light, and looking for some sign of distress in a man whose wife has just been taken away on a charge of murder. But he looked just the same as ever, with his blond head bent over that boot, intent on sewing the leather, as if the only thing in the world that mattered was making that shoe.

I made a little noise to let him know that I was there, and finally he looked up. "I've come for my wages and my things, James."

He nodded. "They have taken Ann away. I guess you'd know about that."

"I was there. They found Laura's body. She had showed me where it was a few weeks back. Did she take on when they came to get her?"

"Ann? No. She turned pale at first, but then she swept out of here like they were taking her off to a dance. She didn't make a sound or shed a tear. She didn't even look back."

It crossed my mind that Ann and Tom were together at last. There was a wall between them in the Wilkesboro jail. I wondered if they could talk through it, or if they would try.

James set the shoe aside, and looked up at me. "Where are you headed, Pauline?"

"I don't know. I'd go back to Watauga County if they'd let me, but they say I must stay here in Wilkes until the trial. I am to be a witness. I might see if other kinfolk will take me in, but they didn't want to last March, and I don't reckon they'll think me any more of a bargain now."

"You can stop on here."

I stared at him for a minute, trying to tell from his face what he had in his mind, but you never could tell what James Melton was thinking by looking at him. "Stay here?"

"I still have the babies to be looked after, and with Ann gone, there's no one to cook or tend to the house." He almost smiled when he said it, because both of us knew that Ann wasn't any more use than a chicken when it came to housekeeping, but that didn't make what he said about needing help any less true. "I reckon I could still pay you just the same."

"All right. I can stay on. But you know I'll be called as a witness in the trial."

"So will I."

I had not thought of that. "What will you say, James?"

"I will tell the truth, whatever they ask me. It's my duty."

"Even if it gets Ann hanged?"

"I don't know anything that could harm her. Or Tom, either, come to that. I was here that night. I saw people come and go. That's all I can swear to."

"Are you going to go see her in jail?"

He was silent for so long that I didn't think he heard me. Finally he looked down at that boot again, and he barely whispered, "I don't think I'll have time. I don't suppose she'll be locked up for very long— one way or the other." He went back to sewing the leather then, as if he had forgotten I was there.

I don't know if James Melton ever went to see his wife in jail or not, or if she even wanted him to. I never went.

That was in September 1866, and the trial was set for the beginning of October, which is when they held Superior Court in the courthouse in Wilkesboro. I thought it would all be over quick. Trials only lasted a day or two at most, for the high court only met twice a year, and they had so many cases to settle that they could not dally over any of them, not even something as serious as a killing. I thought there would be more graves in Reedy Branch before the leaves fell.

I was wrong about that.

The court went and appointed Governor Vance, that was, to defend Tom and Ann, and they ordered him to do it for free. He got his teeth into that case like a terrier cornering a rat. First he moved the trial over to Statesville, so that all the witnesses had to travel forty miles or more to get to court, and nobody thanked him for that, but he managed to drag the proceedings out for another year and a half out of sheer contrariness.

None of us could read, so it's no use asking me what the rights of it were, because I never did know. I just went when they told me to, and said my piece on the witness stand as many times as they asked me to.

One thing did worry me, though. I never understood all the legal twists and turns as the lawyers tried to sort out what a jury could hear, and what some clerk had got wrong in filling out the legal papers. I thought of it as a game of noughts and crosses, and I figured that everybody had just clean forgotten about Laura Foster, who was tucked away by now in a solitary grave on the Foster farm in German's Hill. All she had wanted was to get away from there, and in death they took her right on back there, so now she must stay forever. Unless she went to heaven, if there is one. I never heard it said that anybody had ever seen her ghost lingering about the place.

The one thing that worried me was the one person who knew almost as much as I did. John Anderson. In the weeks leading up to that first day in court, the lawyers from both sides were scurrying around, collecting witnesses, until it seemed like most of Elkville would be congregated in that courtroom, telling what they knew.

I was afraid that someone would think of adding John Anderson to the list, or else that he would hunt them up himself and offer to testify. But when I said something to Wash Anderson about it, he just laughed at me.

"What would they want to talk to him for, Pauline?"

I wasn't about to tell him, so I just hung my head and muttered, "I only wondered because I hear that you and your sister are on the witness list, and your house is right next to the Bates' place. So maybe they think he saw something."

Wash snickered. "You don't know nothing, Pauline. John may be near as light as you are, but to the law he ain't nothing but a darky. He can't testify in court, not when the accused and the dead victim are all white folks. What would he know about it anyhow?"

"I just wondered," I said.

It set my mind at ease somewhat to know that John Anderson could not be a witness in court, but I was still afraid he might go seek out one of the lawyers, and tell them the truth about Laura's elopement. I had not seen him alone since Laura went missing. I think he knew how dangerous it would be for him if anyone guessed the truth. But if he ever got to the point where he didn't care, he could ruin everything, for he could put me squarely back into the case. I didn't want it known that I had lied to Ann. If everyone kept quiet about how it really happened, the law might hang them both.

I waited it out, though. Least said, soonest mended. I was right to do that. They found Tom guilty. The court ordered him to hang in Statesville on November 9, 1866, but the lawyer, Governor Vance, labored on Tom's behalf as if he were being paid in gold instead of working for nothing. He fought and objected and quibbled about every little thing, fighting like he was back in the War again. He was an important man with half the quality folks in the state counting themselves as his friends, so he got his way.

By and by we heard there was to be a new trial for Tom, on account of they hadn't got it right the first time around. I never understood the rights of it. Since the high court only met twice a year, spring and fall, that gave Tom another six months of life, or six more months to spend penned up in a cell, depending on how you looked at it. I remembered what he had said about that Union prison camp, and I reckoned he was burning to get out, one way or another.

Ann continued to bide in the jail, and months went by with nothing done about her. Since Governor Vance had arranged for them to be tried separately, she would have to wait until it was settled with Tom, once and for all, before they would consider her part in it.

The next time the court met, we all got ready to traipse down to Statesville to say our piece all over again, but then we heard that the defense wasn't ready, on account of some of their witnesses not turning up. That was Mr. Vance, up to his old tricks again, we figured, so things got moved along to the fall of 1867. A year in jail for Tom, with that first death sentence hanging over his head. I thought that if I were the Iredell County jailer, I'd invest in a couple of extra guards.

I was back in Elkville in June, visiting folks, and mainly asking around to see what was transpiring in the court case. That's when I heard that Governor Vance was trying to round up new witnesses for the second trial, and I began to worry that he might stumble on to somebody who knew more than he bargained for. He might use his fancy tricks to get Tom off on new evidence, and then turn around and get Ann freed based on her beauty and the Governor having friends in high places.

I decided to pay a call on someone while I was there. I went to see

James Melton first, and found him well and working as hard as ever. He looked older than his years, perhaps from all the worry and from having to run the place all on his own now. The little girls were still too young to be much help.

"I just came by to say how-do," I told him, sipping the tin cup of well water he had given me. "How is my cousin Ann faring in jail?"

He sighed and mopped his forehead with a rag. I thought that I could see strands of gray in his yellow hair. "You'd do better to ask her mother about her. It's a long way to town, and I have no time to go."

"Don't you miss her?"

He thought about it. James never was one for making hasty replies. "She was beautiful, you know. Like having a fairy maiden out of an old ballad come to stay, but you know how those songs end. The fairy always goes back to where she came from. She never stays forever. And after a while it just seems like it was all a dream."

I just looked at him, while I tried to picture lazy, foul-tempered Ann Melton as a fairy queen, but it sounded like pure foolishness to me. One thing was clear, though: as far as he was concerned, she was gone.

I left him soon after that, just as it was gathering dark, and I walked down the hill to the Andersons' house, but I didn't aim to pass the time with Wash or his sister Eliza. Wash was all right when he was sober, but that Eliza was a milk and water miss, and it near 'bout put me to sleep to try to talk to her.

Everything looked just the same as it always had. The Bates' place was as desolate as ever, though I didn't suppose anybody ever gave it a second thought anymore, if they had to look at it every day. Laura was dead and buried, and Tom and Ann were away in jail, so life went on. But there was one person that I thought would still remember, and it was him I had come to talk to.

I found him in the barn, milking the Andersons' one old cow. I was surprised that he had stayed around after what happened, but then the government had set all the slaves free four years back, and he hadn't gone off then, so maybe he was the staying kind. As soon as I thought that, though, it came to me that John Anderson had been wanting to run off with Laura Foster, and maybe he still wanted to get away—more than ever now that she was dead. But he had seen that when Tom Dula tried to run off, it just made everybody think he was guilty of killing Laura. John Anderson couldn't afford to have people wondering things like that about him. Somebody might have seen something while they were keeping company together, and if folks put two and two together, he'd hang for sure.

He glanced up when he saw me, and I saw him startle for an instant. All he could see was a shadow against the bright light outside, and Laura and I were like enough in form and height—both of us little and scrawny—though many would say she was more fair of face. I didn't care, though. Look where it got her. After a couple of heartbeats, he worked out who I was, but he had to finish the milking, so he just nodded how-do, and went back to what he was doing. I stood there just inside the barn until my eyes got accustomed to the light, and I watched him squirting jets of milk into the pail. I could smell it, the hot sweet smell mingling with the odor of fresh-cut hay and cow piles glistening with flies.

He was leaner than the last time I had seen him, and he seemed a little darker, maybe from working in the summer fields—or else the dim light in the cow byre made him seem so. He had a fine chiseled face, though, that put me in mind of a mountain back where I come from that they called The Grandfather. He was handsome enough, but I don't reckon most people bothered to look at him. All they'd see was somebody's slave, good for doing the farm work, and that's all. It's a wonder Laura ever saw more than that, but I reckon she did. He'd not find a woman like her again—and maybe he'd live longer for the fact of that.

When he finished the milking, he stood up and hoisted the pail out of reach of the cow's hoof. He set it down near the door, and turned to look at me. "How do, Miss Foster," he said, quiet and careful, in his white-folks voice.

I smiled. "You don't have to bow and scrape to me, John Anderson. I know you of old."

His face stayed as blank as the cow's. "Was there something I could do for you, ma'am?"

"I kept your secret all this past year, John. Come sit a spell with me, and tell me how you are."

"I can't see how that concerns you, Miss Pauline."

I settled myself on top of a pile of clean straw, and the cow wandered back outside, so after a minute of standing there with his fists clenched, he sat down an arm's length away from me, eying me like I was part rattlesnake.

"You went away," he said.

"I did. I have people up the mountain, and I went back to stay with them. I thought it might be perilous to stop on here for a while. I'll bet you'd have left if you could have."

He nodded. "I used to dream about it. Only in my dream, it would be me and Laura astraddle her daddy's mare, heading up that mountain that looks like it rises up out of the woods behind the back pasture. Reckon I'll never see those mountains up close now."

I took a blade of straw and twirled it between my fingers. "People forget, John. A year has come and gone. Give it another one or two, and nobody will even mark your absence. You are a free man, ain't you? Go as you please."

He leaned back and pointed out the barn door and up at the sky, where a full golden moon was just coming up over the ridge. "See how big the moon looks when it rises? Looks like it's almost touching the ground. When I was little, I used to think that if you climbed to the top of the mountain, you could touch it. But one night I climbed all the way up the ridge, and when I got there, the moon was as far away as ever. Now, I reckon freedom is like that. You think that if you just go someplace else you could touch it, but when you get there, it will still be a million miles away."

"You and Laura might have made it, if you went far enough out west to where they don't care about such things. Indian Territory, maybe."

"Well, that is past praying for. Laura is dead and gone. And I am thinking that once the harvest is over and done with, I will get away from here. At least then I won't have to look at that ridge where they found her buried. Maybe I could sleep better then."

"Where would you go?"

"The Andersons have property over the county line, at German's Hill. I thought I might do some sharecropping on my own over there, if Mr. Washington is willing to let me try. I think he will. It's only Caldwell County—not over the mountain, not Indian Territory, but maybe I can start living again there. Find me another woman."

I smiled at his foolishness. "Another gal like my cousin Laura?"

"No!" He hit the straw with his fist. "As little like her as ever was. I have done with that. I'll find me a good steady woman of color, who can help me tend a farm, and make a life over there, where we don't have to sneak around in fear of our lives."

It was like listening to James Melton all over again. The Foster women seem to have the power to bewitch a man, like the fairy queen in the old ballads, but sooner or later, he wakes up on a cold hillside, with a handful of dust and ashes, and after that all he wants for the rest of his life is a plain ordinary woman who will share his burdens, instead of a moonshine maiden who gives you dreams and leaves you with nothing.

The moon had climbed higher than the ridge now, and it was so dark in the barn that we both looked like shadows. I leaned back in the straw, feeling drowsy and peaceful. Neither one of us said anything for a while. Then I heard John sigh, a heavy, weary sound like a tired old horse.

"What?"

He sighed again. "It's just that you put me in mind of Laura, sitting there in the hay like that, all in shadow. You favor her."

"Laura and me were blood cousins, so we ought to."

"I'll miss her until the day I die."

I thought the day he died might have come sooner if she still walked the earth. I didn't say that, though, because I was mindful of what I had come about. So I leaned close to him in the soft darkness of that summer evening, and I put my hand on his shoulder and leaned close. "She was mighty lucky that she had you to make her happy, John. I never had anybody." I made my voice quaver, and it was too dark for him to see that I shed no tears. Before he knew what was happening, I was in his arms, and then I just let nature take its course. He called me "Laura," and I never said a word, just went on kissing him and running my hands over his body. Never saw a man yet that didn't take to rutting given half a chance. He wasn't but twenty-two or so, and Laura had been dead a year and more. By the time he remembered himself, it was too late to matter.

He turned his back to me when he was done, and I thought I heard him crying softly in the dark. I left him be for a minute or two, while I righted my skirt, and picked straw out of my hair. Finally, I said, "Tom Dula is getting a new trial around harvest time. And then Ann will have her day in court. And I reckon you know more than anybody about what really went on that day."

"I know Laura wasn't running off with Tom Dula. It was me she came to meet. I never told anybody, though."

"See that you don't. I reckon you know what would happen to you if people knew about you and Laura."

"I know. But they already sentenced Tom Dula to hang in that one trial. If the next court does the same thing, they're going to kill him. And he's an innocent man. He had no call to kill my Laura. None at all. I keep thinking I should tell somebody that."

I leaned in close again, but there was no softness about me this time. "You won't tell anybody anything, John Anderson, for if you do, it's you that will hang."

He tried to pull away, and I could hear the bewilderment in his voice. "But—but—I never harmed Laura."

"No. But I can't have you trying to save Tom. I want him to hang."

"But why? Are you aiming to save your cousin—Miz James Melton?"

"Well, no, John. I want them both to hang. And if you try to stop it, I'll see that they lynch you, no matter what. I'll tell them you raped me."

I couldn't see his face in the dark, but I heard him draw breath, and he shuddered like he'd touched a snake. "Somebody should have killed you," he said.

I laughed. "Why, I'm just a servant girl here. People hardly notice me at all."

. . .

When the fall term of 1867 rolled around, wouldn't you know it, this time it was the prosecution that wasn't ready. They claimed that some of their witnesses had not turned up. That there Colonel Grayson from Tennessee was one of the missing witnesses, and I wasn't surprised. A whole year had passed, and by now he must have thought he had better things to do than to travel all the way to Statesville to watch a bunch of North Carolina attorneys waste everybody's time with their legal shenanigans. I hear they fined him eighty dollars, though, for not attending. I wonder if they ever collected it.

They finally had that second trial on January 21, 1868, and mostly the same witnesses went all the way to Statesville to say their piece again. But there were a few changes. In the corridor outside the courtroom I saw Eliza Anderson, Wash Anderson's younger sister, decked out in her Sunday best.

"What did they call you for?" I asked her.

She doesn't care for me overmuch, and I reckon that's because her brother has been tale-bearing, but she answered me civil enough, "Nothing very important, I'm sure. But we live next to the Bates' place, and I suppose the prosecution called me on account of that."

I thought it was odd, because her brother was already down as a witness, and could have answered any questions about that, but I didn't think too much about it, for my mind was occupied with my own testimony, which was a deal more important than hers.

She went into the courtroom while I was still waiting in the hall, wondering if the court was planning to give us lunch. Presently Miss Eliza came storming out of the courtroom, looking like a wet hen.

"What happened to you?"

"Where is my brother?"

"Outside having a smoke. I said I'd fetch him if it was his time to go in. What's the matter?"

There was a pink spot on each one of her cheeks, and her lips twitched. "That awful man who is defending Tom Dula asked me . . . actually, in public . . . asked me if I was kin to—as he put it—'a man of color' named John Anderson."

I sat very still on the bench. "Strange question for a lawyer to ask. What does that have to do with Tom?"

"I haven't the least idea. I did not respond, and in fact before I could, the other lawyers objected, and the judge told me I need not answer."

"Well, as light as John is, I should think there might be a blood tie there somewhere."

Eliza Anderson gave me a cold stare. "Well, it's nothing to do with me!" And she stalked off to complain to Wash about that godless lawyer from Charlotte.

I wondered what prompted Tom's lawyers to ask that. Had he figured out the truth of Laura's disappearance and tipped them off? Well, it didn't matter. John Anderson could not tell what he knew, and I had no intention of telling it, either.

I don't think Tom ever worked it out. I reckon when Ann finally found him on the Friday that Laura went missing, she had said to him something like, "Well, you'll not be running away with Laura Foster now, Tom Dula, for I have killed her."

And poor easygoing Tom must have stared back at her, and said, "What are you talking about?"

But it was too late then, for by that time, Laura was lying dead in the weeds at the Bates' place with a knife wound in her heart.

And what could he do then? Let her hang for a crime she

committed for love of him? He loved her too much for that. So he buried that body, and then he was as guilty as she was.

They found Tom guilty in the second trial, same as the first, and although his lawyers succeeded in getting the execution postponed from February until May, they could not delay it forever.

By then I knew that Ann would likely go free whenever she came to trial, but that didn't matter. However long she walked the earth thereafter, the truth is that she would die the day they hanged Tom Dula.

I don't know why, though. I never did understand what it was that made people prefer one man over another.

I went back to Watauga between the trials, and found me an old man to marry, but that was a matter of business: getting a roof over my head and enough to eat. Besides, I had a baby on the way by then, and I needed to marry before it arrived. I reckon I come as close to caring about that baby as I ever have to loving anybody. Not because of its father—he is the least of it—but because the child is a part of me, and for that reason alone, I value it. But if it is born poxed, I will stifle it.

So I shall get away from Wilkes County for good, and I will take care to steer clear of tragedies, so no one will ever think to ask what became of me. The people who live happily ever after—they don't appear in the history books. They just fade away. I reckon that's what happiness is.

# ZEBULON VANCE

D octors, as a rule, do not attend their patients' funerals, and it is for similar reasons that lawyers absent themselves from public executions: it is daunting to have to face one's professional failure squarely in the cold light of day. In addition to that, I could argue that I was by no means out of the financial mire that the War had left me in, and I had my living to get at my law office in Charlotte, a good fifty miles from Statesville, where my erstwhile client would pay with his life for his crime—or possibly for mine: the arrogance of thinking my rusty legal skills adequate to mount a criminal defense in so serious a matter. I hoped him guilty, and I did not see what good it would do to go and try to offer comfort, when I had none to give. I got him a second chance before a jury, and, when that failed, his consolation could only come from a clergyman, in the hope of heaven.

He had been a soldier, and I hoped he would die like one.

In any case, my duties lay elsewhere, for I appeared before the court not only in Charlotte, but in Salisbury, Lexington, Lincolnton, Concord, Monroe, and even farther afield. I expect to be remembered for my political career, but if I am remembered for any legal case I ever took part in, I expect it will be the Johnston Will case, tried in February 1867, in Superior Court in Chowan County. It was a legal tangle involving a legacy, and no one's life was at stake, Mr. Johnston having already gone on to meet his maker. My chief contribution to that case was an impassioned speech, somewhat off the subject of the case at hand. I'm good at that. If I can entrance a jury with a diverting yarn, or make them laugh, I can often make them like me enough to find in favor of my client. It is sentiment, rather than logic, and the opposing lawyers do not esteem me for it, but it is the best way I know to practice a trade that I was taking up again after a hiatus of a dozen years. As I said, I won that case, and I hope it will suffice to sum up my career before the bar.

But in the Dula case, a young unmarried girl was dead. She was no angel of virtue, to be sure, but people were sorry for her, and that rather cramped my style in the way of misdirecting the jury with tall tales and humorous rhetoric.

Though I am committing my memories to paper, this case will not make it into my memoirs, if I have anything to say about it. It was not a shining hour in my career.

I was not there at the end, and I expected to know no more about it than what was reported in the *Salisbury Watchman* a week thereafter. But some time later I chanced to run in to my former co-counsel, the Iredell County attorney Captain Richard Allison, in the courthouse in Charlotte. He was there on another matter, but, upon seeing me, he delayed his departure for home in order to spend an hour with me, so that I might hear how it all ended in the Dula case, for he had indeed been there.

We repaired to a quiet corner, where we could sit undisturbed and talk without being overheard. After we got the initial pleasantries out of the way, Allison turned somber. "I was there, Governor," he said. "The man died bravely. I thought it my duty to see it through."

I sighed. "I wish we could have saved him. Did you speak to him before the end?"

"I did, yes. He sent for me. I never thought he would, for the jailers were saying how indifferent he was to his impending execution. He laughed and joked about the fact that he was to die the next day, and he refused the offers of ministers who would have offered him spiritual solace. His sister Eliza and her new husband made the journey from Wilkes County to Statesville with a wagon, in order to take the body back home for burial after the hanging. She brought him a note from their mother, imploring him to confess the truth of what happened, so that she could cease to be tormented by doubts and questions, but his only response to this was to ask that his sister and brother-in-law be allowed to see him."

"I don't suppose the jailers agreed to that?"

Captain Allison shook his head. "They had every reason not to trust Tom Dula. Even when he was locked in his cell, they kept him shackled to the wall on a length of chain. He did not mean to die if he could help it."

"One can hardly blame him for that."

"No, I suppose not. That night the jailer took him his supper, and he ate heartily as if he had another twenty years to live instead of only that many hours. But as the jailer got up to leave, he noticed that one of the links on the prisoner's shackles was loose. He called at once for another guard to help him, and together they examined the chain. When they saw that the link had been filed through, they knew that the prisoner had somehow got a weapon in his cell, so they began to search."

"Did they find it?"

"A piece of window glass. He had concealed it in his bed. The jailer told me that he scowled fiercely at them when they found it, but by the time they started to remedy the damage to the chain, his mood had turned sardonic again. He told them the chain had been severed so for some weeks. But he must have realized that their finding the break had ended his last chance to escape before the execution the next day, and at last he accepted the fact that he was going to die. When at last the jailer turned to leave, Dula asked that I be summoned to meet with him as soon as possible."

I considered that, momentarily stung that he had not asked for me instead. Pride is the besetting sin of the public man. "I suppose that was because he knew that you lived in Statesville? No doubt I would have been hard to locate, being down here in Charlotte, and time was short."

"I expect that was the way of it, Governor," said Captain Allison. "They sent a man to fetch me, and he found me at dinner, but I came away as soon as I could, and made my way to the jail. They led me to his cell—and they made sure to tell me about that filed chain, so that I'd be on my guard against any move he might make against me—but I think by then he had given up hope. He sat there on his cot, shoulders slumped, staring at the floor. He did not even look up when I came in. I hoped that he was praying."

"I doubt it."

"No. Perhaps not. I said, 'Well, Tom. I have come. If there's anything I can do to ease your mind, you can depend upon me to do it.' He looked up at me then, and there was nothing of the joker about him anymore. His face was ashen and haggard with worry. I only hoped that he would recover his bravado before the execution. As a soldier, he would not wish to be dragged to the gallows begging for his life."

I shuddered. "There are some things that put dying in the shade."

"Yes. To die like a slaughtered hog would be no end for a brave soldier, no matter what his crimes were. But I was no minister, so I knew he had not called for me to hear tales about repentance and salvation. I warned him, 'There is nothing more that I can do for you under the law. You would be better off making your peace with God, than by trying to struggle any more against the decree of the state.'

"He nodded. Then he picked up a length of the chain that shackled him to the wall, and let it fall again. 'They told you about this, then? Well, I had to try. I reckon I am bound to die, Captain Allison. So there is something I need to leave with you. But first I must have your word—on your sacred honor—that you will keep secret what I am about to give you while there is still breath in my body.'

"I put my hand on his shoulder, to reassure him, I suppose, and I told him upon my obligation as his attorney that it was my duty to do his bidding, within the limits of the law. 'And if it is your dying wish, then I am honor bound as a gentleman to do as you ask, so long as no other person is harmed by your request.' He smiled then, and for an instant there, he seemed to get back a bit of his boldness. 'It won't harm nobody, Captain. Just the other way around. I aim to save a life.'

"He asked me if I had a bit of paper on me. I fished about in my jacket pockets and finally found a rumpled scrap of notepaper, and a stub of pencil, which I handed over to him. He slipped down off the cot and smoothed out the bit of paper on the floor. While I stood there watching, he grasped the pencil, curling all his fingers around the haft. He set his face in a frown of concentration, with the tip of his tongue tucked in to the corner of his mouth—for all the world, the way a child does when it is just learning penmanship. I felt a stab of pity for him then, for he wasn't much more than a boy himself— or he might have been, if the War had not come."

I had lost as much as anybody in that war—a seat in the United States Senate, and the chance to someday be President—but every time I passed a cemetery, or spied a woman in widow's weeds, or met a one-legged man hobbling along on a crutch, I was humbled by the thought that my sacrifice was mere vanity compared to theirs. We lost so much in that infernal war. So much. "Do you think that the War made Tom Dula into a killer, Captain?"

Allison shook his head. "The man was a drummer in the 42nd North Carolina—just a music maker, nothing more. And the records say that he spent half the War on sick call. Indeed, I am still not convinced—well, you must let me finish my tale, Governor. Dula passed a few minutes laboriously carving words on to that scrap of paper, and when he had completed it to his satisfaction, he handed it up to me. 'Not until I am dead, mind,' he warned me as he gave it to me, and I had to promise once again to honor his wish. Only then would he allow me to read what he had written.

"It was the simplest of documents. Only a few short words, but it said everything. He had written: '*Statement of Thomas C. Dula—I declare that I am the only person that had any hand in the murder of Laura Foster. April 30, 1868.*' I read it through twice. My first feeling upon seeing those words was one of relief that we were not sending an innocent man to the gallows through any lack of skill as attorneys. But a moment later I found to my dismay that I did not believe him. I thought that statement was designed to set people's minds at rest—but also to effect the release of the other defendant. He could not save his own life, but it was within his power to save hers.

"He had clambered back up on the cot now, straightening out the heavy chain that bound him fast. He was watching me closely as I read his confession. I slipped the document into my pocket, and fixed him with a stern gaze. 'Is this the truth, Tom Dula? Do you swear to it?'

"He smiled up at me then, and I could see some of the old charm in his countenance. 'The truth is that Laura Foster wasn't worth the forfeit of two lives, and there seems to be no hope of saving mine.'

"'But if you did not kill her, man . . .'

"He smiled up at me then, as if he were speaking to a child. 'I did not care enough about her to kill her. But there is someone that I love enough to save. Let me do this. This confession will break my mother's heart, but at least she will have a measure of peace, believing her questions answered. And I will go to my grave knowing that I did one last thing for the one person I would willingly die for.'

"It was in my mind to tell him that Ann Melton was not worth such a noble gesture, but the words stuck in my throat. I could see that the poor wretch wanted his death to count for something, and this was the only deed that lay within his power. 'I will do as you ask,' I told him.

"He nodded and said, 'Thankee, Cap'n. And if it sets your mind at rest any, I'll have you to know that I am not entirely blameless in this. I dug that grave, and I carried the corpse up the ridge to it. I reckon they'd hang me for that, same as if I'd killed her.' I could not dispute the point, and when I told him so, he seemed more pleased than anything. 'Well, then, let them take my life, and welcome to it. But mind—I told you—one life and no more for that of Laura Foster. That's a fair enough trade. I'll hold you to that, sir.'

"As I turned to go, he asked if he could have more paper to write down his thoughts, and from that I surmised that he intended upon making a last speech from the gallows. 'Keep the pencil,' I told him, 'and I will instruct the jailer to bring you paper.' He thanked me again, and then, in a soft voice, muffled, I thought, with unshed tears, he said, 'I don't suppose they would let me see Ann again—one last time?'

"I hesitated—not because there was any chance of it, but only because I was trying to decide how best to soften the blow of refusal. 'She is another man's wife, Tom,' I reminded him, as gently as I could.

"He smiled at that, and then he said, 'We have belonged to one another all our lives, and nothing either one of us ever did with anybody else amounted to a hill of beans.'

"I looked away. 'Shall I tell her that, then?'

"He shook his head. 'She knows.'"

I told Captain Allison that I had read an account of the hanging in the *Salisbury Watchman*. "May the first. *May Day*. There's a sad irony in that. A day when maypoles should be garlanded with flowers, but instead in Iredell County they erected a pole and suspended a man from it until he died. Strictly speaking, both customs are barbaric, but I prefer the former."

"Well, we both saw worse in the War, Governor."

"That's so. I fought up in Virginia at Malvern Hill—that was like a thousand hangings all at once. But at least there is some dignity to a battlefield death. People don't crowd around to watch a man die, and cheer for his passing."

"Not everyone cheered, Governor, but there were too many that did. I only went because I thought it was my duty to attend. I found it difficult to sleep that night after my interview with Dula in his cell, and after a restless night, I went along to the jail again about seven to see the prisoner one last time, in case he had changed his mind about that confession.

"The jailer took me along to his cell. 'He paced near the whole night, Captain,' he told me. 'He was like a caged bear, lumbering to the length of that chain on his leg, back and forth, back and forth across the floor. I looked in on him towards daybreak, and he had stretched out on his cot with his eyes closed, but I don't think he was sleeping. I took him in his breakfast, and told him there were preachers a-waiting to see him, and he allowed as how I could send them in.'"

"He found the Lord at the end? That eases my mind, Captain Allison—though I never thought to see it happen."

"I had the honor of seeing him baptized by the Methodist minister. Once the prayers were concluded, I was able to speak to him privately. 'This is a fine thing you have done, Tom,' I told him. 'It will be of great consolation to your mother and sister to know that you sought salvation at the last.' He gave me a grim smile. 'I don't reckon my mother sets much store by the promises of preachers, Captain. But the baptism was free, and it seemed like a chance worth taking. I would like to believe there is a heaven. It's the only hope I have of ever seeing Ann again.'

"I thought of his confession, resting still in my pocket. 'But if she has done the murder, and if she dies unrepentant and unconfessed of the crime, then she will not go to heaven.'

"He smiled again. 'Why, she'll have to, Captain. It won't be heaven without her.'"

Richard Allison and I passed the next few moments in silence, while I lit a cigar, and thought about what he had said. I was trying to pity the prisoner, but that sentiment kept getting mixed up with something very like envy. I revered my Harriette, and stood in awe of her piety and her devotion to our boys, but all the same . . . I wished I loved anything or anybody as much as that raw mountain boy loved Ann Melton.

Finally I said, "I suppose there was a carnival atmosphere in Statesville on gallows day?"

Captain Allison nodded. "Well before noon the crowds began to gather. The sheriff had called out guards to keep order, and the saloons were closed so that drunkenness should not make matters worse. People must have traveled forty miles to come—rustic-looking hill folk, sunbronzed and chewing cuds of tobacco."

"Yes, I came from those hills, Captain. Those are my people, and you should not be deceived by their outward appearance. They are the salt of the earth."

"Begging your pardon, Governor. I spoke as I found. Some of the ruffians I encountered were soldiers who had served with Dula in the 42nd. They seemed to think that he was a desperate character, and they meant to see with what bravado he would meet his death. And I was dismayed to see how many women had come to see the execution."

I smiled. "Dula was—what? Twenty-three? Tall and wiry, with a head of thick dark curls. I reckon if we had female juries he might have gone free on the strength of that."

"That's true enough." Captain Allison sighed. "Unjust, but true. Beauty absolves a great many sins. Since juries are comprised of men, I think Ann Melton might well have prevailed even without her lover's confession."

"We shall not risk it, though. When Mrs. Melton comes to trial in the fall term of Superior Court, we must offer Dula's confession in to evidence, and request a dismissal of the charges. He wanted to save her, and I think we must allow him to do it."

"She isn't worth it, Governor, though I shouldn't say such a thing of a client. Still, it's the truth. She is a vain and proud woman, who thinks she is worth any sacrifice a man may make on the altar of her beauty. And I firmly believe that she killed that girl, even if we never find out the reason why. She ought not to be saved."

"No. But neither should poor Tom have died in vain. Try to look at it that way. You were with him to the end, Captain?"

"Yes, and no one ever more heartily wished themselves elsewhere than I did that day. They took him out of his cell about half past twelve, and Sheriff Wasson and some deputies led him out to the town square. They had a cart waiting there to convey him to the place of execution. They meant to hang him from the back of it, too, of course."

"Yes, it is a distressing sight, watching a man ride off to his death in a cart, sitting upon the very coffin in which his body shall rest in an hour's time. His coffin was with him, I suppose?"

"Yes. He sat upon it. But at least his sister was permitted to ride in the cart with him, and, perhaps for her sake, he smiled and spoke calmly to her as the procession went along. His sister and her husband had brought the coffin with them from Wilkes County—a heartbreaking errand for the poor young woman, but at least he had someone to claim his body. I was seated next to the minister, keeping my balance in the cart as best I could, but we were engulfed by the multitude of spectators—black folk and white, men and women, even children, and I cannot imagine what their parents were thinking to allow them to attend such a spectacle. There were people in carriages, on horseback, or simply walking in the throng alongside the cart—a sea of eager, cruel faces. I hope never to see the like again. Tom seemed oblivious to all these strangers, though. He kept talking about how he had been saved, and assuring his sister that he would see her in heaven. He seemed more concerned for her peace of mind than for his own fate."

"Did you have far to go?"

"No. Only to that open field beside the train depot, but the accompanying crowds so impeded our progress that it took us nearly half an hour to get there. There were even more people waiting around the gallows—and some enterprising young boys had climbed in to the trees surrounding the field, in hopes of getting a better view of the proceedings. It was barbaric. I shouldn't like to die in the midst of all that."

"Nor will you, Captain. Rest assured. You and I will die in our beds like gentlemen, and no one will be singing broadside ballads about us after we're gone."

"Well, if they do write any songs about Tom Dula, I suppose he has earned them. He died *game*, as he would have phrased it. When they pulled the cart up underneath the gallows, we all got out, leaving him there alone with his coffin. This must have been Sheriff Wasson's first hanging, for he had erected a shoddy excuse for a gallows that couldn't have taken an hour to put together. Two upright posts of cheap pine, with a crosspiece set across the top. I was afraid the thing would not hold his weight, and that he would topple to the ground still alive. It sickened me to think of it."

"I daresay it might have broken under *my* weight," I said, patting my substantial girth. There had been lean times during the War, but I had been making up for it since, and it showed. "But I take your point about Sheriff Wasson. There are problems with North Carolina's one-term sheriff law, and you have hit upon a major one. It is the county sheriff who must hang the convicted prisoners, but in a four-year term, a sheriff is not likely to perform enough executions to become proficient at it. We ought to follow England's example and have one well-trained hangman to service the whole state. It would be a kindness to all concerned not to have our executions turned into botched exercises in torture through the incompetence of the hangman."

"Well, Governor, if you ever get elected to office again, perhaps you could suggest such a plan. And you might consider limiting the condemned man's last words, while you're about it."

"Oh, I don't know. I'm famous for my speech making. If I had a rope around my neck, I believe I could talk for a week."

"Yes, perhaps it was the fear of death that made him talk at such length. Or perhaps he thought that if he could stall long enough, a rider would come tearing up the road, waving the Governor's pardon— but of course, no such thing happened. He talked about his childhood in Happy Valley, and he talked about his experiences in the War. He even touched on politics in his harangue. Apparently, he is not fond of our new governor Holden. Called him a secessionist."

"Yes, they weren't fond of the Confederacy in Wilkes County. That's why I moved the trial to Statesville. As the former Confederate Governor, I thought I could win with a sympathetic jury in a county where I was personally popular—or at least not vilified as a secessionist."

"We agreed with you, though, Armfield and I. As we had no evidence to refute the charges, it did seem the best course."

"Did Dula get around to talking of the murder in his oration?"

"He did. He protested his innocence loud and long, but he also commented on the physical evidence presented in the trial. Something about the roads leading to the Bates' place. Oh, and the map that the prosecution put in to evidence. He cursed Colonel Isbell, who drew it, and he insisted that there were errors in the map. And he accused some of the state's witnesses of swearing falsely against him."

"Did he mention the servant girl, Pauline Foster? I'd agree with him there. What was it the newspaper called her? A monster of depravity?"

"Well, a woman who has recently given birth to a black child, although her husband is as white as she is . . . one can hardly call her faithful."

"He may only be a common-law husband at that. Some poor old wretch from up the mountain who thinks a simpering young woman is a prize. I wonder what she told him about the child. I'd give worlds to know who its father is myself."

"I doubt she would ever say, if indeed she knows."

"The Foster women have an uncommon gift among the fair sex: they can hold their tongues. In the two years she has languished in jail, Ann Melton has not said one word in her defense or to accuse anyone else of the crime. She is a sphinx. And it has served her well. She will go free. I have no doubt of it."

"Tom Dula talked enough at the end, but he said nothing at all about her. Anyhow, I don't think his preaching made him any converts. Nobody cared about the fine points of evidence by then. Most of the crowd believed him to be guilty, and they were ready to see him hang. At last, he ran out of words, and, giving his sister a tender farewell, he indicated to the sheriff that he was ready to proceed. It was half past two o'clock by then. A deputy threw the rope over the crosspiece of the gallows and tied it in place. Then at a signal from the sheriff, another deputy took hold of the horse's bridle, and they led it away, so that the cart slipped out from under the prisoner's feet."

I shook my head. "Wasson made a hash of it, didn't he?"

"Oh, yes. It was torture to watch. The drop was less than three feet—not enough to break the prisoner's neck. So the end was not quick—or kind."

"We don't know how to hang people in this country, I tell you. In England, now . . ."

But Allison wasn't listening. He was staring at the marble floor, but seeing the hanging happen again. "He did not struggle. It must have been agony for him to hang there while the rope slowly throttled him. I have wondered how long he was conscious during the ordeal, and if he could hear the roar of the crowd as he strangled. I hope not. I hope he passed out quickly. When I could no longer bear the sight of it, I closed my eyes and whispered a prayer for the repose of his soul. After thirteen minutes, Dr. Campbell pronounced him dead, but Wasson left the body suspended there on the gallows for ten minutes more, to make sure. And all the while, the rabble was cheering as if it were a horse race."

I shuddered, trying not to envisage it myself. "He is out of it now, poor devil. I suppose the sister and her husband took him back to Wilkes County for burial?"

"Yes. They were going to bury him a mile or two from his mother's place, on the farm of a prosperous cousin, I think. So he is at rest a good seven miles from the place where Laura Foster lies buried now."

"Oh, he won't care about that, Captain. He always said that she meant nothing to him, and I believe him. This was always about Ann. I wonder where there'll bury her. At a crossroads with a stake through her heart, if they are wise."

"She is but twenty-four, though. She may live to see the new century come in."

"No, Captain. Like Jezebel and Cleopatra, I think she will die young. And, like you, I see no hope of heaven for her, but I can well imagine their reunion in the hereafter—two troubled souls reuniting after death . . . Ann Melton and Tom Dula, together in the mists of that ridge next to Reedy Branch."

Captain Allison smiled. "You have grown fanciful, Governor Vance. If you knew Wilkes County as I do, you would never be able to imagine restless spirits in that quiet earth."

I would have been content to let it rest there, with Captain Allison's comforting epitaph ending the matter in a bucolic haze, but life is seldom so accommodating as that. Much as I might have wanted to forget the whole Wilkes County incident, and return to more profitable endeavors elsewhere, there was still the matter of the second defendant, Mrs. Ann Melton. Her trial was set for the court's fall term, and, while it would be a brief and perfunctory appearance, thanks to Tom Dula's confession, I was still obliged to attend and to confer with the prisoner about the state of her case. I took the train to Statesville to meet with her.

All was peaceful at the depot when I arrived, with flies buzzing in the late summer sunshine. I found it hard to imagine that only a few months earlier thousands of spectators had thronged in the adjacent field to watch a man die. I shuddered to imagine it, and made my way as quickly as I could to the county jail to see my remaining client.

The years of incarceration had been kind to Mrs. Melton. Her beauty was as striking now as it had been when I had first set eyes on her in October of 1866. Her hair was glossy and well brushed, and her skin glowed like polished ivory. The simple blue dress she wore was not new, but it was clean and well-kept, and I wondered who did her laundry and her mending. If she missed her children or her lover, I saw no evidence of the ravages of grief. She received me with that same regal courtesy that I remembered, as if she were a duchess and I a courtier come to do her bidding.

I sat down across from her at the little oak table in the jail, and prepared myself for a difficult interview with a distraught woman. I did not get it.

"Mrs. Melton, I am here to speak to you about your forthcoming trial, and I hope to effect your release shortly thereafter."

She nodded, as if this was no more than she expected. "Thank you, Mr. Vance. I hope you will send word to my husband, so that he will bring the wagon to Statesville to collect me."

"I will see to it. Have you been keeping well?"

She shrugged. "I get mortally tired of soup beans and corn bread. Have the apples come ripe yet?"

I considered it. "I think they lack a week or more yet, but the last of the summer tomatoes are still to be had. Perhaps I could arrange for a bag of tomatoes to be sent to you here."

"Thank you, Mr. Vance. I'd be partial to some hard candy as well. There ain't much to do in here."

I nearly offered to send her some books, but then I recalled that, elegant as she was, Ann Melton could neither read nor write. In a way, all the world was her prison. I wondered what I would have done in my own incarceration if the pleasures of reading and correspondence had been denied me, but, as she knew no better, she would never miss it. I promised to get her some penny candy, mostly as expiation for all the pleasures my education had afforded me that she would never know.

I waited for her to ask after her family, or for some news of the outside world, but she remained silent, without a trace of distress or anxiety, patiently waiting for me to state my business.

"Let me tell you what you can expect when we go to court. Your trial will be so brief that it hardly merits the name. We will present the new evidence to the court and ask for your release."

"New evidence?"

"Yes." I hesitated to bring up a sensitive matter, for fear of disturbing her elegant serenity. "You know that Tom Dula was executed in May?"

Her expression did not change. "Yes, I do know that. They ought not to have done it. They had no witnesses, nor ary weapon, nor one whit of proof. We never said one word to those lawmen, and we ought to have been safe. It ain't fair."

Technically, I agreed with her, but as an officer of the court it did not behoove me to speak ill of its decisions. "Tom Dula died bravely, though," I told her. "They tell me that he spoke for nearly an hour, exhorting people to live right, and that in his final moments he died like a soldier." I had thought to quote lines from Macbeth—*Nothing in his life became him like the leaving it*—but Shakespeare would have been lost on her, for all that she might have had in common with the lady of Glamis and Cawdor.

I waited for a storm of weeping, but Ann Melton only shrugged.

"No point in fighting what you can't change. At least he didn't give any satisfaction to them that come to see a sorry spectacle."

"He left a confession, you know. He dictated it on the eve of his death to my colleague, Captain Allison."

"He'd have done better to use the time trying to escape."

"He had already tried that. They found a sliver of glass in his cell, and took it from him. He had been trying to wear away the iron shackles with it. It was only when they took it away from him that he sent for Captain Allison. He wrote a few words on a scrap of paper, saying that he alone was responsible for the death of Laura Foster."

"Well, he was. He shouldn't have been having to do with her in the first place. He had no call to go chasing after Laura Foster, when he had always sworn that he loved me."

"His confession will save you, though. His dying declaration proclaimed your innocence."

Ann nodded, satisfied. "He owed me that. I have spent two years of my life locked away in this cell, and if he hadn't fallen in with that no-account Laura Foster, none of this would ever have happened."

I tried again. "He did a noble thing, Mrs. Melton. He gave his life for you."

"Yes. But it doesn't matter to him anymore, does it? He couldn't save himself. He is dead and buried, back in Wilkes County. No use in both of us dying for the likes of her." She twisted a stray lock of her dark hair. "You won't forget about those sticks of candy you promised to send me, will you? I'm mighty partial to peppermint sticks."


The next day I stood up in open court, and, in as steady a voice as I could manage, I read out Tom Dula's confession, exonerating his codefendant Ann Foster Melton. The court dismissed all charges against her, and pronounced her free to go. I saw a fleeting smile of pure triumph cross her face, and then she resumed her expression of cold indifference. She swept out of the courtroom on my arm, amid murmurs from the spectators. No one cheered or approached her as she passed.

Once outside, I handed my client over to a subdued and somber James Melton. Without a word, she linked her arm in his, and they walked away without a word of thanks or a backward glance.

But people will remember that she was beautiful.

Ann Foster Melton was released from prison, but died of an illness—perhaps syphilis—a few years later. Local legends say that on her deathbed she screamed that she saw flames and cats around her bed. After her death, in 1875, her widower James Melton married Louisa Gilbert, and lived on peacefully into the twentieth century. John Anderson moved back to Caldwell County and married a woman of color named Jane, with whom he had a son. Laura Foster is buried in a marked grave in a pasture on the site of her father's tenant farm in Caldwell County. No one knows the name of the man Pauline Foster married. After the second trial of Tom Dula, Pauline left Wilkes County and vanished from history.

# AUTHOR'S NOTE

I do understand and sympathize with the reader's reaction to any
novel based on a true story: *What in this book is true?* And the
answer is: *As much as I could possibly verify.* Where I differed from
traditional accounts of the case, it is because I chose to place weight
on certain statements in the trial record that other people had dismissed—*but the evidence for my version is there.*

The first thing to discount in the study of this incident is the
catchy but irrelevant Kingston Trio version of the folk song, "Hang
Down Your Head, Tom Dooley." The young man's name was Dula,
not Dooley. He was not hanged in a lonesome valley from a white oak
tree, but from a specially constructed T-shaped post in a field beside
the train depot in Statesville, North Carolina. The song mentions
someone named Grayson—"If it hadn't been for Grayson, I'd a been
in Tennessee." That is true enough, but Grayson was simply the farmer
who hired Tom as a laborer when he fled in June 1866. A more au-
thentic version of the song, made famous by North Carolina mountain musician Doc Watson, is more faithful to the facts of the story,

although it, too, supposes that Tom Dula is guilty. Most people who are familiar with the case think otherwise.

When a story has become as steeped in legend as the Tom Dula incident, the first thing a writer has to do is question all the assumptions that have become attached to the narrative over the years, because rumor, conjecture, and wishful thinking taint the story. Over the years dozens of people have offered to tell me the "real story" of Tom Dooley—the one their grandmother heard from the storekeeper/ the postman/the doctor, etc. No two are the same. The story as it is generally told did not ring true to me. When I worked on an article about "Tom Dooley" for *Blue Ridge Country* magazine, my travel companion and I went through all the possibilities inherent in the love triangle. None of them worked.

- *Tom killed Laura Foster because she gave him syphilis.* There is no evidence that she did. Patient Zero was Pauline Foster, with whom Tom had sexual relations. It is more likely that he gave the disease to Laura instead of vice versa.

- *Tom killed Laura Foster because she was pregnant.* There is no evidence that she was. Dr. Carter did not note the presence of fetal bones in the autopsy. Besides, Laura had a reputation for promiscuity. Judging by the example of Ann's mother, who had five children and no husband, pregnancy in that place and time would not have made marriage compulsory. If Tom had dallied with a planter's daughter or a lawyer's sister—sure. But not with an unchaste tenant farmer's daughter.

- *Ann Foster Melton killed Laura Foster because Tom loved her and was planning to elope with her.* Tom said more than once that he "had no use for Laura Foster," and I believe him. If Ann had killed the woman he truly loved, would he have written a confession exonerating Ann on the eve of his execution?

- *Tom and Ann killed Laura Foster. Motive unspecified.* Why? She had no money, no hold over them, and apparently no malice toward them.

- *James Melton or Pauline Foster killed Laura Foster.* Neither was ever suspected of involvement in the death of Laura Foster, and neither of them had the slightest motive to dispense with her. Besides, if either of them had done it, Tom Dula and Ann Melton would certainly have saved themselves by denouncing the real killer. They did not.

I concluded that there was a missing piece of the puzzle, because one could not construct a plausible scenario with the traditional collection of facts.

When I read the trial transcripts and the newspaper coverage of Dula's execution, I found three references to a black man, a detail roundly ignored in other studies of the case—but he was real, and he was there.

- As depicted in the novel, when Laura Foster went missing, Pauline Foster says to Wilson Foster: "Maybe she ran off with a black man." You might dismiss this as a taunt, except that instead of becoming angry Laura's father agreed that this might be so. In the 1866 Reconstruction South, Wilson Foster's reaction is astounding. He should have been enraged by that suggestion. Why wasn't he?

- When Eliza Anderson, Wash Anderson's sister, takes the stand in the second trial, a defense attorney asks her if she is kin to a man of color named John Anderson. She says no. Census records show that John Anderson had been a slave of her family, and that in 1866, he was still working on their farm. John Foster West interprets the kinship question at the trial as an attempt to discredit the witness, a young, unmarried white woman. This question is too volatile to be used in 1868 on an unimportant witness, especially if the witness is an unmarried girl who is suspected of nothing. *Why was John Anderson mentioned at all?* I considered this for a while, and then I asked Wilkes Community College research librarian Christy Earp to find out where the Andersons lived in 1866. We found them—living on property adjoining the Bates' place, where Laura Foster was killed.

- When a New York newspaper reporter came to Statesville to cover Tom Dula's trial, he dismissed the state's chief witness, Pauline Foster, as a depraved woman, commenting that she had recently married a white man and had given birth to a black child. Whose child was it? We will probably never know for sure, because the name of Pauline's husband is never given, and she vanishes from history after the second trial. But she worked as a servant girl on a farm within sight of the Andersons' place, where John Anderson lived and worked. This is not proof of their involvement, but it is a plausible theory.

- Pauline's suggestion—that Laura Foster ran off with a black man—makes more sense than speculating that she was eloping with Tom. Both Tom and Laura were of legal age and unmarried: there was no reason for them to elope. No sneaking around was required. Laura's father, who had caught her in bed with Tom, would have been relieved. If Laura really was sneaking off to get married, what bride-groom would require such subterfuge? *Not Tom.*

- But if Laura wanted to plight her troth to a man of color, they would be forced to go elsewhere. I think that John Anderson, who was listed on the census records as mulatto, was light-skinned enough to pass for white in an area where he was not known—in other words, anywhere but Wilkes County. The elopement of John Anderson and Laura Foster makes perfect sense.

- *And another thing*—if you were running away with Tom Dula, would you arrange to meet him a mile away from his house and five miles from your house, but *within sight* of the home of his jealous married lover? But John Anderson lived right beside the Bates' place. It was the logical place to meet him.

Most romanticized versions of the Tom Dula legend make a dewy heroine of Laura Foster. I don't see any evidence for that. When she went missing, her father declared that he didn't care if he ever saw her again or not, but he did want his horse back. Tom Dula said he had no use for Laura Foster. The people who searched for her seemed to be disinterested community members who were inspired by the thought of an unmarried young girl who had come to harm. Within days of her disappearance, the real Laura Foster vanished into a moonlit haze of sentimentality, in which she remains to this day. I saw her more as a situation than a person: *a springe to catch woodcocks.* Inciting jealousy over the casual sexual relationship of Tom and Laura would be the perfect weapon for someone intent upon destroying Ann Melton.

Pauline Foster is generally dismissed as "the servant girl," and some people I talked to thought that she might have been mentally deficient, but—since she managed to bring about the deaths of three people, and to emerge unscathed from the incident and the trials—I decided to take her seriously. If Pauline had intended to harm those people, she succeeded admirably. If she had been a malicious and scheming malcontent, she could easily have manipulated the vain and passionate Ann into precipitating the downfall of everyone. After months spent studying the heartless Pauline, who brought venereal disease and tragedy to Wilkes County, and the cold narcissist Ann Melton, who cared for nothing but herself, I ended up feeling deeply sorry for Tom Dula, and I wish his sacrifice could have been made for a more deserving person.

One of the most underestimated characters in the story is James Melton, the husband of Ann. Because he seemed indifferent to his wife's affair with Tom Dula, storytellers have cast him as an elderly man, a mere farmer who was no match for Tom the soldier. The facts indicate otherwise. As I noted in this novel, James Melton was only six years older than Tom and Ann—still in his twenties at the time of the murder. His war record was far more impressive than that of

Tom, the malingering musician. James Melton did, indeed, carry the colors of the 26th North Carolina at Gettysburg, where he was wounded. He did spend the waning weeks of the War in a prison camp at Point Lookout, Maryland, and, as I said in the novel, he was incarcerated there at the same time as Tom Dula. Here is a synopsis of the war record of James Melton. (Note that in 1866 he would have been only twenty-eight.)

*James Melton, of Wilkes County, NC, enlisted at the age of 23 on June 12, 1861, mustered in as a private in Company C, 26th North Carolina Troops. Present or accounted for until wounded in the left shoulder and right leg with the colors of the regiment at Gettysburg, Pennsylvania, July 1, 1863. Melton returned to duty sometime between July and December 1864. Present or accounted for until wounded in the right leg at Hatcher's Run, Virginia, March 30, 1865.*

*He was hospitalized in Richmond, Virginia, where he was captured by the enemy on April 3, 1865. Transferred to Point Lookout, Maryland, May 2, 1865. Released at Point Lookout on June 26, 1865, after taking the Oath of Allegiance.*

Once I began to study it in depth, one of the most striking facets of this story was its close parallel to Emily Bronte's classic English novel *Wuthering Heights*, set in a similar remote and rugged place. In my construction of the paradigm, Heathcliff and Catherine, the star-crossed lovers of *Wuthering Heights*, are Tom Dula and Ann Foster Melton, so that James Melton is cast as the gentle and patient Edgar Linton, and Laura most closely corresponds to Isabella Linton, whom Heathcliff wooed and tormented (to punish Catherine for marrying Edgar), but did not care for. The narrators, the servant girl Nellie

Dean and the aristocratic tenant Mr. Lockwood are, of course, Pauline Foster and Zebulon Vance. Alert readers will find echoes of Emily Bronte's prose, deliberately inserted here and there in *The Ballad of Tom Dooley*.

Zebulon Vance was exactly who he said he was: a poor mountain boy who became Governor of North Carolina, fought in the Civil War as Colonel of the 26th North Carolina regiment, and ended his days in Washington, representing his home state as one of its most beloved Senators. When the funeral train brought his body back to Asheville in 1894, a detachment of National Guard troops was needed just to unload the accompanying funeral wreaths. In his brief hiatus from public service in 1866–68, when he practiced law in Charlotte with Clement Dowd, Vance did indeed spearhead the defense of Tom Dula and Ann Foster Melton. It was the inspiration of Vance's meteoric rise from poverty, his success as a statesman, and his wisdom and humanity that made me decide to write this story. For those cynics who characterize Appalachia as a land peopled only by the likes of Tom and Ann, I offer the remarkable life of Zebulon Baird Vance as evidence to the contrary.

I'm sure that a great many superficial readers will see this work as a crime story and spout a lot of nonsense about "solving the case," as if it were an episode of *CSI*, but I wish they wouldn't. It can hardly be a mystery when practically anybody in Wilkes County will tell you on first acquaintance that "Ann did it." I agree. So there was no case to solve. My concerns lay elsewhere.

While I wanted to understand the motivation for the tragedy, I was more interested in the characters of the persons involved, and in re-creating the world of the post-War mountain South. As a writer, I relished the challenge of crafting a novel in which the principal narrator is a sociopath—one who feels nothing—and the beautiful heroine is a narcissist linked with an amiable ne'er-do-well. If the resulting narrative appears effortless, I assure you that it was not.

I did want to know what really happened in Wilkes County, North Carolina, in 1866, and, although my version of the events can never be proven, I am satisfied with the answers I got. Whether or not you agree with my findings, I want you to understand that I did not invent anything: every conclusion I made stems from a fact in the original trial transcript, which is on file at the North Carolina Archives in Raleigh.

# ACKNOWLEDGMENTS

The story of Tom Dula, Ann Melton, and Laura Foster has been a carefully tended legend in Wilkes County, North Carolina, for well over a century. To sort out the real story at the heart of the folk song, I needed to go to the source.

Appalachian State University historian John Foster West wrote two nonfiction accounts of the Tom Dula story, and I consulted these books as the basis for further investigation. Although West's account of the case was thorough and meticulous, his research, conducted more than thirty years ago, did not have the benefit of the resources that modern technology has made available and accessible to scholars today. When I began to study Mr. West's scenario, I felt that the facts did not add up to a satisfactory explanation, and I went back to the original trial transcripts and began to put together a theory that would make sense of the case.

Ever since I first began writing novels about the history and folklore of the Southern mountains, people have been asking me to tell the story of Tom Dula, but I had thought that the story was too sordid and unexceptional to make a good novel. I revised my opinion in

2005 when Cara Modisett, editor of *Blue Ridge Country* magazine, asked me to research the legend for an article for the magazine. One summer day, armed with maps and a copy of John Foster West's book, I traveled to Wilkes County, North Carolina, with my old friend David McPherson, and together we tried to make sense of that long-ago incident. Thank you, David, for listening, and for agreeing with me that what we had been told wasn't making sense.

A few miles from where it all happened, Edith Ferguson Carter has kept a "Tom Dooley" museum within the grounds of her Whippoorwill Academy for the past half century. Besides preserving artifacts from the case—a lock of Laura Foster's hair, Tom Dula's fiddle, and his original headstone—Ms. Carter also keeps track of the genealogical records, and her museum is a repository for all the stories that have grown up around the case. It was to the Whippoorwill Academy that I went when I began to study the case, and I owe a great deal of thanks to Edith Ferguson Carter for her time, her generosity, and her patience. The Zebulon Vance part of the story was enriched by the encouragement and assistance of David Tate and the staff of the Zebulon Vance Birthplace in Reems Creek, Madison County, North Carolina.

Three scholars at Wilkes Community College shared their expertise and gave me the pleasure of their company in the course of my research. Professor Julie Mullis, chairman of WCC's Department of Arts & Communication, who teaches a course on the Tom Dula story, led the expedition to Ferguson one bright fall day, and we visited the places where the Dula, Foster, and Melton houses once stood. We photographed the Bates' place, climbed Laura Foster Ridge, where the body was originally interred, and scaled a high fence in order to get in to the pasture that contains the grave of

Laura Foster. WCC Research Librarian Christy Earp searched genealogical records and census data to pinpoint the residences of the
Andersons, the Scotts, etc., and to track the people in the case through
the years. The most exciting moment of the research was when I
asked Christy to locate:

- a light-skinned man of color (mulatto), probably named
  John Anderson;
- in 1866 he would be younger than thirty, probably early
  twenties in age;
- he would live either close to Laura's home in German's Hill
  or close to the Bates' place.

Within hours, Christy Earp had found him in the 1870 Caldwell
County census. John Anderson, mulatto, was twenty-one—the same
age as Laura—in 1866, and at the time he lived on the Anderson farm
(Eliza's, with her widowed mother and her brother Wash, who was
Tom's best friend). When we discovered that the Anderson farm ad-
joined the Bates' place, I got chills. We knew we had found a crucial
piece of evidence.

WCC-Ashe professor Shannan Roark was my connection to
the experts in Wilkes County, and she went along on our trek to
Ferguson, photographing sites and measuring the distance from one
place to another, as we tried to make sense of what really happened.

Mr. Zelotese Walsh of Wilkes County has amassed detailed genealogical records of Wilkes County's people, and he sorted through
the Foster "begats" for me, in an attempt to pinpoint the lineage of
Pauline Foster.

Dr. Randy Joyner of Wilkes County, a descendant of the Andersons, checked family records for me in connection with Wash and Eliza Anderson, provided me with a number of physical details about the county that helped me to construct the narrative, and took me to the grave of Tom Dula. My thanks, too, to genealogist Andy Pilley for his help with the background and photographs relating to the people in the story and to attorney David Hood of Hickory, North Carolina.

Michael Hardy, North Carolina's Historian of the Year for 2011, is an author of North Carolina regimental histories and an expert on the Civil War. It was he who tracked down the war records of Thomas Dula and James Melton, discovering connections between them that had not previously come to light.

My thanks to my son Spencer McCrumb who spent a morning at the North Carolina Archives in Raleigh, obtaining for me the trial transcripts and any relevant documents concerning the case of Tom Dula.

When I realized that the Tom Dula story was an Appalachian parallel to *Wuthering Heights*, Elizabeth Baird Hardy, a Western North Carolina English professor and author, heard me out, leaping to the connections as fast as I did, and we had a wonderful time finding a literary template for this most famous of mountain legends. I am grateful for her encouragement and her friendship.

The psychological aspects of the story were important. While most people have dismissed "the servant girl" as a minor character in this incident, I concluded that the catalyst in this story was Pauline Foster, and that her malice and discontent caused the deaths of Laura Foster and Tom Dula. Ann Melton's narcissism made her indifferent to the suffering of other people. To understand Pauline's sociopathic disorder and Ann's narcissism, I was fortunate to receive guidance from Forensic and Consulting Psychologist Dr. Charlton S. Stanley of Tennessee, who helped me understand the psychology of these two pivotal characters, and to determine how their mind-sets would be manifested in their behavior. Dr. Martin E. Olsen, director of OB/GYN at East Tennessee State University, helped me to determine whether an autopsy would have showed if Laura Foster was pregnant.

It took many hours of talking to a great many people to enable me to sort out the facts and the personalities that shaped this story, and I am grateful to everyone who listened.